Elizabeth Gail

and the frightened runaways

Hilda Stahl

Tyndale House
Publishers, Inc.
Wheaton, Illinois

Dedicated with love to
Kay, Tammy, Shauna, Melody, and Andrea

The Elizabeth Gail Series

Third printing, September 1983

Library of Congress Catalog Number 80-53246
ISBN 0-8423-0728-1, paper
Copyright © 1981 by Hilda Stahl. All rights reserved.
Printed in the United States of America.

Contents

One
A noise
in the barn

Libby gripped the wire handle of the red plastic bucket of grain as she slowly turned away from Snowball's stall. Had she heard a sneeze? Her heart seemed to stand still, then almost to leap through her jacket. Would her real mother dare to sneak up on her and kidnap her so that the Johnsons couldn't adopt her?

Snowball nickered and pawed the dirt floor of her stall. A barn cat mewed. Libby held her breath and cocked her head, listening intently. What was wrong with her? She had no reason to fear. Mother had signed the papers saying the Johnson family could adopt her. Mother had said she would never bother Libby or the Johnson family again.

Slowly, painfully Libby released her breath and turned back to Snowball's stall.

"I shouldn't be jumpy, Snowball," she said as she poured the grain into the white filly's feed container. "Dad said we have nothing to fear. He said everything was going to be all right. I believe him, Snowball. He loves me! All the Johnson family love me even if I am only an aid kid."

Libby rubbed her hand down Snowball's neck. "They won't change their minds, Snowball. I know they won't!" She hesitated and tried to stop the shiver that ran up and down her spine. "Will they? I just wish I could be good all the time! Then I wouldn't have anything to worry about."

Snowball lifted her head and nuzzled Libby's shoulder. "I love you, Snowball. I'm glad you belong to me."

With a smile Libby pushed her short brown hair out of her face and walked out of the stall. Suddenly she stopped, her hazel eyes wide. That had not been a cat sneezing! Someone was in the barn! Ben, Susan, Kevin, and Toby were in the house watching Saturday morning cartoons. Chuck was in town at his store and Vera was getting ready to go to town.

Who was in the barn? Should she run to the house to get Ben? He was always brave. She dare not stay out much longer. Vera would be waiting to take her to her piano lesson with Rachael Avery. And she would not miss her piano lesson!

"Who's in here?" Libby's voice sounded weak and scared. She'd meant it to come out loud and demanding. She cleared her throat

8

and tried again. Oh, what if it was Mother?

With her back pressed against Snowball's stall door, Libby looked around. Whoever was in there had to be in one of the stalls. Had she imagined the sneeze because she was worried about Mother taking her?

She forced her legs to support her as she slowly walked down the concrete aisle of the barn. She stopped, her heart racing wildly, and stared at a stack of baled hay. Someone could be behind the hay. She had hidden there just last night when they'd played hide-and-seek after school. Kevin had finally given up and called her in free.

Slowly Libby walked around the bales of hay and peeked down in her favorite hiding spot, then jumped back in surprise. Someone was hiding there! But it was not Mother.

Libby wanted to run away screaming, but she stood beside the hay and forced her body to stop shaking. "I see you! I see you in the hay. Come out right now!" She waited, poised for flight.

A girl just a little taller than Libby slowly crept from her hiding place and stood up. She had light brown hair and brown eyes. She stared at Libby as she rubbed her hands down her jeans, then stuffed them in her green jacket pockets. "Hi, Libby," she said in a small voice.

"April?" Libby whispered, stepping back until she bumped against the wall, "April Brakie?"

The girl shook her head. "No. I'm May. April's over there."

Libby jerked her head around to see another girl on the other side of the hay.

"Hi, Libby." April grinned sheepishly as she walked around the hay and stopped beside Libby. "Are you mad?"

Libby stared at the girls, then slowly shook her head. "What are you doing here?"

"We came to find you," said May urgently. "We need help."

"We heard you're going to be adopted," said April. "We said if Elizabeth Gail Dobbs can find herself a family, then maybe we can too."

"You mean you ran away again?" Libby stared at the girls, remembering the first time she'd seen them. They'd all three lived with the Mason family for about four months. April and May had always dressed exactly alike so that no one could tell them apart. Mrs. Mason had beat them both for any wrongdoing in order to make sure that the offender had been punished.

April sneezed, then wiped the back of her hand across her nose. She looked pale and too thin, thinner than May. "We had to get away, Libby. We couldn't stay there."

"But how did you find me?" Libby had not seen the girls for almost three years.

"We heard Mrs. Blevins talking about you," said May with a giggle. "She said she didn't know how such a wonderful family would want

10

you. We said if Libby can do it, we can too. We came to meet your family and see if they'd take us."

"Oh! Oh, dear!" Libby shook her head. "I don't know. I don't know what they'd say if they knew you had run away. Who were you living with?" She saw the hard look on April's face and the fear in May's eyes. "Tell me, girls."

April nervously pushed her long brown hair back from her thin pale face. "Remember Morris and Evelyn Stern?"

Libby's stomach tightened into a hard knot and the barn seemed to spin. "No. I don't remember them."

"Yes, you do, Elizabeth Gail Dobbs!" cried May, catching Libby's icy hand in hers and squeezing it. "You remember living with them."

"No!" She pushed the memory back and would not let it out. "No!"

April shrugged. "If that's the way you want it, then that's the way it'll be."

"You must remember, Libby," cried May in alarm. "Then you'll know how much we need you to help us or hide us or something! We can't go back to them! We can't!"

Libby jerked free and turned to run from the barn, but May grabbed her again and knocked her into the corner of the stall, where she struck her arm. Pain shot through her and she cried out.

11

"Don't hurt her, May," said April sharply. "She'll help us. I know she will."

"Will you, Libby?" May's voice was low and soft and pleading and Libby wanted to shout No! "Please, Libby."

Slowly Libby stood up, holding her throbbing arm protectively. "I'll think about it. I have to go to town right now. When I get back, I'll tell you my answer."

May's thin hand reached out pleadingly. "You won't tell on us, will you?"

Libby shook her head, glad that she could help erase the fear from May's eyes. "I promise not to tell. You girls stay hidden in here. I'll be home by noon and I'll bring you something to eat."

"Thanks, Libby," said April, wrapping her arms around herself and hunching her thin shoulders. Pieces of hay clung to her hair. Dark circles around her eyes made them look large in her pale face.

Libby wanted to take both girls into the house and ask Vera to mother them and give them a home forever. Finally she turned away and walked out of the barn into the cool September day.

She lifted her pointed chin and squared her thin shoulders. Goosy Poosy honked from the chicken pen. Rex barked a short, sharp bark and ran to Libby's side. She rested her hand on his head, then cried out in pain. Gingerly she rubbed her arm.

12

Determinedly she ran to the back door of the house. She would not think about her arm or the girls right now. She had to take a piano lesson with Rachael Avery.

She opened the back door and stepped inside, leaning weakly against the closed door. She would *not* remember Morris and Evelyn Stern!

Two
Piano
lesson

Libby tried to ignore the pain in her arm as she followed Rachael Avery into the music room. The baby grand piano gleamed brightly where the sun shone through a window onto it.

"I hate to see winter come," said Rachael with a smile as she waited for Libby to stand her books on the piano and take off her jacket. "I'd like to see fall last until spring." Rachael laughed with her head back, her long black hair flowing down her back and over her slender shoulders. Several pictures in the grouping on the wall beside the piano showed her in concert. Libby had often stared at the pictures, seeing herself in concert instead of the famous Rachael Avery.

Libby bit back a moan as she hung her jacket on a wooden hall tree next to the door. Vera had asked her why she was pale but she'd answered that she was excited about the lesson. Once she started playing, her arm would stop hurting.

"Did you practice your hour a day this week, Elizabeth?" Rachael sat on her stool beside the piano and smiled across at Libby.

Libby nodded and was able to smile. "I had a little trouble but Mom helped me." Libby sat on the bench and opened the first book. A groan escaped and Rachael asked if anything was wrong. Libby quickly explained that it was nothing, maybe a little cramp.

"I heard Mrs. Johnson play in church last Sunday. I was visiting your church with my husband's sister. Mrs. Johnson is very talented."

Libby smiled and flushed with pleasure. "I want to play as well as she does."

"You will—and better." Rachael patted Libby's shoulder and told her to play.

Pain shot up her arm as she pressed the keys and she could not move her hand.

"What is it, Elizabeth? Have you forgotten the notes in that piece? It's very simple."

Tears stung Libby's eyes as she forced herself to play the song. Rachael must not think she wasn't good enough to keep as a pupil! Someday she would be Elizabeth Gail Johnson, a concert pianist, and everyone would come to listen to her play. Rachael had said that she was good enough to become a concert pianist because she had the dedication, the determination, and the dream. The past several weeks of lessons from Rachael had improved her playing a lot. Nothing was going to stop the lessons! Especially not a little pain in her right arm!

As she played, the pain increased until she could barely sit still. Several times she fumbled and Rachael made her repeat the notes.

"Are you sure you practiced enough this week, Elizabeth?" Rachael looked at her with a slight frown, a question in her blue eyes. "I know with the work in seventh grade that you don't have the time you had during the summer, but you insisted you could make the time. You wouldn't tell me that you'd practiced just to keep me from being upset, would you?"

Libby shook her head hard. "I did practice! I'm just having a little trouble right now. I'll be fine next week."

Just then something crashed in another room and a baby wailed loudly. Rachael jumped up, saying that she'd better see what her young son had done this time. "I left the little neighbor girl in the nursery with him, but he is getting to be quite a handful."

Libby slumped forward with a sigh as Rachael hurried away. Carefully she rubbed her arm, looking at it with a frown. She felt a hard lump but she could not see a bruise. It would be all right. It had to be.

She walked around the music room, then stopped in front of the pictures of Rachael in concert. Libby remembered the time she'd come to be interviewed to see if Rachael would take her as a student. Vera and Chuck had brought her and waited in the living room, almost as anxious as she was. Chuck had told her that having a dream was nothing unless you set about fulfilling that dream. And she was determined to!

Someday she would sit in front of hundreds of people and play the piano and they would stand and clap until their hands were sore and they would say, "Can this really be the little aid girl whose father deserted her when she was three and whose mother beat her and deserted her? How can such a nobody become somebody so important, so talented?"

Libby smiled dreamily. She could almost hear the applause for her. The Johnson family would be proud of her and glad that they had prayed her into their home, then adopted her.

She gasped and turned away, her eyes wide. They had not adopted her yet. They were waiting for their day in court. What if she did something that would make them change their minds? What if they got mad at her for trying to help April and May Brakie?

Slowly Libby sank down on the piano bench. She pressed her hands against her legs and felt the rough corduroy of her blue pants. The pain in her arm shot almost to her shoulder and she moved it until the pain eased. If she held it just right in front of her, close to her body, it didn't hurt.

Rachael walked in with a laugh. "Seth was investigating again." She sat down, her dark green skirt falling over her knees. "Ready to try again, Elizabeth? I want you to work on this one." She moved the book so that Libby could see the page. "Your mother will be here soon and we don't want to keep her waiting."

Libby bit the inside of her lower lip and forced herself to play the song. Tears stood in her eyes and she would not turn to look at Rachael as she said that it was much better and that she should go over it again for next week.

"Your first recital is in November. Keep up the good work and you will make me very proud of you."

"I will."

"Are you all right? You look pale."

Libby shrugged. "I'm anxious to get my songs just right for you."

"You'll do just fine as long as you practice." Rachael showed her the new songs that she'd have and helped her through them once. "If at any time you get tired of practicing, just remember your dream, Elizabeth. You can't reach the top without working at it."

"I'll work hard." Libby reached for her jacket with her left arm. She could not slip it on without Rachael knowing about her injured arm. She carried her music and her jacket to the front door, then turned with a forced smile. "See you next Saturday."

"Tell your mother hello for me."

Libby nodded with a real smile. It felt great to have Rachael call Vera Johnson her mother. Rachael knew that she was a foster girl, that her real mother was Marie Dobbs.

"Better put on your jacket. It's chilly today, Elizabeth."

"It'll be warm in the car, Rachel. 'Bye." She hurried out the door before Rachael insisted she put on her jacket.

The cool wind cut through her flowered blouse and she thankfully slid into the warm car at the curb.

"How did it go, honey?" asked Vera with a wide smile. Her blonde hair was pulled back and pinned in a knot at the nape of her neck. She looked young and pretty to Libby, not hard and worldly the way Mother always looked. She smelled like the roses that she grew in the backyard. Mother's perfume had made her sick to her stomach.

"Rachael said to practice more. She said my first recital is in November."

"Does that worry you?" Vera pulled away from the curb and drove down the street, then turned onto the highway toward home.

"It doesn't worry me, Mom. I just wonder if. . . ." Her voice trailed away.

"Wonder what?" Vera looked over at her and lifted her eyebrow.

"Will I be a Johnson by then?" She waited without breathing.

"I don't know. I hope so. Toby's adoption

went through fast and there's no reason that yours won't, too."

Libby sighed in relief and leaned back, holding her arm carefully against her.

"How about going for a hamburger for lunch, Elizabeth?"

Libby was ready to agree when she remembered April and May waiting for her. "I want to get right home, Mom."

"Are you sick? I've never had you turn down a burger, fries, and a chocolate shake before." Vera laughed, but Libby caught the concerned look she threw her.

"I'm all right, Mom. I want to work a while with Snowball and do some other things." Like feeding the Brakie twins!

Oh, what was she going to do about April and May?

Three
A big decision

Libby flicked on the barn light and quickly shut the door, leaving Rex outdoors whining to be let in. "Go away, Rex," she said sharply.

Taking a deep breath Libby walked down the aisle to the back of the barn where the bales of hay were stored. Snowball nickered. The smell of the food in the bag she carried almost overpowered the pungent odor of the barn.

"April. May. I brought you something to eat." Libby stopped beside the bales of hay and waited, her heart suddenly racing. Maybe they'd left already. Maybe they'd thought she wouldn't help them. It might be better that way. They could talk to Mrs. Blevins and ask for other foster parents.

Libby turned to go, then decided she'd better call once more. "April. May." Her voice was sharp and impatient and she wished with all her might that they would be gone. "April! May!"

Two heads popped up from behind the hay. April smiled hesitantly and May rubbed sleep from her eyes.

"I brought food," said Libby as she sat the bag of food on the hay. "I thought you'd gone."

She watched the girls dig into the sloppy joes. Libby waited impatiently while the girls wolfed down the food, then drank the milk she'd poured into two covered plastic glasses. Susan had almost caught her fixing the food, but she'd only been looking for a pencil and had left the kitchen as soon as she'd found one.

Red juice dripped down May's chin and she rubbed it with the back of her hand. "We were hungry," she said finally. "We were very hungry."

"Will you help us, Libby?" April's eyes were sharp as she turned to Libby.

Libby bent to pick up a gray barn cat that rubbed around her legs. Absently she stroked his dusty fur and he purred loudly.

"Are you going to help us, Libby?" asked May sharply, her face gray.

Libby licked her dry lips and hugged the cat tighter. "I thought about it a lot, girls. Honest. I can't do it. I can't take a chance of messing up my life. I want this family to adopt me. They love me! I love them."

"Won't you help us?" cried May as tears filled her eyes, then rushed down her cheeks, leaving stains on her dirty face.

"Can't you understand?" Libby's voice rose
and she had to force it back down in case
someone was in the yard and heard her. "I
can't do anything! Do you really think the
Johnsons would take you in just because I asked
them to? Do you think the family you were
staying with will give you up? Go back to them
and tell them you're sorry for running away and
you won't do it again." The cat squirmed in her
arms and she released him. He jumped to the
floor and streaked out of sight into another
stall. "I'm sorry, April. I'm sorry, May." She
wanted to run away at the looks in their eyes.

April grabbed Libby's arm and she cried out
with pain until finally April released her.
"Libby! Libby, it's Morris Stern! Do you really
mean you'll send us back to him?"

"I would rather die," whispered May
fiercely, holding her green jacket tightly
around her thin body. "Morris Stern, Libby!"

The name bounced around inside her head
until she wanted to scream. She backed away,
her face white, her eyes wide. "I don't know
him."

May stepped toward her, hay clinging to her
jeans and jacket. "You know him, Libby. You
wish you didn't, but you do."

Libby numbly shook her head. "No," she
whispered. "No!"

"Miss Miller got you away from him, Libby.
You told us all about it. Miss Miller couldn't

prove he'd done anything to you, but you know what he tried." May's eyes blazed as she clamped her hands on Libby's shoulders. "Morris Stern! He touched me, Libby. He touched me all over just the way he did to you, only Mrs. Blevins won't believe me and won't let us leave them."

"He tried with me, Libby," said April sharply. "But I kicked him and bit him and he left me alone."

Libby's legs gave way and she sank to the floor, her back tight against Jack's stall. She covered her face with her hands as wave after wave of shame broke over her. She would not remember Morris Stern! She dare not! She would think of Miss Miller taking her from that home and finding another home for her. She would remember the day Miss Miller had brought her to the Johnson farm. She had not wanted to come, but soon she'd found that she was wanted. They had said they'd prayed her into the family. They believed in praying. She had learned to love Jesus. He was with her always, helping her, loving her.

Finally Libby lifted her head. She saw the concern on the girls' faces as she slowly stood up. "I will help you. I will hide you until I know how I can help you."

Tears spilled down May's cheeks again and April knuckled her eyes, then smiled.

"We weren't able to bring any clothes with us," said April, looking down at her dirty

26

jeans. "We haven't had a bath since we left two days ago."

"I'll get you to the house and hide you in my room. You can take showers when I do." A doubt about getting the girls into the house tried to push its way in, but Libby refused to allow it to stay. She would find a way.

"Elizabeth!"

Libby jumped, ready to tell the girls to hide before Ben found her in the barn, but they were already diving out of sight.

"What are you doing, Elizabeth?" Ben stood in the open barn door. The sun shone on his red hair, making it brighter. His blue jacket made his hazel eyes look almost green. "I've been looking all over for you."

She hurried toward Ben, wondering anxiously if she should tell him about the twins. If he knew, would he help? She could not take the chance. He might think it was wrong to hide the girls.

"Why do you want me?" she asked as she turned off the light and closed the door. She stood beside him in the barnyard. He was a little taller than she was and just as thin. Chuck called them his two string-beans.

"I wanted you as my partner in Ping-Pong. Susan and Kevin want to see if they can beat us." He laughed and she liked the sound of it. "They sure don't like to lose."

"Neither do we." She walked along beside him and tried to act as cheerful as he expected her to be. "We beat them a lot but they beat us a few times, too."

On the back porch she started to pull off her jacket, then stopped as pain shot through her arm. "I forgot, Ben. I have something important to do. I can't play with you."

He frowned. "What's wrong?"

"I just can't play with you. Maybe tomorrow afternoon."

He begged her and Libby wanted to give in, but she couldn't because of her arm. Finally he walked away in a huff and she was afraid he'd be mad for a long time.

Slowly Libby pulled off her jacket and hung it up with her left hand. How much longer would her arm hurt like this?

Piano music drifted from the family room. Libby stood quietly, listening to Vera play. Libby leaned against Chuck's red plaid farm coat with a sigh. If her arm stayed the way it was, she'd never learn to play as well as Vera.

"It will be just fine," she whispered fiercely. "I know it will!"

She looked out the porch window toward the horse barn. Right now she had more important things to think about. She had to find a way to smuggle two girls into the house and up to her bedroom. Oh, what had she gotten herself into this time?

Four
Trouble

Libby held the telephone receiver tightly
against her ear. "Answer your phone, Adam,"
she whispered urgently. She didn't want
Grandma Feuder or Adam's parents to answer.

As Adam answered, Libby sank in relief to
the kitchen chair next to the phone. "Adam, I
need your help."

"Sure. What?"

"I need a few minutes to myself. Could you
invite the others down for a while this
afternoon? Is Grandma there? Could you ask
Vera to come too?"

From the silence on the other end Libby
knew Adam was trying to think ahead of her to
figure out why she was going to need time
alone.

"What are you up to this time, Elizabeth?"
He sounded very suspicious and Libby forced a
laugh.

"Will you do it for me, Adam? Please?"

"First tell me what you're up to."

"I can't." She wanted to tell somebody, but she couldn't. Adam would probably keep her secret, but she couldn't take a chance. "Please, Adam."

He sighed and she knew he would do it. He had been her friend ever since she'd taken care of Teddy, the big brown teddy bear, for Grandma Feuder. Teddy was sitting on her bed beside her toy dog Pinky right now. She would keep him forever!

Several minutes later Vera found Libby in the family room. "Are you sure you want to stay here while we go to Feuders, Elizabeth? We won't be long. You can practice when we get back."

"I want to stay home, Mom." She stood with her back to the burning logs in the fireplace. She smiled and Vera kissed her flushed cheek, telling her she'd see her later and to call if she needed them home for any reason.

When the door closed behind them Libby sighed in relief. Grandma Feuder lived down the road with her great-grandson Adam. She wasn't really related to Libby or the Johnsons, but everyone called her Grandma.

Finally Libby rushed to the barn with Rex at her heels. She called to the twins and hurried them from the barn and into the house. Had anyone seen them?

"Oh, it's warm in here!" cried April with a laugh. "I've been cold for so long I forgot what it felt like to be warm." She sneezed, then sneezed again.

"I brought the bag of garbage in from our lunch," said May, holding up the bag.

"Come into the kitchen and have something to eat before you go upstairs. I won't be able to get food to you after supper." Libby's legs trembled as she led the way to the kitchen. How could she get by with this? With all the people who lived in this house, someone would see the twins. If it were summer she could have left them in one of the barns.

"What a house!" cried April, looking around the kitchen with wide brown eyes. "I see why you like living here. Me and May would like this place."

"Do you have a bedroom of your own, Libby?" asked May as she poured herself a glass of milk.

Libby told them about her red, dark pink, and pink bedroom and about the big pink dog that Susan had given her because she was so excited about having a sister.

"What's Susan like?" asked April as she sat at the kitchen table. She bit into her peanut butter and jelly sandwich as Libby sat down across from her.

Libby smiled and shrugged. "Susan is twelve, the same as we are."

"We're thirteen now," said May, sitting

down with a large sandwich in her hands.

"I'll be thirteen February 14th," said Libby, remembering all the times she was teased for being a Valentine sweetheart. "Susan is a nice sister to have. She's short and cute and has long red-gold hair. She gets mad at me sometimes."

Libby hurried the girls with their snack, then took them upstairs to her room. "If you hurry, you can both take showers while I find clean clothes for you." Her hands shook as she rummaged through her drawer for clean clothes. What if the family came back sooner than she thought they would? "Please, girls, hurry with your showers."

April sneezed and pressed her hand against her head. "Do you have an aspirin, Libby?"

"Look in the medicine cabinet, April. Just hurry!" Libby pushed the clean clothes into the girls' arms, then watched them walk down the carpeted hallway. Quickly she picked up their jackets and shoes and pushed them behind a box in her closet.

"What am I doing?" she whispered in agony. "Oh, dear! What am I doing?"

Slowly she walked to her desk and rubbed her finger across the shiny top of the puzzle box that her real dad had sent her. He was dead now but she had been able to forgive him for deserting her when she was three. Jesus had helped her forgive and love him.

Libby stiffened. Had the door downstairs

opened and closed? Was anyone home? She waited tensely, listening with her head cocked, her left arm supporting her sore right arm.

The grandfather clock in the downstairs hall bonged four and Libby jumped nervously. A car drove past on the road, then all was quiet except for the sound of running water in the bathroom. When the water stopped Libby only heard her own breathing.

Libby sank to the large red hassock and gently rocked backward and forward. What if Vera and Chuck learned about April and May and got so angry with her that they wouldn't want to adopt her? It wasn't too late for them to change their minds. They could call Ms. Kremeen to come and get her and find another foster home for her. Ms. Kremeen would love to get her away from this Christian home. The social worker had often said that she didn't like all the religious teaching Libby was getting from the Johnsons.

Just then April and May walked in, carrying their dirty clothes with them. Both girls had towels wrapped around their heads. Libby's clothes fit them as well as their own. April had on Libby's yellow sweatshirt and blue jeans and May was dressed in a red sweatshirt and blue jeans. Their feet were bare.

"I'm clean!" cried May, dropping her clothes and holding up her hands. "I'm clean again!"

"Not so loud," said Libby with a frown. "What if someone heard you?"

"Is someone here besides us?" asked April, looking around in alarm.

"No," said Libby sharply. "But you will have to get used to the idea of being quiet. I could get in bad trouble if anyone found you here."

"We're already in bad trouble," said April sharply.

Libby flushed. "I know you are. You stay in my room while I clean up the bathroom and kitchen. Lock the door. I'll take the key and let myself in when I come up later. But hide when you hear it because someone might be with me."

Just as she reached the door May said, "Libby." She turned around. "Libby, thanks. You saved my life."

"You did, Libby," said April. "Thanks."

Libby nodded, then rushed from the room before she burst into tears. Why couldn't April and May find a good home? Why didn't Mrs. Blevins hunt until she found a family like the Johnson family? Why couldn't all the foster kids find Christian homes with people who really loved them and helped them? Oh, she had a lot to be thankful for!

And how was she repaying her new family? She was bringing them trouble! She would have to ask April and May to leave Sunday while they were in church. Mrs. Blevins would believe them if they insisted that they wanted another foster family.

Libby worked fast in the bathroom, then

rushed down to the kitchen. She remembered how Mrs. Blevins had tried to take baby Amy away from Lisa Parr. Mrs. Blevins wouldn't believe that Lisa could take care of her baby.

Libby leaned against the sink as she washed out the dirty glasses. Mrs. Blevins wouldn't help April and May. She would force them to live with Morris and Evelyn Stern no matter what May told her.

Tears stung Libby's eyes and she bit the inside of her lower lip. She couldn't send the twins back to that family. She would face whatever trouble came! The Johnsons would not let her down.

Five
More
pain

"I'd still like to know who used my shampoo," muttered Susan to Libby as they carried dirty dinner dishes into the kitchen.

"You know Mom said to drop the subject, Susan." Libby could barely concentrate on what Susan was saying. Her arm was hurting again from carrying the pile of dessert plates. She wanted to get Susan's mind off the missing shampoo but her brain wouldn't work fast enough.

"Who would use my shampoo? Who would use Kevin's hairbrush? I think something funny is going on." Susan piled the dishes in the dishwasher with a thoughtful frown. "I think we should investigate this. What do you think, Libby?"

Libby pressed her sore arm against herself. "What's to investigate? We have better things to do." What if Susan started snooping around? What if she found the twins upstairs? Had Vera missed the food they'd eaten while the family was at church?

"Oh, Libby! You're no fun at all today! Go get the rest of the dishes off the table. At least Mom won't let you out of that."

Libby hurried to the dining room. She knew Susan was upset because Vera had said that Libby could stay in bed a little longer if she really didn't feel well and Susan would do her chores. And she hadn't felt well. The twins had kept her whispering long past bedtime and during the night she'd had a nightmare that she wouldn't let herself remember. Her arm had been very painful when she'd dressed in her orange and brown dress. April had had to help her with the zipper.

Impatiently Libby pushed aside her thoughts and carried the dishes to the kitchen, making several trips so that her arm wouldn't ache too much. She reached for the last item on the table, Vera's favorite white ironstone platter that had held the roast.

"How's my girl?"

Libby jumped, then looked over her shoulder at Chuck. His red hair was mussed from running his fingers through it. He'd changed from his church clothes into a dark blue pullover shirt and faded jeans. "I thought you were taking a nap, Dad."

"I couldn't yet. I wanted to talk to you."

Her heart zoomed to her feet. Had he seen

the twins in her bedroom? "Have I done something wrong?" she asked in alarm.

Chuck laughed and turned her to him, resting his hands on her shoulders. "Why would you think that? I wanted to make sure you were feeling better, that's all."

"Oh."

"And are you?"

She shrugged. "I guess so." Her arm was still very painful, but she couldn't tell Chuck about it or he'd insist that she rest it and not play the piano. Maybe she'd have to stop lessons altogether.

He smiled and laugh lines spread from the corners of his eyes to his hairline. "You don't seem sure." The smile faded and he looked deep into her eyes. "Elizabeth, never be afraid to share your feelings with your mom and me. We want to help you with any problem you might have, large or small. We care about you, about what hurts you, what makes you happy. I can see that something is bothering you a great deal. Would you like to talk about it?"

Oh, she wanted to! She opened her mouth, then closed it and slowly shook her head. She had to find a way to help the twins without Chuck's help. He would not approve of helping runaways, of hiding them from Mrs. Blevins and the Sterns.

"What is it, Elizabeth?" His voice was low and tender and she wanted to rest her head on his broad shoulder and tell him everything.

"I have to take this platter to the kitchen," she said stiffly.

He kissed her cheek and smiled. "I'm ready to help with your problem anytime you're ready."

Tears stung her eyes as she bent her head and picked up the heavy platter. She knew he was watching her, giving her another chance to talk to him, but she turned toward the kitchen. The platter was heavy and the pain in her arm increased.

"What took you so long?" asked Susan sharply as she reached for the platter. She bumped Libby's sore arm and the platter fell into the sink, shattering loudly.

"Look what you made me do!" cried Libby, shoving Susan hard enough to send her staggering across the room to land against the kitchen table.

"I didn't do anything!" screamed Susan, her hands on her hips, her blue eyes blazing. "You're so touchy today that I can't even look at you without making you mad."

"I am not!"

"What trouble are you in this time, Libby?"

"Shut up!"

"Did you use my shampoo and Kevin's hairbrush?" Susan stepped closer and glared up into Libby's pale face. "Did you?"

"What if I did? What will you do to me? Who cares about your stupid shampoo and Kevin's brush? Who cares about anything?"

"You sure don't, do you? You're acting just like you did when you first moved here. You think you're such hot stuff just because you're an aid kid. You want everyone to feel sorry for you and baby you."

Libby slapped Susan's cheek, then cried out with pain just as Susan did.

"Girls! Girls, what's going on in here?" Vera stood in the doorway with a frown on her face and her hands at her waist. "I want this fighting stopped right now. Settle it and apologize to each other. I mean it!"

"*She* started it!" cried Susan, pointing at Libby. "She broke your good platter."

"What?" Vera rushed to the sink where Susan pointed and Libby wanted to run and hide. "Oh, Libby! That was my grandmother's platter. Oh, dear!"

"Susan bumped my arm," snapped Libby, lifting her pointed chin high. "It was her fault that it fell in the sink. Susan's just trying to make trouble for me because she's mad at me."

Slowly Vera lifted the broken pieces from the sink. She turned to Libby and Susan. "Girls, broken platters can be replaced. Broken relationships are much more important. Don't let anger keep you from being kind to each other and loving each other. This platter was important to me, but you both are much more important. Settle your argument and apologize."

Libby hung her head, fighting against the

tears. "Mom, I'm sorry about your platter."

"I am, too," said Susan barely above a whisper.

"I know. I'm going to put it in the garbage while you girls settle your problem."

Libby peeked at Susan to find her looking sheepishly at her. "Susan, I'm sorry. I shouldn't have pushed you or yelled at you."

"I'm sorry, Libby. I did bump your arm. I didn't think I bumped it that much."

"You didn't. It . . . it hurts a little. I bumped it yesterday." She wanted to take back the words but it was too late. Maybe Susan wouldn't ask about it.

"You didn't really use my shampoo, did you?"

"No."

"Then who did?"

"Can't we just drop it, Susan? I'm sick of talking about your shampoo. I have to shake out the tablecloth and slide the chairs up under the table." She turned away before Susan could read the guilt that she knew was in her eyes.

Just as she finished, Toby ran in to tell her that Adam was waiting outside to talk to her. "He said he couldn't come in because Grandma Feuder wants him right back home," said Toby breathlessly. "Do you and Adam have a secret?"

Libby stared in surprise at Toby. His freckles seemed to stand out more in his excitement. "Why do you ask that?"

"He said I couldn't hang around and listen to him talk to you." Toby grinned and Libby wrinkled her nose at him. She envied Toby because he'd already been adopted by the Johnsons. At first he'd been afraid of her because she'd looked a lot like his real sister who had been mean to him. Now they were good friends even though she was twelve and he was only nine.

"Go find Kevin and play with him," said Libby. "I'll go talk to Adam." She had a feeling that he wanted to find out why she'd needed the family out of the house yesterday.

Adam was standing beside his bike in the backyard and he smiled at Libby. The wind ruffled his brown hair. His brown eyes looked dark with excitement. She would have been very glad to see him if he had wanted something else.

"I can only stay a few minutes, Elizabeth. Tell me about yesterday. I tried to ask you between Sunday school and church but you wouldn't let me."

"I sure didn't want you asking me in front of anyone!" She looked across the yard as Goosy Poosy swayed back and forth in a lazy walk across the yard.

"Then it is a surprise!" He caught her hand and she cried out, making him drop it immediately. "What's wrong?"

"You hurt me."

He frowned. "How?"

"Oh, never mind. Just go home and mind your own business."

"Elizabeth, what's wrong with you? I thought we were friends. You said we were."

"We are, Adam. But right now I can't tell you anything about anything. Can't you understand?" She pressed her sore arm against herself and tried to think of something to say to make Adam feel better. "When I can tell you, I will."

He sighed and stuffed his hands into his jacket pockets. "I could tell Ben that you asked me to get all of you out of the house."

Her eyes widened in fear. "No!"

"Hey. I'm sorry, Elizabeth. Don't look like that. I was teasing. I wouldn't do that to you."

Her shoulders sagged in relief and she managed a shaky smile.

"I'd better get back home. Grandma's waiting." He lifted his hand and smiled, then turned his bike to go down the long driveway to the road. He looked over his shoulder and Libby could see him looking up at the upstairs windows. She froze with fear at the look on his face.

"Elizabeth, I just saw a girl looking out of your window. It wasn't Susan. Who was it, Elizabeth?"

She managed a shaky laugh. "You must be seeing things, Adam. Who would be in my room? Maybe it *was* Susan."

"I know what I saw." He walked his bike

44

toward her. "Are you in some kind of trouble?"

"Of course not!"

"Then why won't you tell me who I saw in your window?"

She stamped her foot. "You didn't see anybody!" The words almost caught in her throat. How could she lie? She was a Christian. She should not lie. "Adam, go home. I can't tell you anything."

"Tell me this. Was there a strange girl in your room just now?"

She bit her lip nervously. "Yes," she whispered hoarsely.

"When you can tell me about it, I'll help you all I can."

"Thank you. Please, don't tell anyone what you saw. Please!"

"I promise." He smiled and she managed to smile back. "See you on the bus in the morning. You will be going to school, won't you?"

She nodded.

"See you." He pedaled his bike away and she watched until he reached the road and turned toward his house. She had to trust him. She had no choice.

Slowly she walked back into the house, her head down, her sore arm carefully pressed against herself. How long could she keep April and May hidden? How long before everyone knew her secret?

Six
Snoopy
Susan

Libby sat cross-legged in the middle of her bed
with Pinky in her arms. She looked at April on
the large red hassock and May on the floor
with her back tight against the closet door.
Both girls were dressed in Libby's nightgowns.
"I hope you aren't too hungry," said Libby in a
low voice. She didn't want anyone who might
be walking past in the hall to hear her.

"I don't feel much like eating," said April
with her hand pressed against her forehead.
Her face was flushed red and her eyes had dark
circles around them.

"I'm glad you brought the cookies up." May
reached for another cookie from the bag sitting
on the floor.

"We have to think of a plan," said Libby
earnestly. "Mom is going to start noticing
missing food. And she'll wonder how I could
get so many clothes dirty in one day."

April sneezed and said she was cold. Libby tossed her a bathrobe and she slipped it on. May ate another cookie and said she'd had enough.

"I heard that Miss Miller married Luke Johnson," said April. "If she was still at Social Services she'd help us."

Libby nodded. "I didn't like her at first, but I was wrong about her. I call her Aunt Gwen."

May giggled. "Aunt Gwen! And you once spit in her face and called her all kinds of dirty names."

Libby looked down at her multicolored bedspread. "I'm different now, girls." She looked up at them and watched the questioning looks pass between them. "I'm a Christian now. I accepted Jesus as my personal Savior. I'm learning how to love others with Jesus' love."

The ticking of the clock on the desk seemed loud in the quiet room. Finally April said, "I knew you were different. May and I once stayed at a home where the folks were Christians. We thought about becoming Christians, but before we could we had to move. They couldn't afford to keep us."

"Sometimes I read my Bible that the Gideons gave me in the fifth grade." May twisted her long fingers together. "I can't always understand what I'm reading, but I read anyway."

"Chuck reads the Bible to the family each

evening, then we pray and sing and worship together. At first I didn't like it. I thought it was kind of crazy, but I like it now." Libby rubbed her hand on Pinky's soft fur. "I've had my prayers answered. I didn't think God would listen to me at first since I'm nothing but an aid kid, then Chuck said that God loved me just the way I am. Chuck said that I am important to God, that I am his creation." She laughed self-consciously. "Me! I'm important to God! It doesn't matter to him that I'm tall and skinny and ugly."

Just then the doorknob turned and Libby's voice died in her throat. Wildly she motioned for April and May to hide under her bed.

"Libby, open the door."

It was Susan and Libby wanted to scream at her to go to her own room and leave her alone. "What do you want, Susan?"

"I heard you talking to someone."

"Go to bed, Susan." Libby stood beside the closed door, her heart racing.

"I'm going to tell Dad if you don't let me in right now." She rattled the knob impatiently.

Quickly Libby looked to see that the girls were out of sight, then she unlocked the door and opened it. "Do you always have to snoop around to see what I'm doing, Susan?"

Susan sailed past Libby and looked around the room. "I heard you talking to someone, Libby. Who's in here? Is that why you've been acting so terrible since yesterday afternoon?"

49

"What do you mean?" Libby wanted to shove Susan out the door and lock it behind her.

"I know you didn't have a cassette playing, Libby. I know you were talking to someone." Susan opened the closet and peered inside.

Libby grabbed her arm. "What are you doing? Get out of here. I'll tell Dad if you don't!"

Susan's blue eyes flashed angrily. "And I'll tell him that you were talking to someone in here. I'll tell him you have a secret that he needs to know about."

"Oh, Susan! Please, please go to your room. Don't get involved."

Susan clasped her hands in front of herself. "I just want to know your secret, Libby. I won't tell. Honest, I won't. Please, tell me. I'm sorry for getting mad at you. I get so tired of having nothing exciting happen to me. Everything exciting happens to you. Please, please, please, tell me what's going on!"

Libby sighed and shook her head. "You wouldn't want to know."

Just then April sneezed and Susan dived under the bed with a gleeful laugh. "Come on out. I know you're under there."

Libby closed and locked her bedroom door, then told April to come out. Susan laughed, looking from Libby to April. Then May crawled out and Susan's mouth dropped open.

50

"Girls, this is my new sister Susan. She's all right. She won't tell on you."

"Twins?" whispered Susan in awe.

"I'm April and this is May."

Susan giggled. "April and May? Where's June and July?"

May rolled her eyes. "We're always asked that. Our mother had April just before midnight April 30 and me a few minutes after midnight on May 1. So she named us April and May."

"How did you get here?" asked Susan, pulling her bathrobe tightly around herself.

"Mostly we walked. Sometimes we rode. Not many people will pick up hitchhikers." April sank down on the edge of the bed and sneezed again. "Oh, my head!"

"Are you sick?" asked Susan in concern.

"Just a cold," said April. She pulled a hanky out of her pocket and blew her nose. "I'll be all right."

Susan sat in the chair beside the desk. "How did you girls know to come here?"

Libby looked nervously at the door while the twins told Susan their story. What if someone stopped outside her door just as Susan had done and heard them? "Girls, we have to get to bed. Dad will come up in a little while."

"Where will you sleep?" asked Susan with a frown.

"Under Libby's bed," said May.

"Libby, why didn't you put them in the guest room? Nobody would think of looking in there." Susan walked to the door. "Come on. We'll take them there now."

Libby caught her arm. "Wait. How do you know no one will look in there?"

Susan shrugged. "Who would? They can lock the door and if someone tried to open it, they could hide under the bed. Come on." She opened the door and peeked out.

Libby's heart raced. What if one of the boys walked out into the hallway just then? Her mouth felt dry as she followed Susan and the twins to the guest room. She let her breath out in a loud sigh once they were in the room.

"I'll like sleeping on a bed tonight," said April, pulling back the covers. "Now I can get warm and get rid of this cold."

"I hope you girls can stay out of sight tomorrow while we're in school," said Libby anxiously as the girls climbed in bed. "I don't know what Mom would do if she found you in the house."

"Mom is going to be gone all day tomorrow," said Susan, smiling. "You girls will have the house to yourselves. You can watch TV and eat when you're hungry, and everything."

May smiled. "Thanks. We'll make sure we clean up after ourselves."

"How long are you staying?" asked Susan.

"Not long," cut in Libby before April could

say what she'd started to say. "We're going to find a way to help them, then they'll leave."

May wrinkled her nose. "Or we'll ask the Johnson family to take us in. If they can stand Libby, they can stand us."

"Thanks," said Libby, but she laughed, knowing that May was teasing. "We'll see you right after school tomorrow. Stay out of the way of the boys. They won't keep a secret."

"It was nice to meet you, April and May," said Susan. "Sleep well." She smiled and Libby could tell she was loving every minute of what was happening.

Libby turned off the light and twisted the knob so that when she closed the door it was locked. She sighed in relief. The twins were taken care of for now.

"Why aren't you girls in bed?"

Libby almost jumped out of her skin at Ben's question. Had he seen them come from the guest room? Did he suspect something? "We're going to bed right now, Ben. Good night."

"Good night, Benjamin," said Susan with a giggle that made Libby want to shake her. Why couldn't she act normal? What if Ben questioned her and got the story out of her?

Ben shook his head. "Girls. Always giggling." He walked to his room and Libby breathed a sigh of relief.

"Stop that, Susan," whispered Libby. "Go to bed and forget this whole thing."

"I'm going to bed, but I won't forget any of

it. I can't wait to get home from school tomorrow afternoon to talk to them again."

Libby clenched her fists at her sides and started to snap at Susan, then stopped herself. "Good night, Susan. Don't talk in your sleep."

"You either. You probably have a lot more to say that I would." Susan walked into her room and closed the door.

Slowly Libby walked to her room and climbed into bed, thankfully pulling the covers up under her chin. Susan was right. She did have a lot of things that she could say in her sleep, but she wouldn't.

She turned on her side, then back on her back to keep from hurting her arm. If it wasn't better by tomorrow, she'd have a hard time holding a pencil and writing.

Just as she was drifting off to sleep her mind clicked back to Morris Stern and she could not lock it back in place. She moaned and covered her eyes but the picture was behind her eyelids and it refused to leave.

Suddenly she was with Morris Stern and he was holding her on his lap and hugging her and kissing her and she was liking it. She wanted a daddy to love her. But all at once it wasn't like a daddy's hold. He was touching her where he shouldn't have and for a minute she liked it, then she was embarrassed because she did, and she hated it. She tried to break free but he was too strong for her. She could smell his stale tobacco breath and feel the stubble of his

54

whiskers. She screamed but he easily silenced her with his mouth. Her stomach had churned and a bitter taste had filled her mouth. She thought she was going to get sick.

Then a door had slammed and she knew Evelyn Stern was home. He had pushed her away and told her to get into bed immediately. He had said if she ever told, she'd be sorry. But she'd told Miss Miller and Miss Miller had believed that something was very wrong and had taken her from that home.

Libby clutched Pinky tightly. She was safe. She was not with Morris Stern. Chuck Johnson was her dad. He didn't do what Morris Stern had done. Chuck loved her and treated her like a daughter.

Tears filled her eyes and streamed down her cheeks and the bed shook with her sobs. She would not think about Morris Stern again! She would not! She would push that memory back in place and lock it in her head and it would stay hidden forever!

Seven
Ms. Kremeen

"I finally figured it out, Elizabeth." Adam leaned close to Libby so that no one else on the school bus could hear him. "Somebody is blackmailing you. You have to keep quiet about that girl or you'll be killed in your sleep."

"Adam!" Libby didn't know whether to laugh or scold.

"Am I right?"

"No!" She frowned and stared out the window at the passing countryside. She had tried to avoid Adam, but he'd caught her on the bus and she didn't know how to stop him from asking questions.

He nudged her. "Are you in danger?"

She turned to him in exasperation. "Of course not! Will you just drop it? I said I'd tell you when I could. I can't yet."

He shifted his English and math books. "You know you're driving me crazy. Just try to tell me when you *can* tell me what's going on."

She leaned her head back wearily. "Tomorrow. The next day. At least by Saturday."

"I can't wait," he groaned, sliding lower in his seat. "You're turning me into an old man."

She knew what he meant. She felt like an old woman, at least forty. Vera had asked her if she was sure she felt well enough to go to school, but if she'd stayed home, Vera would've stayed with her. That would have been too nerve-wracking.

Libby smoothed her blue plaid skirt over her legs, then carefully laid her arm in her lap. She had been able to write in school as long as she hadn't gripped her pencil too tightly. At home she planned on practicing the piano no matter how much it hurt her arm. She had to keep her evening as normal as possible. And she'd have to keep Susan from popping wide open and telling everything. Several times in school Susan had whispered something about the twins and she had had to shush her. Susan had a very hard time keeping a secret.

Just then Susan nudged Libby from behind. "We're almost home," she hissed. "I can't wait."

Libby closed her eyes tightly. Why couldn't Susan keep quiet? Would Adam realize that Susan knew something?

"Libby. Libby, what's wrong?" asked Susan. "Aren't you excited? How can you just sit there. I feel like jumping up and down."

Libby jerked around with an angry frown. "What's so special about tonight? We're going to do our chores and homework same as usual."

Susan seemed to shrink inside herself and she mumbled something Libby couldn't catch.

"Why are you mad at her?" asked Adam sharply.

"Mind your own business," snapped Libby, then softly, "Adam, don't talk to me right now. I have too much on my mind."

"I can see that." He opened his English book and started reading. When the bus stopped at the Johnsons' driveway he looked up. "If you need any help, call me."

Tears stung Libby's eyes. "Thanks," she whispered. She stepped around his legs and followed the others out of the bus.

The warm sun shone down on her and she pulled off her jacket carefully, making sure she didn't twist or bump her right arm. The others ran on ahead, but Susan stayed with her, walking quietly beside her.

A small yellow car stood in the drive near the front door. Libby stopped, her heart racing. The car belonged to Ms. Kremeen!

Libby turned and glared at Susan. "You told! You told, and she's come to take me away and take the twins back to the Sterns. Mrs. Blevins is probably with Ms. Kremeen!"

"Libby!" Susan grabbed her arm and she winced in pain. "Libby, I did not tell anyone.

Ms. Kremeen is probably here for her usual visit to see about you."

"Why today?"

"I don't know. Let's find out."

Libby licked her dry lips. "Oh, what if Mom found the twins and called Ms. Kremeen? I thought you said Mom would be gone for the day."

"But she had to come home to be here when we got home. Calm down, Libby. You're getting upset for nothing." Susan's red-gold hair bounced around her slender shoulders and hung down her back over her yellow jacket. She was almost a head shorter than Libby.

Libby rubbed her hands down her skirt and nodded. "Maybe you're right. I'll talk to Ms. Kremeen and find out what she wants. I don't dare walk in there expecting her to know about the twins because if she doesn't know, she'd see I have a secret."

"I'll stay with you, Libby. If she does know about the twins, I'll try to get them out of the house and away so they won't have to go back to that terrible family."

Libby managed a smile. "Thanks, Susan."

She wrinkled her small nose. "I want to help."

Libby's legs felt almost too weak to carry her into the house. She smelled fresh-baked cookies and wondered how long Vera had been home.

"Elizabeth." Vera stood in the study door

60

and motioned for Libby to join her.

Slowly Libby walked to the study with Susan close behind her. A shiver ran down her back. The grandfather clock bonged four o'clock.

"Ms. Kremeen wants to talk to you, Elizabeth." Vera slipped her around Libby's shoulders. "Susan, run to the kitchen and have milk and cookies with your brothers."

Libby saw Susan hesitate, then turn away.

Inside the study Ms. Kremeen sat on a chair behind Chuck's large oak desk. She nodded to Libby and asked her to sit down.

Thankfully Libby did. She knew her legs wouldn't support her another minute. Vera sat beside her and crossed her legs, her red skirt falling over her knees. Libby could see Vera's hands clasped tightly together in her lap. What had they been talking about?

"How was school, Libby?" asked Ms. Kremeen in a brisk, businesslike voice. Her gray eyes looked cold and hard. Her long auburn hair waved attractively around her pretty face.

"It was all right," said Libby, dropping her eyes to the tips of her stockinged feet.

"I hear that you're having trouble in reading."

Libby's head shot up. "I am not!"

"Libby," warned Vera, patting Libby's leg. "Don't get upset."

"Who said I was having trouble in reading?" she asked, forcing her voice to sound normal, not angry or rebellious. Ms. Kremeen was trying to find a way to get her away from the Johnsons.

"I called the school and talked to Mrs. Kayle." Ms. Kremeen folded her hands on the desk and leaned forward. "She said you haven't been doing the work she assigns you."

Libby opened her mouth but Vera interrupted.

"Elizabeth is taking special tutoring to help her reading, Ms. Kremeen. She is doing the best she can. I work with her at home also. I don't think you have to worry about her reading."

Ms. Kremeen cleared her throat. Libby could see the anger boiling inside her. Did Vera know how angry she was? Libby peeked at Vera, then away. If she knew, she didn't care. Libby tried to relax, but couldn't.

"Mrs. Johnson, I would like to talk to Libby alone."

"No, Ms. Kremeen. I'm staying here with her. Whatever you have to say to her, I want to hear."

Libby hid a smile. She knew it had been hard for Vera to say that. Chuck would have said it without any problem, but Vera wasn't as brave as Chuck.

"I must insist, Mrs. Johnson." Ms. Kremeen stood up, her fists knotted tightly at her sides, her head high. She was dressed in gray pants and jacket with a white tailored blouse. Libby thought she was going to explode.

Vera leaned back with a smile. "Insist away, Ms. Kremeen. I am staying. I know that you don't approve of Libby living with us because of our belief in God. I know that you want to get her away from us before the judge can rule in favor of our adopting her, but nothing you can say will stop it from happening. Elizabeth is ours."

Libby watched the struggle Ms. Kremeen was having with herself. What would happen if she ever lost her poise and control?

Finally Ms. Kremeen sat down. "Libby, I want to know again if you want to stay here."

"I do."

"I have a family in the city who would very much like to have you live with them."

"I'm staying here." Libby's heart raced and she was glad when Vera's hand closed over hers.

"This family has only one daughter," continued Ms. Kremeen in an even voice. "They could give you more time and advantages than the Johnsons can with four children—five counting you."

Libby bit back a giggle as she thought of April and May hiding upstairs. The family had seven children, but only she and Susan knew it. Oh, she was glad neither Ms. Kremeen nor Vera had discovered them!

"Elizabeth is going to stay with us, Ms. Kremeen. We prayed her into this family, and she is going to stay. I will work harder with her on her reading and on whatever else she needs help with. You don't have to worry about her at all."

Ms. Kremeen opened her case and pulled out a folder. "I will drop this discussion for now. I am not giving up, Mrs. Johnson. I am only pulling back." She opened the folder and looked at it, then lifted her cold, gray eyes to Libby.

Libby squirmed uncomfortably.

"Mrs. Blevins told me that you once lived with the Mason family when April and May Brakie lived there."

Libby sat very still and forced the panic away. She knew Ms. Kremeen's sharp eyes wouldn't miss a flicker of her eyelash. She nodded.

"The twins have run away again. Do you know anything about them?"

"How can she?" asked Vera sharply. "Libby has been here all the time except when she's in school. How can she help you find two runaway girls?"

"We're asking everyone who knew them," said Ms. Kremeen impatiently. "I told Mrs. Blevins I would ask Libby."

Libby did not move. She would not answer unless Ms. Kremeen asked again.

Ms. Kremeen stuffed the folder back into her case and stood up. "I had some business to discuss in private with Libby, but since I'm not allowed to, I'll leave."

Libby was too weak to move.

"Ms. Kremeen, we will not allow you to upset Elizabeth. We know that you wanted her back with her real mother. We know that you will try anything to get her away from us, but you will not succeed. She belongs to us!" Vera held her head high. Her blonde hair curled around her head and hung down onto her slender shoulders. Libby could smell her perfume as she walked to the study door with Ms. Kremeen.

Libby sat still for a long time, then finally pushed herself out of the chair. A smile spread across her face and lit up her hazel eyes. "Thank you, Jesus. Thank you for this wonderful family."

Eight
Double trouble

Libby wanted to grab Toby and shake the freckles off his face. She scowled down at him angrily. "I can't do your chores, Toby! I can't!"

"But I want to watch the 'After-School Special'!" He looked as if he would burst into tears. "You help Kevin and Ben and Susan whenever they ask you. Why won't you help me? Do you hate me because the Johnsons already adopted me and not you?"

"Leave me alone, Toby." She walked toward the cow barn where Ben was milking. She had three calves to feed. If she did her chores, Toby's chores, and practiced her piano she knew her arm would start hurting so much that someone would notice.

"I bet you won't because of the secret you have in your room," shouted Toby and Libby whirled around in fear.

"What secret?" she whispered hoarsely. She

had been very careful when she'd gone to her room to change after Ms. Kremeen left. She had talked in whispers to April and May. They had said the day had gone just great. May had said that once the phone had almost rung off the hook and she'd had to slap her hand to keep from answering. April had said she'd slept most of the day. She hadn't been able to eat anything but May had said she made up for it.

Toby made a face. "I know you have a secret. I heard Susan talking about it. Kevin knows you have a secret and Ben knows it and if you don't do my chores for me, I'll tell Mom."

"You go right ahead and tell! And when Mom doesn't do anything about it, you sit in the corner and pout and suck your thumb!" Libby watched his face turn as red as his hair. He was trying very hard to stop sucking his thumb.

"I hate you, Libby! I hope you never get adopted into this family! I hope you have to go live with the meanest family in the whole world!" He spun around and ran across the yard to Kevin at the chicken house.

Libby slowly walked to the barn. After the Johnsons learned about April and May, would they send her away? What if she had to live with Morris and Evelyn Stern? She moaned in pain and shook her head. That could not happen to her! But she could not take a chance on Chuck or Vera learning about the twins.

Tonight they would have to leave after everyone was in bed. No matter what! Where would they go? What if they starved to death or worse because she wouldn't help them when they needed her?

She walked into the barn, her head down, tears stinging her eyes. Toby would stay mad at her forever. She couldn't do anything about it. Before long maybe everyone in the whole world would be mad at her.

"Here's the milk, Elizabeth."

Libby looked up with a start as Ben held out the pail of foaming milk.

"What's wrong?" asked Ben as she quickly put the milk down on the concrete floor.

"It's heavy." She wanted to rub her arm but she knew Ben would want to know why.

"I'll help you pour it in the calves' buckets." He smiled and the pain around her heart eased a little. Ben was always very patient with her. He'd taught her to ride a horse when she'd first come to the farm. He'd helped her learn to do outdoor chores when she'd been afraid to try because she'd never lived in the country before.

She watched as he divided the milk equally between the three buckets. Steam rose from the milk and Libby wrinkled her nose at the smell. How could the calves drink warm milk without cocoa mix in it?

Libby carried the buckets one at a time to the large stall where the calves were impatiently waiting. She leaned against the wooden gate across the stall and watched as the calves drank the milk, butting against the buckets as they finished. Quickly she pulled the buckets away from them and carried them to the faucet and rinsed them clean. A cat rubbed against her leg as she stood the buckets upside down on the shelf made for them.

She turned around to find Ben watching her with a puzzled frown. Her heart skipped a beat and before she could stop herself she flushed guiltily.

"Elizabeth, you haven't been yourself since Saturday. Can't you tell me what's wrong?" He walked toward her and she pressed her thin lips tightly together. It was going to be hard to keep her secret from Ben.

"I see that stubborn look on your face, Elizabeth. I won't force you to tell me, but I can't help you if I don't know your problem."

She turned away, her eyes wide to keep the tears from falling. Oh, she wanted to tell him! She wanted him to help her!

"Has Brenda Wilkens been causing more trouble for you?"

Libby shook her head.

"I didn't think so, since she's a Christian now. Have you noticed how different she is?"

Libby nodded. She had to get away from Ben before she told everything about the twins and her arm and the Sterns. "I'm going to the house, Ben," she said in as normal a voice as she could.

She walked to the barn door, waiting for him to call her back, hoping that he might force her to tell him what was bothering her. Outside the door she lifted her face to the evening breeze and breathed in deeply.

Rex barked from where Kevin had tied him to his doghouse for the night. A horse neighed from inside the barn. It sounded like Apache Girl.

Libby squared her shoulders and walked to the house. She had to face the family at supper, help with the dishes, practice her piano, and then she'd be free to go to her room to talk to April and May. Was Susan with them now? Would she get overexcited and expose the twins?

Libby picked at her supper, causing Vera to ask her if she was feeling sick. She said she wasn't very hungry and thought that she might never be hungry again if she had to keep worrying about the twins.

By the time she walked to the family room to practice piano, her arm hurt badly enough to make her cry. She wanted to go to her room and lie down, but she forced herself to sit down and open her piano book. She had to practice! Rachael Avery had said that if ever she didn't keep up with her practicing, she couldn't continue as a student. Vera had said Rachael was one of the best teachers around, that Rachael would help her turn her dream into a reality.

Pain shot up Libby's arm as she pressed the keys. "I will not give up!" she muttered.

"Did you say something, honey?" asked Vera from the doorway. She was drying her hands with a dishtowel and a flowered apron was tied around her narrow waist.

"I was talking to myself," said Libby. She played the songs in the first book, then opened the second book. How long would her arm feel this way? Would she ever be without pain? Her hands froze on the keys. What if she could never play again? What if she ruined her arm by using it too much while it was hurt? She could not play another minute. Maybe tomorrow her arm wouldn't hurt and she could practice two hours.

Wearily she climbed the carpeted stairs, her hand sliding along the shiny banister. She stopped outside her closed bedroom door. She heard giggling and she looked quickly around in alarm. What if one of the boys heard the giggling? She turned the knob, her heart almost dropping to her feet. It was unlocked! How could they forget to lock it?

She rushed in, slamming the door shut behind her. Susan and May jumped from the bed, then sank back down.

"You scared me silly," said Susan.

"You forgot to lock the door," snapped Libby.

"Sorry," said May. "We came in here to talk. April wanted to take a nap. I don't think she feels very well."

"Neither do I!" Libby plopped down on the chair at her desk. "I can't wait until you girls get out of here away from me."

May picked up Teddy and rubbed his furry arm. "Me and April were making plans today. We could leave the state and live on our own."

"You can't do that!" cried Susan, shaking her head until her pony tails bobbed hard.

May sighed unhappily. "Libby, you've been good to us. I wish we could stay here in this family, but I don't think they can keep us. They don't need two more girls. We've decided to leave when we can, tomorrow after you go to school."

Libby sagged back in her chair, then sat up straight. "But how can you live on your own?" She remembered the terrible stories she'd heard of girls on their own. She didn't want anything bad to happen to April and May.

Susan jumped off the bed. "I think we should tell Dad. He'll know what to do. I think we should ask him to find a home for April and May." She turned toward the door but May caught her arm.

"You can't! Your dad would turn us in. He wouldn't believe us about Morris Stern. I couldn't live if we had to go back there! I would kill myself first." Her brown eyes were wild with fear and her face was as white as the pillowcase on Libby's pillow.

"She won't tell," said Libby softly. "She's only trying to help." She turned to Susan. "You won't tell, will you?"

Susan stared at May, then slowly shook her head.

"I'm going back in with April," said May quietly. "We'll leave in the morning for sure."

Libby wanted to scream and cry and make someone change the terrible things in life. She wanted the twins to have a good home to live in with wonderful people to love them and take care of them. Slowly she opened the door and peeked out. She motioned for May to follow her. What would she do if she came face to face with one of the boys or with Chuck or Vera? It was too scary to think about. Her heart raced as she hurried down the hall.

In relief she closed the guest room door, then walked with Susan and May to the bed where April lay. She looked thinner than the day before. She opened her eyes and tried to smile through her cracked lips.

Libby leaned against the bed, her hands on the fuzzy gold blanket. "How do you feel, April?"

"I'm all right." Her voice came out in a croak. "Did May tell you that we're leaving in the morning? We don't want to get you in

74

trouble. You got it made here and we don't want to mess it up for you."

"How can you leave?" asked Susan in alarm. "You're sick. You can't leave while you're sick."

"I'll be all right in the morning." She tried to smile and failed.

Just then the doorknob made a noise as it slowly turned. May dove under the bed but April couldn't move. Libby dashed across the room and grabbed for the door to slam it shut.

Toby slipped into the room and looked around with wide eyes. "I knew you had a secret!"

"Get out of here, Toby!" cried Susan angrily. "You get out right now!"

Libby caught at his arm but he jerked away and ran to the bed. "I know you. You're April Brakie. My sister Janis once stayed in a home with you and your sister."

May climbed out from under the bed. "Hi, Toby. We heard you were adopted."

"You won't tell, will you, Toby?" asked Libby breathlessly. She nervously rubbed her hands down her jeans.

Toby walked to the door and opened it. "Yes, I'll tell!" He slammed the door and Libby could hear him running down the hall.

She stared at Susan and the twins, her heart racing wildly.

Nine
Tattletale
Toby

With a cry Libby jerked open the bedroom
door and leaped into the hallway just in time to
see Toby disappear into Ben's room at the head
of the stairs. Susan pushed against her but she
told her to stay with the twins and keep them
out of sight.

Supper smells still lingered in the air as
Libby raced to Ben's room. Oh, no, now
she'd never be adopted! She'd probably end up
living with the Sterns along with April and
May.

Outside the bedroom door Libby could hear
Toby's voice loud with excitement. Libby's
chest rose and fell and her hand trembled as
she reached for the doorknob.

She jerked open the door and stepped
inside, closing the door with a sharp bang. She
leaned against it as Toby jumped behind Ben
and peeked out from behind him. Kevin stood

beside Ben's desk, his eyes wide behind his glasses. He stepped toward Libby, then stopped abruptly.

"Toby, you can't tell," said Libby in agitation. "You can't tell! You don't know what's going on. You'll hurt the girls. You'll hurt me!" She saw the triumph on his face and her heart sank. He was determined to tell because he wanted to hurt her.

"Do you really have two girls hidden in the other room?" asked Kevin in a hushed voice.

"She does!" cried Toby, nodding hard. "She sure does!"

"Toby!" snapped Ben, gripping his arm. "Let Elizabeth talk."

Toby jerked free, his eyes blazing. "Sure. Libby can talk all she wants. Libby can do anything! I don't care what you say. I'll tell Mom and Dad! And I'm telling them right now." He rushed toward the door, but Libby caught him and held him tightly. He squirmed and almost got away.

"Stop it, Toby," she said as she shook him. "The girls are leaving in the morning. There is no reason to tell. I was helping them, Toby. You can understand that, can't you? Remember how bad Janis was to you? You had to have help to get away from her—your own sister. April and May are in trouble and they need help." She saw his hesitation, then his firm decision that no matter what she said he

78

was going to tell. She looked across the room at Ben and silently begged him to help her with Toby.

"Don't tell, Toby," said Ben softly. "We'll help Elizabeth with those girls."

Toby stood quietly and Libby smiled in relief as she loosened her grip. He brought his arms up hard and jerked free, pushing her. She stumbled and fell against a tall chest, striking her sore arm. She cried out in pain, doubling up on the floor and sobbing in agony.

"Look what you did, Toby," cried Kevin as he knelt beside Libby.

"I don't care!" Toby crossed his arms and glared back at them.

"Where do you hurt?" asked Ben as he helped her to sit up. "Is it your arm?" He touched it and she cried out again, cradling it against her thin body.

"My arm's broken. I know it. I'll never play the piano again." She rocked back and forth, trying to ease the pain.

"I'm glad!" Toby stood beside her, glaring down at her. "I hope they have to cut it off!"

"Toby!" Kevin grabbed for Toby but he jumped back. "Can't you see she's hurt bad? Stop being mean."

"She doesn't like me so why should I like her?" Toby backed against the bed, his face white and his freckles standing out boldly.

Just then the door opened and Chuck and

Vera walked in. Libby wanted the floor to open up and swallow her.

"What is all this yelling?" asked Chuck sternly.

"We heard you clear down in the study," said Vera. "Have you boys hurt Elizabeth?"

"Toby knocked her against the chest and hurt her arm," said Kevin breathlessly. "It might be broken."

Chuck knelt beside Libby and carefully examined her arm. "It isn't broken, just bruised on the muscle right here." He pointed to the swollen place and Libby felt fresh tears run down her cheeks.

"It looks like you won't be able to use that arm for a few days, honey," said Vera. "I'll fix a sling so that it'll rest completely."

Chuck gripped Toby's shoulder. "We'll go to my study and have a talk, young man."

"No!" cried Libby, struggling to her feet.

"Why?" asked Chuck with a frown. "What is going on, Elizabeth?"

She moistened her dry lips and knuckled the tears from her eyes. "It was my fault. I was fighting with Toby. He didn't mean to hurt me. Honest, Dad."

"Ben, was it an accident?" asked Chuck, turning to Ben.

Ben nodded.

"Toby was going to tell on Libby," said Kevin. "And she tried to stop him and he pushed her."

80

"What was he going to tell?" asked Vera, looking from one to the other.

Libby silently pleaded with Toby not to tell on her. She saw by his face that he was hesitating. Ben's clock ticked loudly in the silence.

"Elizabeth. Toby. Both of you come with me to my study." Chuck walked to the door and waited for them. His white pullover fit snug against his muscled chest and arms.

"I won't let you beat me!" cried Toby, hanging back in fear.

"Toby, have I beat you since you've come to live with us? Has Vera beat you?" Chuck stood with his hands lightly on his narrow hips.

Toby hesitated, then shook his head.

"I will never beat you, Toby. Vera will never beat you. But I do insist on the truth from you. I insist on right behavior or I'll punish you the same as I punish the other children in this family."

Libby walked toward the door, her head down. Soon everyone in the family would know what she'd done. She would never be Elizabeth Gail Johnson. She'd be Elizabeth Gail Dobbs forever. She'd be put in a juvenile home, or worse, in the Sterns' home. Her dream of becoming a concert pianist was gone forever! April and May had come to her for help and she'd failed them.

Vera touched her shoulder and Libby jumped. "Are you sick, honey? You look ready to collapse." Vera turned to Chuck. "Why don't we let Libby go to bed. You can talk to her in the morning."

"You'd let Libby off but not me!" cried Toby, his fists doubled at his sides. "You love her more than you do me. Everybody loves Libby more!"

"Let's talk in my study," said Chuck, slipping his arm around Toby but Toby jerked away and glared at Libby. She knew he was going to tell and there was no way she could stop him.

With a moan Libby leaned against the door frame, her head down, her sore arm against her body.

"I see that we have a real problem here," said Chuck softly. "I think that we need to talk right here, right now. Toby, you start."

Libby bit the inside of her bottom lip to keep from crying out. It was over. She could not stop Toby now. Chuck wouldn't let her.

Vera looked around with a frown. "Where's Susan? It isn't like her to miss out on anything." Before anyone could answer, Vera stepped to the door. "Susan. Come here, Susan." She waited, then called louder.

Libby heard a door open and close and she knew Vera had seen Susan come from the guest room.

Ben cleared his throat and Libby looked up at him to find him studying her in concern.

She dropped her gaze and stared at Chuck's stockinged feet.

Susan walked guiltily into the room. "Don't blame Libby, Dad. She was only trying to help them. They had to run away. I helped them, too."

Libby stifled a groan as she stared at Susan.

"What are you talking about, Susan?" asked Chuck with a frown.

Susan looked around helplessly. "Didn't Toby tell?"

"Not yet," said Vera. "But he's going to. It looks like this is a family affair, something we'll all want to hear about." She walked to the chair beside Ben's desk and sat down. Libby could tell that she was prepared for anything.

"I think we'd all better sit down," said Chuck as he sat on the edge of Ben's bed. He waited until the others were seated on the plaid carpet.

Libby smiled weakly at Susan beside her. Susan managed a weak smile in return.

"Toby, I think you should start," said Chuck, reaching over to tap Toby's red head.

Libby's heart dropped down. She forced herself to sit still. Running wouldn't do any good now.

"I don't want to tell," said Toby in a low, tight voice.

"You sure wanted to a while ago," snapped Ben.

"Since you want to talk, Ben, you tell me," said Chuck sternly.

Ben squirmed uncomfortably and shook his head.

"Toby, I want to hear what was so important that you had to hurt your sister," said Chuck in a voice that Libby knew meant business.

Toby's eyes seemed large in his face. "Libby is. . . . Libby is hiding. . . ." His voice trailed away.

Libby's heart pounded loudly enough that she was sure everyone could hear it. Her stomach cramped tightly. The pain in her arm seemed like nothing now.

"Continue, Toby," commanded Chuck.

"Don't make him, Dad!" cried Susan, twisting her fingers tightly together. "You don't want to know!"

"Oh, dear," said Vera.

"I insist on knowing," said Chuck. "Toby."

Libby wanted to die on the spot.

Toby's eyes filled with tears and slowly the tears slipped down his pale face. "April and May Brakie are here," he whispered.

"April and May Brakie?" asked Vera with a frown.

"Twins," said Susan. "Libby's helping them run away."

"Oh, dear," said Vera again.

"My, my," said Chuck.

Libby sat very still and stared at her knees.

Ten
Discovery

Libby pulled up her knees and pressed her face against them. She heard Ben's clock and her own breathing. Wasn't anyone going to say anything? She jumped as a hand closed over her shoulder.

"Look at me, Elizabeth."

Slowly she lifted her face and looked up at Chuck. He didn't look as if he hated her. Her hopes rose a little, then crashed back down. It might be out of his hands. Ms. Kremeen would love to hold this against her and place her in a different home.

"Tell me about April and May Brakie," said Chuck, sitting in front of her on the carpet.

Libby's hand brushed back a stray strand of hair. "They're twins. Twin girls. We lived together with the Mason family. They're thirteen." What more could she say? Chuck would not know about men like Morris Stern.

"Why did they run away?"

Libby closed her eyes, then opened them wide. "They want to live somewhere else. They heard I was being adopted and they came to find me to see if you would adopt them too."

"Why did they run away, Elizabeth?" Chuck caught her left hand and held it firmly.

Libby looked quickly around the room, then back at Chuck. "The man was mean to them."

"Did he beat them?"

She shivered. "No." Oh, she could not think about it, could not let herself remember again! "I told April and May I would help them find a place to live. I thought I could tell Mrs. Blevins to place them with a nice family, a family like this one."

"I think we should talk to the girls," said Vera, standing up. She tugged her gray sweater down over her black pants. A gold chain hung around her neck.

"I want to see them," said Kevin excitedly.

"Did they come Saturday?" asked Ben, a knowing look on his narrow face.

"Yes," said Susan. "Libby said they were hiding in the horse barn. She said she thought Marie Dobbs was hiding and waiting to grab her, then she found the girls."

"I can see you children think this is a great adventure," said Chuck, rubbing his red hair back, then letting it fall over his wide forehead. He looked at them and shook his head.

"I never have anything exciting happen to me," said Susan defiantly. "It was fun helping Libby hide them."

"I wondered what happened to the food in the refrigerator," said Vera. "And cookies seemed to disappear right before my eyes."

Chuck caught Vera's hand in his. "Let's go talk to Elizabeth's runaways. But I don't think they need all these listening ears and watching eyes at our first encounter."

Kevin groaned and Ben begged to go along. Toby asked what the fuss was about, since they were only two girls who looked alike. Susan looked as if she'd burst into tears. Chuck told Libby to lead the way.

Libby's legs felt like melting marshmallows as she walked ahead of Chuck and Vera to the guest room. It was already dark inside and she flicked on the light. May stared back at her with wide, fearful eyes. She had on Libby's jeans and a gold sweatshirt. Her hair was in two pony tails, one over each ear. April tried to push herself up in the bed but then she lay back down.

"Don't make us go back!" cried May in alarm as she stared from Chuck to Vera.

Chuck reached out to pat her arm but she cringed away from him. He dropped his hand at his side. "We came to talk to you."

Vera touched April's forehead. "How long have you had this bad cold?"

"A couple of days. I'm all right," said April

in a weak voice. "We're leaving in the morning."

Chuck shot Libby a look and she explained that the girls knew that they couldn't live off the Johnson family, that they were going out of the state.

Chuck raised his eyebrow, then shook his head. "Who is April and who is May?"

"I'm May." She pointed to the bed. "She's April. Are you going to call Mrs. Blevins tonight?"

Libby rubbed her arm to ease the pain. What would ease the pain in her heart, in the twins' hearts?

"When did April last eat?" asked Vera, looking from May to Libby.

Libby shrugged and May said she didn't know. "She hasn't been drinking anything," said May. "I told her she should."

"I can't," said April.

"You must have fluids," said Vera. "I'm going to get something for you right now." She hurried from the room, a worried frown on her pretty face.

Libby moved close to Chuck and looked up into his face. "You won't call Mrs. Blevins to get them tonight, will you?"

"Don't! Please, please don't!" cried May.

"Girls, I will call her to let her know that you're safe, but I'll ask her to leave you with me until tomorrow." He smiled. "Relax. We aren't in this alone. God is the head of this house. He guards our lives and our actions. He loves both of you girls and he wants what is best for you." He rested his hand on April's forehead and she tried to pull away. "Don't be afraid of me. I won't hurt you."

"He won't," whispered Libby.

"Are you sure?" asked May barely above a whisper, and Libby nodded.

Vera hurried into the room. "Here's a glass of orange juice. April, you must drink a little of it." She helped April drink, then set the glass on the nightstand beside the bed. "I want you to drink a little as often as you think of it."

"April, the Bible says that God really cares about our problems," said Chuck. "We'll pray for you, if you don't mind."

"All right," she whispered.

Chuck rested his hand on her forehead and she didn't move away. Libby caught May's hand and held it as she bowed her head.

"Heavenly Father, thank you for sending Jesus to us. We ask you, Lord, to take care of April's cold. We know that you want her to be well and strong. Help April to know that you love her and will help her get well. Help May to know you love her, too. Thank you that you are answering the girls' needs for a place to live. Thank you that they came to our Elizabeth for help, and that you are showing us how to help them the most."

When he finished praying, Libby felt a smile tug at her lips; she hadn't known she could smile. She saw the tension leave May's face. April drank another swallow of juice and dropped off to sleep.

Chuck smiled at May. "Jesus will take care of April. You don't have to worry about her."

May smiled hesitantly at Chuck, then backed away from him.

"May, when did you last eat?" asked Vera. "Come downstairs with me and I'll fix you something nutritious."

May hung back, her eyes on Chuck. "You won't let Mrs. Blevins take us tonight, will you?"

"No. I'll call Mr. Cinder and he can contact Mrs. Blevins. He will let you stay here."

"Thanks, Dad," said Libby. She wanted to hug him and tell him she loved him very much, but she followed May and Vera from the bedroom. She stopped in the hallway and waited while Susan introduced May to the boys.

Chuck slipped his arm around Libby's thin shoulders. "I'd like to talk to you in my study while May's eating," he said in a voice too low for the others to hear.

Libby's heart sank. She should have known that she wouldn't get out of it that easily.

"Where's April?" asked Kevin with a chuckle.

"She's asleep," said Vera. "Please don't disturb her. You can meet her in the morning." Her voice was firm and the boys knew they had to obey. They walked to their rooms and Susan followed May and Vera downstairs.

Libby walked with Chuck and he stopped her outside Toby's room. "We can't settle for the night until we have this problem solved between you and your brother."

Reluctantly Libby walked into Toby's room. He was lying on top of his covers sucking his thumb. He jumped up and quickly hid his hand behind his back.

"Toby, I know it's almost your bedtime," said Chuck. "I don't want you to go to sleep feeling bad toward your sister."

"She's not my sister!"

"Yes, she is." Chuck sat on the bed and pulled Toby close to him. "Son, we love you. We prayed you into our family. You are part of us. Elizabeth is part of us. What has happened to cause this trouble between the two of you?"

Libby stood quietly beside the dresser. She watched Toby's eyes fill with tears.

"Libby doesn't love me," he whispered.

"I do too!" cried Libby. "Why do you say I don't?"

His chin trembled. "You won't ever help me like you do the others. You wouldn't do my chores when I asked you and you wouldn't play a game with me and you yelled at me."

Libby flushed.

"Is that right?" asked Chuck.

She nodded. "I was thinking too much about the twins. I was scared and I'd hurt my

91

arm and I didn't know what to do." She walked to him. "I'm sorry, Toby. I won't yell at you again and I'll help you when you need help." She remembered the times when she hadn't been able to say she was sorry when she'd wanted to. Jesus was helping her.

"I'm sorry, too, Libby." Toby grinned self-consciously. "I didn't really want to get you in trouble."

"Elizabeth, because you couldn't trust enough to share your problems, Toby was hurt. And Toby, because you looked too much at your own hurt, you couldn't look past it and see if Elizabeth was acting the way she was for a reason. We're here to help and love each other. No one is alone. I want you both to remember that." Chuck kissed Toby and told him to get ready for bed.

Libby touched Toby's arm. "Good night, Toby."

"Good night, Libby." He smiled and she did, too.

Chuck tugged Libby's hair. "Let's get out of here so Toby can get to bed."

She walked with him down the hall to the stairs. What would he say to her when they were alone? He wouldn't break his word and force the twins to leave tonight, would he? He wouldn't call Mr. Cinder and tell him to come pick all of them up, including her—would he?

Eleven
A talk
in the study

Libby sank wearily to the sofa in the study. It seemed later than nine o'clock. She watched the door for Chuck. He'd gone to the kitchen to tell Susan and May good night. Was he in secret telling Vera that the first thing tomorrow the girl they'd prayed into their family would have to go?

Libby moaned and rocked gently back and forth, protecting her sore arm. Her dream was dead. She might as well get used to it. Why try to fool herself any longer? This whole life with the Johnsons, this whole way of living was a fake. God didn't love her. She wasn't important to him at all.

Tears stung her eyes and she defiantly brushed them away. When Chuck walked into the study, Libby glared at him, defying him to fool her a minute longer. She was past fooling. Nobody loved her and no one ever had!

"I can see by your face that we have some talking to do," said Chuck, standing before her.

She leaped up, protesting, "We don't have anything to talk about! Go right ahead and make me leave here. See if I care!"

"Elizabeth." His voice was soft and gentle and tugged at her heart. "Satan is a deceiver. He wants you to think bad thoughts about this family—that we don't care for you, that you're not wanted or loved. Just yesterday we read the Scripture that said we are to put down all vain imaginings and trust only in what God's Word says about things." He caught her hand and she allowed him to seat her on the sofa. He slipped his arm around her and pulled her close, his head on hers. "You belong to this family, Elizabeth. This family belongs to you. God gave us to each other. We prayed you here and here you'll stay. God loves you. I love you."

The words melted the ice that seemed to be around her heart and she leaned against him thankfully. How many times would he have to reassure her before she believed him?

"Elizabeth, your problems are our problems. You can trust us. You can trust me." He held her away and looked down into her face. "You've been worrying yourself sick because of April and May. I would have helped them, honey. Vera would have helped them. You are not alone! Please, please remember that."

"I'll try, Dad. I'm glad you don't hate me."

He tapped the end of her nose. "I love you. No matter what you do, my feelings will not change. My love doesn't change because one day you're good and one day you're bad. I love you with God's love. We are learning to love everyone with God's love. His love never changes."

She tried to understand what he was saying, but it was hard. In all her years she had never been loved. There were times when someone liked her for a while, then hated her when she got mad at the person or did something mean. She didn't know what to say to Chuck. What did he want her to say?

He smiled and sat back once again with his arm around her. "Can you tell me why the twins ran away from the family they were with?"

She stiffened and she knew he felt it. "They want a family who loves them."

He was quiet for a while and she could hear his heart beating. "Did you ever live with that family?"

She closed her eyes tightly. "Yes," she whispered.

"And did you run away?"

"Miss Miller came and got me after I called her."

"Why didn't you want to stay?"

She jerked away from him and jumped up, her chest rising and falling. "I don't remember!"

He caught her hand. "Yes, you do."

She shook her head hard. Her mouth was cotton dry. "No. No!"

"All right. All right, Elizabeth." He stood up and rested his hands on her shoulders. "I won't ask you again tonight. I can see you're very upset by whatever happened. Just remember what I've told you before." He tipped her chin up until she finally looked at him. "You can give those bad memories to Jesus to heal. Never push the memories back inside yourself and lock the door on them. When you remember something that hurts you, ask Jesus to heal the pain it brought you then and now."

"It . . . it hurts too much to even remember," she whispered hoarsely.

"No matter how much it hurts, it's better to let it out. Once Jesus takes care of it, it won't hurt you again."

"I won't remember, Dad. Don't make me."

He pulled her close and held her. She could smell his aftershave lotion. "Honey, I won't make you. Just remember that God knows everything about you. He knows what is bringing you pain. He wants to take care of it but he can't until you allow him to."

She slipped her arms around his waist and hugged him, then cried out in pain. "Oh, my arm!" She held it in front of her and rubbed it.

Chuck gently took it between his large hands. "Tonight we prayed for Jesus to heal April of her cold. We will do the same for your arm." He carefully touched the bruised area. "Father, please take care of Elizabeth's injured arm. Help the arm to heal quickly so that Elizabeth can use it normally. Thank you, Father, that you love us. We trust you always. We love you. In Jesus' name, Amen."

Just then the study door opened and Vera walked in. "Did you call Mr. Cinder yet, Chuck?"

He shook his head. "I'll do it right now. Elizabeth, you sit down again so you can listen to the call. I don't want you going to bed with a single worry on your mind." He smiled as he lifted the receiver to his ear. "Did May get off to bed all right?"

Vera nodded. "I know she'll sleep well after the soup I fed her. She was very hungry. She hadn't wanted to bother anyone for food." Vera sat beside Libby and patted her knee. "I'm so glad the twins came to you for help. What if they had gone somewhere where they would have been hurt, or worse?"

Libby smiled, glad that Vera had said that. Then her head snapped around as Chuck explained to Mr. Cinder about having the twins.

"No, I don't want Mrs. Blevins to pick them up tonight," said Chuck firmly. "You know you can trust me, Mr. Cinder. The girls refuse to return to the foster family they were with. I'd like you to investigate that family."

Libby shivered and Vera squeezed her hand.

"Are you sure that they are a good couple for foster children to live with?" Chuck frowned as he thoughtfully looked at Libby. She wanted to scream at Mr. Cinder and tell him that the Sterns were bad. "I know foster families are hard to find, Mr. Cinder. I also know that you want good homes for the children under your care. Mrs. Blevins could be mistaken about them." He hesitated and Libby's heart raced. "Mr. Cinder, why don't you leave the girls with us for a few days until you can check into this. I'll take full responsibility for them. They won't run away from us." He listened a while, then hung up with a satisfied smile.

Libby leaned back, weak with relief.

"I am believing God for the right family for the twins," said Vera softly. "God loves April and May. I know he has a family for them."

"I believe that with you," said Chuck. "How about it, Elizabeth, my girl?"

"I will believe that, too," she said with a smile. She jumped up. "I'm going to tell May about Mr. Cinder letting them stay a while. She'll be happy. I know she will."

"If she's asleep, tell her in the morning," said Vera. "Both girls need rest."

Libby kissed them both good night and

hurried upstairs. Just a short time before, she'd felt unhappy about everything. Now she knew everything was going to be just fine.

Susan stopped her outside her bedroom door. "Tell me, Libby. I can't get to sleep until I know!"

Libby laughed softly as they walked into Susan's room and closed the door. "The twins get to stay a few days while Mr. Cinder looks into the home they were in. I know he'll find them a better home."

Susan bounced around gleefully. "I can't wait to tell the twins."

"Come with me now and we'll tell them." Libby walked down the hall with Susan. "Mom said that if they're asleep not to bother them until morning. Oh, I hope they're awake!"

"Me, too." Susan giggled and her blue eyes sparkled with excitement. "I wish the twins could live here always. Then we'd have four girls and three boys."

Libby eased open the guest room door, glad that they didn't have to lock it tonight. She peeked in, then shook her head sadly. "They're asleep," she whispered as she pulled the door shut. "I'd like to wake them up and tell them."

"Let's do." Susan reached for the doorknob but Libby stopped her.

"We'll tell them in the morning, Susan." She yawned wide. "I'm going to bed. See you in the morning."

"Good night, Libby. I'm glad you didn't get in trouble with Mom and Dad."

"They love me, Susan," Libby said in awe.

"I know."

Libby flushed and ducked into her room. Susan poked her head into the still dark room.

"I love you, too, Libby. I'm glad you're my sister."

Libby wanted to hug her but she felt too shy. "I love you, Susan." Susan whispered good night again and left. Libby whirled around the room, her arms stretched wide.

Suddenly she stopped and dropped to her knees beside her bed. "Heavenly Father, I'm sorry that I thought you didn't love me. I know you do. I love you and I love this family you gave me. Thank you for helping me and helping the twins."

She prayed quietly for a while longer, then quickly slipped on her nightgown and climbed into bed. She smiled into the darkness. Was this really Elizabeth Gail Dobbs? She felt like a different girl than the one who had moved into the Johnson farm almost a year ago. How different would she be next year?

But what if she wasn't here next year?

Abruptly she pushed the thought aside. She would be! "Thank you, Father, that I will be here next year and the year after and I will be more like Jesus all the time."

With a contented smile Libby turned on her

side and closed her eyes. God would help find a home for the twins that was just as great as this home.

"In the morning I'll tell them," she whispered.

Twelve
April
and May

Libby sat up in bed with a start. Rain lashed against her window. The dim light from the hall cast dark shadows in her room. What had made her wake up? She frowned thoughtfully. Then the nightmare rushed back on her and she moaned in pain, covering her face with her hands.

Why had the nightmare started again? She had pushed Morris Stern to the back of her mind and had refused to think about him. In her dream, she had run from him, run until she was weak with exhaustion. Then he'd caught her and no matter how hard she had tried, she couldn't get away.

A bitter taste filled her mouth as she once again felt his hands all over her.

"I won't think about it!" she whispered urgently. "I won't!"

The bed shook with her shivers, then she

relaxed as she forced her mind to dwell on playing the piano for Rachael Avery.

Libby wiped the perspiration off her forehead. She needed a drink of water.

After her drink Libby stopped outside the guest room door. Did May ever have nightmares about Morris Stern? Libby rubbed her hands down her flannel nightgown. May probably had worse nightmares.

Slowly Libby pushed the half-opened door wide and stepped inside. She would not wait until morning to tell the twins that Chuck would help them and that they could stay here while Mr. Cinder investigated Morris Stern.

Libby walked to the side of the bed, then gaped in dismay. The bed was empty! The twins were gone! Libby's heart sank.

She flicked on the light and looked around the empty room, making sure to look under the bed in case they'd hidden. A piece of paper on the nightstand caught her eye. She picked it up and read, "Libby, thanks for helping us. We couldn't wait until morning. We will not go back to the Sterns." It was signed April and May.

How far could they go in the rain? When had they left? She looked at the clock. It was eleven-thirty. She had thought it was at least three or four in the morning. She hurried breathlessly to her room.

Quickly Libby tore off her nightgown and slipped on jeans and a sweatshirt. Where would she look first? Had they gone down the road hoping to hitch a ride? Oh, why hadn't she told them the good news before she'd gone to bed? It would have been better to wake them and tell them.

She rushed downstairs, then stopped, her hand on the newel post. Chuck had often said she should not solve her problems alone when he'd gladly help her. Should she call him? Was he already asleep? The rain was loud against the house. The twins were out in that rain right this minute. Chuck might be able to find them faster than she could.

Libby ran to Chuck and Vera's bedroom. She peeked in nervously. She could tell by the breathing that they were asleep. Should she wake Chuck? Oh, she had to!

She touched his arm and he jerked awake.

"Who is it?" he asked sleepily.

"Me. Libby."

He sat up. "What's wrong?"

"The twins are gone."

He reached for his jeans on a chair next to the bed. "Wait for me in the hall. I'll be right out."

She practically ran from the room, anxious to start looking for the girls.

Chuck hurried out of the bedroom, tugging a sweatshirt over his head. "Are they out of the house?"

"I only looked in the spare room, but they left a note saying that they couldn't wait until morning. They won't go back to the Sterns."

"Elizabeth, why won't you tell me about that man? I have all kinds of wild ideas, but I need to know the truth about him so that I can really help the girls."

Her eyes widened in fear and she backed away, bumping into the wall. "I can't tell!"

He studied her face, then slowly shook his head. "I won't make you. Let's find the girls." He led the way to the back porch, then stopped. "Elizabeth, God knows right where the twins are. Let's ask him to lead us to them immediately."

Libby nodded, once again thankful that she'd called Chuck to help her. His hand closed around hers and she bowed her head next to his as he prayed. Would she ever remember to ask God to help her the way Chuck and the others did? Usually she remembered only after she was really in trouble. Chuck had often said that they should depend on God to help them in the first place, before the trouble came.

Chuck handed Libby Ben's raincoat. "Slip this on over your jacket. That rain will be cold and uncomfortable."

"I wonder what time the girls left the house," said Libby as she pulled on a wide-brimmed rain hat.

"I checked on them about eleven, so they can't have got very far. I just wonder if they walked outdoors, then decided to sleep in the barn until the rain lets up."

"Do you think so?" asked Libby excitedly. "We could look in the horse barn where they first hid in the hay."

"Let's go." Chuck smiled as he reached for the doorknob.

The rain whipped against them as they ran to the barn. It sounded extra loud to Libby as it hit against her hat and coat. Without raingear the twins would be soaked to the skin before they reached the barn.

Thankfully Libby followed Chuck into the dry barn. He turned on the light and she blinked against the brightness.

Jack and Dan moved restlessly in their stalls. Libby remembered when she'd first seen the matched greys. She'd never seen such big horses in all of her life. At first she'd been frightened of them, then when she learned how gentle they were, she had lost her fear.

She could not think about the girls not being in the barn. It would be terrible if they'd already hitched a ride and were long gone.

Chuck touched her arm and motioned toward the hiding place in the hay. The girls were curled up together, sound asleep, their green jackets bright against the dull yellow hay.

Libby gripped her hands together as Chuck bent and gently shook the girls awake. They leaped up in fright. May started crying and April glared first at Libby, then at Chuck.

"We're leaving this place and you can't stop us!" April lifted her chin high, her eyes dark with anger.

"Girls, listen to me," said Chuck firmly. "I talked to Mr. Cinder tonight. He said you could stay here while he checks into Mr. Stern's actions. He doesn't know what he's looking for, he said, but he'll do what he can."

"And we can stay here?" asked May, dabbing at her tears.

"Yes," said Libby. "I told you Dad would take care of it."

April sank to a bale of hay and covered her face with her hands. May wiped her nose with the back of her hand. "You wouldn't lie to us, would you, Libby?" asked May.

"No." Libby smiled and touched May's arm. "Dad will make sure you get a nice home away from Morris Stern."

"Honest?"

April looked up. "Do you really trust Chuck, Libby?"

Libby looked quickly at Chuck and he smiled reassuringly. "I trust him. He won't let us down."

Chuck cleared his throat. "Not all men are like Morris Stern. You must know that." He took off his hat and shook off the rain. "I think you girls had better get back to the house and into bed. Unless you want to sleep here all

108

night." He laughed and Libby saw his eyes twinkle.

"It's too cold," said April, shivering. But she grinned, and there was a sparkle in her eyes.

Libby stared at her in surprise. "April! You're better!"

She gasped. "I forgot all about being sick!" She turned to Chuck. "My head doesn't hurt anymore. I don't feel as hot." April put her hand to her forehead. "I *am* better!"

He smiled. "April, Jesus is healing you just like we said he would. Jesus loves you, girls. He wants what is best for both of you."

May twisted the toe of her soggy tennis shoe in the loose hay. "Me and April once wanted to become Christians. I sure would like to now."

"Me too," said April quietly, tears sparkling in her eyes. "I love Jesus. He's helping me. He must love me."

"He helped us find you right away tonight," said Libby.

"Girls, we can pray right now," said Chuck. "Would you like to?"

Libby's eyes filled with tears as the girls nodded.

"Romans 10:9 and 10 says that if you confess with your mouth that Jesus is Lord and believe in your heart that God raised him from the dead, you will be saved." Chuck held his hands out to the twins. They hesitated, then each reached out to him. "Pray with me. Jesus, I

109

want you as my Savior and Lord. Forgive me of my sins and take them away. From this day forward I will live for you, Jesus. You are my Lord. I love you. My life is yours. I belong to you and you belong to me."

As they prayed Libby remembered the day she'd given herself to Jesus. It had been a wonderful day for her. She remembered praying with her former enemy Brenda Wilkens as she asked to become a Christian. Now she and Brenda were friends. Libby smiled and wiped tears from her eyes. Her friends were Christians now, too.

"Girls," said Chuck with a smile for April and May. "This is a very special night for you. You are not alone any longer. Jesus is with you, will always be with you. Read the Bible to learn more about Jesus. And as you do, you will become more like him. While you are here with us, we'll learn together along with Elizabeth."

Libby felt like dancing around the barn. What a perfect way to end this day!

"Let's go to the house," said Chuck. "We'll have some hot cocoa and get to bed."

Libby led the way from the barn, her heart singing with joy.

Thirteen
Morris and Evelyn Stern

Libby looked around the classroom. She smiled
at Susan, then looked down at her math book.
At least she didn't have trouble with math.
Susan did and Libby often helped her.

Libby doodled stars around her paper as she
thought about April and May. They'd been at
the Johnson farm almost a week. Already they
loved and trusted Vera. They were learning to
love and trust Chuck.

What had Mr. Cinder done about Morris
Stern? Had Mr. Cinder found a home for the
twins? Oh, it would be wonderful if they could
live with the Johnsons! Adam had been
surprised and excited to learn of the twins.

"Libby Dobbs, come to the office." The
voice crackled over the intercom, startling
Libby.

"You may be excused, Libby." The math
teacher smiled and nodded and Libby tried to

111

walk out of the room without letting everyone know how upset she felt. Her legs felt like rubber and she shivered as she walked down the quiet hall toward the office. She pulled her blue sweater tightly around herself and tried to believe that the call to the office was nothing that important.

Miss Richie looked up from behind the desk. "You have a visitor, Libby. He said it was very important to see you. Mr. Page said you could use his office."

"Thank you." Libby's mouth felt dry as she walked to the small office next to the main office. Her hand trembled as she turned the knob and pushed open the door.

The room seemed to spin as she looked up at the tall, good-looking man dressed in a gray business suit. He smiled but his blue eyes were ice cold. She tried to leave but he caught her arm and pulled her into the room and closed the door with an ominous snap.

"I had to talk to you, Libby."

Fear pricked her body as she stared silently at Morris Stern. His dark hair was combed neatly back from his suntanned face.

"You have nothing to fear from me," he said with a smile. "Shall we sit down and talk? Mr. Page said to take all the time we needed."

Libby's legs gave way and she dropped to a chair next to the small steel desk. She watched as Morris Stern sat in a chair across from her so that he could watch her face. She rubbed her corduroy pants, then pulled her sweater protectively around her. Why didn't someone come in and rescue her?

"Mr. Cinder talked to me a few days ago. He has the impression that I'm an unfit foster parent. I believe that you've been telling stories, Libby. Am I right?" He lifted a well-shaped eyebrow questioningly. "No matter. Mrs. Blevins said that April and May have taken refuge with you and your family. She said she tried to get them back to us, but Mr. Cinder wouldn't allow it."

Libby swallowed hard and looking quickly toward the door.

"Don't try it, Libby. I'm much faster than you." He crossed his legs and leaned back, his arms resting on the arms of his chair. "Listen carefully to me, Libby. If you tell anyone about what happened between us, I'll call you a liar. I'll say that you wanted me to be your boyfriend, not a foster father. I will make your new family believe whatever I want them to believe. Mrs. Blevins tells me that they're going to adopt you. If you say anything bad about me, I'll make sure they never adopt you."

She tried to cry out but no sound came from her throat. She could smell his aftershave lotion and she thought she was going to be sick.

"Do as I say, Libby, and you'll be happy with the Johnsons. But if you say anything against me, you'll be sorry for the rest of your life." He stood up and walked toward her, towering over her, and she cringed away from him. "I mean to have the twins stay with me. Nothing you can do will stop me from getting them back in my home."

Libby closed her eyes against him, but his image remained inside her head.

"Remember my warning, Libby." He rested his hand on her shoulder and she jerked violently, cracking her elbow against the wall. "You always were a little fighter. The fight is over and I have won."

She stared at him as he walked to the door and out. The smell of him stayed long after he left. Libby could not force herself to stand up and leave.

Mr. Page walked in, then stopped in surprise. "Are you still here? Didn't you hear the bell ring? It's time to go home."

She tried to stand, but fell back in her chair.

"Are you sick or hurt?" he asked in concern, hurrying to her side.

"I'm . . . I'm all right." She pushed herself up and forced her legs to support her. She had to get her jacket from her locker and get to the bus before it left without her.

Hurrying students jostled her as she almost ran to her locker. Ben stopped her and asked if she was all right. She mumbled that she was,

114

but he stayed with her to the bus, then sat with her.

She shivered and he asked if she was cold and she said she didn't know. She felt his questioning look but she leaned her head back and closed her eyes. How could she push Morris Stern out of her mind now? Oh, she hated him!

She could not race with the others up the muddy driveway, but walked slowly toward the house. A strange car stood in the driveway and her heart skipped a beat. How silly! She didn't need to be afraid of every car that parked in their drive.

April met her on the back porch as she hung up her jacket. The house smelled like fresh-baked bread.

"Oh, Libby!" April caught her hand and held it tightly. "They're here—with Chuck and Vera in the study!"

"Who?" whispered Libby with a shiver.

"Morris and Evelyn Stern. They got here about five minutes before the bus. May's hiding upstairs."

Libby wanted to run upstairs and hide with her. "What are they talking about?"

"I don't know. Chuck shut the study door." April pressed her hands together in front of her. "Libby, will Chuck let them take us?"

"No. He promised."

"Will he keep his promise?"

"Yes, April." Libby walked slowly toward

the study door. Oh, what were they talking about? Would Morris Stern convince Chuck not to adopt her?

"Your face is white, Libby. You're as scared as we are, aren't you?" April stopped Libby outside the family room door. "Do you think we'll have to live with them again?"

Libby remembered how sure Morris Stern was that he'd have the girls back with him, but she would not tell that to April. "I wish we could hear what they were talking about."

"I tried to listen through the door, but the kids came in and I ran away from it."

"Let's go listen." Libby walked softly to the study door and stood barely breathing. She could hear voices but not make out the words spoken. How she wanted to rush in and demand to know what was happening. Unhappily she led April back to the family room. How could they stand around and wait to know what was being said?

Just then Vera walked from the study and Libby rushed to her side, asking anxiously what the Sterns were saying.

"They want the twins back," said Vera. "But Chuck says no and they demand to talk to the girls." She turned to April. "Where's May?"

"Upstairs."

"Get her, please. We'll all talk together." Vera waited until April was gone then turned back to Libby. "I want you to come to the study with the girls. Chuck seems to think all three of you have something important to say."

"No." Libby backed away, her eyes wide in fear.

"We'll be right with you. Mr. Cinder said that he would allow Chuck to question the Sterns and the girls, then tell Mr. Cinder his impression of the situation. What Chuck says will help Mr. Cinder decide what to do."

Libby nervously pushed her hair away from her thin face. "Can't he tell Mr. Cinder that the girls can't go back just because they don't want to?"

"It's more than that, Libby. Mr. Cinder wants Chuck to help him find out if Morris Stern's license to have foster children in his home should be taken from him."

"Oh!" Libby's heart leaped. If Morris Stern had his license taken from him, no other foster girl would be in danger from him. Dare she speak up and tell what she knew? But what if he convinced Chuck that she was lying? What should she do?

The twins stopped in front of her and she knew they were as scared as she was. Maybe all three of them together could stop Morris Stern.

Fourteen
Help

Libby trembled as she followed the twins and Vera into the study. Chuck had told her often that she wasn't alone, that Jesus was always with her. Now, more than ever, she needed his help and his strength. What she was about to do might stop her from ever being Elizabeth Gail Johnson. And if she wasn't with the Johnson family she would have to give up her dream of being a concert pianist. She squared her shoulders and lifted her chin high. No matter what happened she was going to tell just what Morris Stern had done!

She felt his eyes on her and she looked right at him, daring him to threaten her again. Evelyn Stern smiled a charming, easy smile and said hello. Libby managed to speak to her, wondering if she knew what kind of man she was married to.

Chuck sat behind his desk and asked them all to sit down. The twins and Libby sat on the sofa and Vera sat on a chair beside the Sterns.

"Girls, we're anxious to have you back home where you belong," said Morris Stern with a wide smile that didn't touch his icy blue eyes. "We've missed you."

"We have," said Evelyn Stern in her quick, low voice. "The house is very quiet without you."

"We are not coming back," said April sharply.

"Never!" said May and Libby saw Evelyn cringe as if she'd been slapped.

"We'll talk about it, girls," said Chuck, leaning forward with his hands clasped on his large oak desk. "May, why don't you want to go back?"

Morris Stern jumped to his feet. "Since when do we ask a child why he or she does or does not want to go home? The girls live with us and we have every right to take them now."

"Sit down!" commanded Chuck in a voice that Libby knew the man had to obey.

Morris Stern finally sank to his chair, a frown puckering his wide forehead.

"May," said Chuck, smiling encouragingly at her.

May's face flushed red and she twisted her long fingers together. "Do I have to?"

"Yes, May. You said you don't want to live with the Sterns. Do you want other girls living with them even though you might not have to?" asked Chuck softly.

Libby sat with her back stiff. Could she talk after May told her story?

May's hand trembled as she pushed her long brown hair away from her pale face. Slowly, in a low, tense voice, she told what Morris Stern had done to her, had tried to do to April.

"That's a lie!" cried Evelyn Stern, jumping up. "My husband would not do that!"

"Please, sit down," said Vera, catching Evelyn's hand and tugging her down. "Wouldn't you rather know the truth?"

Evelyn sagged in her chair, suddenly looking very old and tired.

"Must we continue this?" asked Morris Stern icily.

"We must," said Chuck.

May finished her story and everyone was quiet. Libby could barely breathe. Now it would be her turn. She looked at Morris Stern to find him looking at her, defying her to tell what she knew.

"Elizabeth, I hate to make you do something that hurts you, but I want you to tell what you know," said Chuck.

She licked her dry lips and locked her fingers together tightly. May nudged her from one side and April from the other. Taking a deep breath, Libby told her story, and as she told it, the nightmare that was locked inside of her seemed to fade away. She heard Vera gasp and

Evelyn moan. Finally she finished and Chuck smiled reassuringly at her.

"Mr. Stern, do you have anything to say? I do want you to remember that Mrs. Johnson and I already believe the girls. I already know what I will say to Mr. Cinder."

The man's face sagged and he slowly stood to his feet. "At least keep this quiet until my wife and I can move away from this area. It is a terrible story to follow a man around."

"But a true one," said Chuck.

Morris Stern did not answer. He walked from the room, his broad shoulders bent, his head down.

Evelyn Stern slowly stood up, her purse clutched tightly to her. "I didn't know," she whispered. "I really didn't know. I'll see that he gets help."

After she left, the room was very quiet. The hall clock bonged five. Toby shouted something from upstairs. A car drove away from the house.

"It's over, girls," said Chuck.

Libby leaned back weakly.

"Now, we'll help you twins find a home," said Vera, smiling. "Mr. Cinder will allow you to stay with us until a good home opens up."

"Thank you," they said together.

"I'd like to talk to Elizabeth alone for a while," said Chuck. "Do you girls mind going with Vera to fix supper?"

Libby's head felt fuzzy as the girls and Vera

left, closing the door behind them. What would Chuck say now? She watched him walk to the sofa and sit beside her.

"Honey, thank you for telling that," he said. "It was terrible to have to do it, but it's done. But you have one more step in getting rid of it."

"What?" she whispered.

"Jesus will heal the pain that those memories brought you, just as he healed April, and just as he is healing your arm."

She rubbed her arm. "My arm *is* better! It doesn't hurt nearly as much."

"Wonderful!"

Tears filled Libby's eyes and she laughed with joy.

"Listen, Elizabeth. Jesus will heal the pain Morris Stern brought you just as he healed your arm."

"How?"

"You have to do something first, honey." He took her hand and held it in his warm hand. "The bad feelings that you have toward that man have to be released. You must not hate him."

"I hate him!" she cried. "I always will!"

He shook his head. "No. The Bible says that you are to love. You are to forgive."

She shook her head hard. "I won't forgive him! He's terrible!"

"Elizabeth, the hurt that he caused you will stay and fester and turn into something terrible

123

if you hang onto it. You must be willing to give up those bad feelings and take Jesus' love and healing. If you do this you will be able to think about Morris Stern without fear or pain."

"Oh, Dad. I can't do it."

"Yes, you can. We have been learning to live the Bible. We are to be like Jesus. Jesus loves Morris Stern as much as he loves you." Chuck slipped his arm around her shoulder and pulled her close. "You don't have to forgive on your own. Remember how hard it was for you to forgive your real dad for leaving you? Jesus helped you to forgive him. Jesus healed the pain you felt toward your dad. He gave you love for your dad. Jesus will do the same with Morris Stern. Jesus wants you to forgive the man. Jesus wants to heal that emotion."

Libby leaned weakly against Chuck, listening to his heart beating against her ear. "Do I have to, Dad?"

"Do you want to obey the Word of God?"

"Yes."

"Then you have to."

She closed her eyes and sighed. "Help me pray, Dad."

Chuck prayed with her and she felt the bitterness and hatred leave. And when Chuck prayed for Morris Stern to find Christ, she was able to agree in prayer with him.

Finally Chuck held her away from him. "You have grown a little more today, Elizabeth."

"I have?"

"Yes. Every time you obey God's Word, you grow spiritually. The stronger you are spiritually, the more you are like Jesus." Chuck stood up and Libby followed him. "It's time we found the rest of our family. They're probably wondering what happened to us."

Libby felt as light as Vera's fresh-baked bread that she could smell in the kitchen. She looked up at Chuck. "I think I'd better practice my piano. I haven't practiced an hour every day the way Rachael Avery wants me to."

"I think you'd better. I'm going to help Ben finish the chores. I asked all of them to do your share."

"Thanks, Dad."

Just as Libby finished the first song on the piano she thought of Toby. He had felt bad a few days ago because she always had others help her or she helped everyone but him. She smiled. He would be gathering the eggs right now. She would help him.

The cool wind blew against her jacket as she ran to the chicken house. Toby looked up with a frown.

"Hi," she said. "I'd like to help you, Toby. If you want, you can go watch TV and I'll finish for you."

He stared at her in disbelief. "What do I have to do for you?"

"Nothing. See my arm? Jesus is healing it. I can use it more now. It still hurts a little, but I

125

just want you to know that I really do love you. I'm glad you're my brother."

Slowly he handed the egg basket to her. "What about April and May?"

"What about them?"

"Are they going to hang around here?"

"For a while."

Toby grinned. "Good. They can learn to do my share of the chores. That will give me more time to watch TV."

Libby laughed. "And do you think Mom and Dad will let you?"

He pushed his hands deep into his pockets and hunched his shoulders. "No, they won't."

Goosy Poosy honked from inside the chicken pen.

Libby laughed again. "I think Goosy Poosy is agreeing with you. How about doing chores together?"

"All right." Toby grabbed the basket and walked into the chicken house with Libby right behind him. It was warm and smelled bad to Libby. She liked the smell in the barn, but the chicken house made her sick to her stomach.

Toby knocked a hen off the nest and sent her flying to the floor, squawking noisily. Libby stepped close to Toby, wondering why he wasn't scared of the chickens.

Finally they walked into the yard and Toby looked up at Libby, "I'm glad we live with the Johnsons, aren't you?"

Libby nodded. She looked across the yard at

126

the big house where seven kids lived now, instead of five. "We have the best family in the world, Toby. I know God will find a family for April and May that is almost as nice as ours."

Just then the twins, with Ben, Susan, and Kevin, ran from the barn. Libby watched them come, her heart leaping with love.

Vera opened the back door. "Supper's on, kids. Come and eat."

Libby rushed to the house to have supper with her family, her very own family who loved her.

"Ally," Chris whispered, the sound slowly filtering though the erotic haze around her, and she shivered at hearing her name on his lips.

She opened her eyes to find him staring intently at her, his fingers still tangled in her hair and his thumbs gently stroking her temples.

"If you plan on actually having dinner tonight, we should probably stop." His fingers slid out of her hair, a rueful smile played on his lips.

Dinner? She didn't give a tinker's damn about dinner. The only thing she was hungry for was the man plastered against her like some kind of fantasy in the flesh.

She should let him go. She should go on to dinner. She should act nonchalant about what had just happened. A lifetime's experience of responsibility and rationality told her to backtrack to the getting-to-know-you steps they'd leapfrogged over with that kiss.

I don't want to.

The realization shook her to the soles of her plain brown sandals. And it was her sandals that were the tipping point. They were practical, boring and suddenly symbolic of her entire existence. She didn't even have sexy, pretty shoes in her life—much less men like Chris.

He hadn't moved since she'd tightened her hold on him and when she looked up to meet his eyes she saw the heat and the question there, and her decision became crystal clear.

"I'm not in the least bit hungry. But if you are I do know a place that delivers to my hotel."

Dear Presents Reader,

Happy Valentine's Day—and if you're in the mood for hot steamy romance, look no further than these exciting new stories from the Harlequin Presents® line! Two books a month that offer you all that you expect from Presents— but with a sassy, sexy, flirty attitude!

All year you'll find these exciting new books from an array of vibrant, sparkling authors such as Kate Hardy, Heidi Rice, Kimberly Lang, Natalie Anderson and Robyn Grady. This month there's sizzle and sass from talented new Atlanta author Kimberly Lang with *Magnate's Mistress…Accidentally Pregnant!* And for sun, sea and sex, don't miss *Marriage: For Business or Pleasure?* by Australian author Nicola Marsh.

Next month, there's the first in Kelly Hunter's saucy new duet, HOT BED OF SCANDAL, set on a French vineyard and entitled *Exposed: Misbehaving with the Magnate.* And there's an exciting and dramatic pregnancy story from hot British talent Heidi Rice in *Public Affair, Secretly Expecting.*

We'd love to hear what you think of these novels—why not drop us a line at Presents@hmb.co.uk.

With best wishes,

The Editors

Kimberly Lang

MAGNATE'S MISTRESS...
ACCIDENTALLY PREGNANT!

TORONTO • NEW YORK • LONDON
AMSTERDAM • PARIS • SYDNEY • HAMBURG
STOCKHOLM • ATHENS • TOKYO • MILAN • MADRID
PRAGUE • WARSAW • BUDAPEST • AUCKLAND

Recycling programs
for this product may
not exist in your area.

ISBN-13: 978-0-373-23661-9

MAGNATE'S MISTRESS...ACCIDENTALLY PREGNANT!

First North American Publication 2010.

www.eHarlequin.com

Printed in U.S.A.

All about the author...
Kimberly Lang

KIMBERLY LANG hid romance novels behind
her textbooks in junior high, and even a Master's
program in English couldn't break her obsession
with dashing heroes and happily ever after. A ballet
dancer turned English teacher, Kimberly married
an electrical engineer and turned her life into an
ongoing episode of *When Dilbert Met Frasier.*
She and her Darling Geek live in beautiful north
Alabama with their one Amazing Child—who,
unfortunately, shows an aptitude for sports.

Visit Kimberly at www.booksbykimberly.com for
the latest news—and don't forget to say hi while
you're there!

To my beautiful, clever, and all-around Amazing Child—although it will be many years before you are old enough to read this book *(thirty, at least, if your father has any say in the matter),* let me remind you that tonight, at dinner, you told me you wanted to be a romance writer like me when you grew up because it was "cool." You know what? I think you're cool, too, and you can be anything you want to be when you grow up—well, except maybe a flamingo.

CHAPTER ONE

NOTE TO SELF: never prepay your honeymoon.

Ally Smith sat on the beach under a tattered umbrella nursing her watered-down piña colada and wondered why that caveat didn't make it into any of the wedding planning books. *Probably because no one plans a wedding with escape clauses.*

She should write her own book for brides-to-be. She'd definitely include a chapter on cancellation clauses, the folly of prepayments and how to mitigate the financial toll of lost deposits. Oh, and some fun stuff like how to build a nifty bonfire with three hundred monogrammed cocktail napkins.

And a chapter on how to know you're marrying the wrong guy.

She dug her toes into the warm sand and watched the sailboats bobbing on the waves as they made their way into and out of the marina just down the beach. Why hadn't she pushed harder for the trip to Australia where she could at least be snow skiing right now? June in Oz was supposed to be fabulous.

Why had she let Gerry talk her into this when they
lived just twenty minutes from the Georgia coast—
a popular honeymoon destination in and of itself?
She could go to the beach anytime she wanted. She
didn't have to fly to the Caribbean for sand and
surf.

Because I was too happy to finally be engaged.

In the four months since she'd happened home at
lunchtime to find Gerry having a nooner with their
travel agent—which explained why he'd insisted
they use her to begin with, and probably also why
Ally was booked into the worst hotel on the island—
she'd come to realize some hard truths: she'd picked
good looks and charm over substance, and she should
have dumped Gerry-the-sorry-bastard four years ago.

Now, two days into her "honeymoon," she was
bored out of her mind.

"Is this seat taken, pretty lady?"

The low, gruff voice pulled her out of her reverie.
Shading her eyes from the late-afternoon sun, she
turned to find the source of the question.

And nearly spit out her drink as she ended up
eye level with the smallest swimming trunks ever
made, straining over a body they were never
designed to grace.

In any decent movie, the voice would have
belonged to a handsome tennis pro with a tan and
bulging biceps. This was *her* life, though, so while
her admirer did sport a tan, his body bulged in all

the wrong places—like over the waistband of his Speedo. Ally bit her lip as her eyes moved upward, past the gold chain tangling in his furry chest hair to the three-day salt-and-pepper stubble, the ridiculous iridescent blue wraparound sunglasses and wide-brimmed Panama hat.

She was being hit on by a bad cliché. This horrible vacation experience was now complete. "I'm sorry, what?"

"You look like you could use some company. How about we have a drink and get to know each other?" Without waiting for her response, the man lowered himself into the adjacent lounge chair, took off his sunglasses and stuck out his hand. "Fred Alexander."

With no excuse to deny the tenets of her proper Southern upbringing, she shook the proffered hand. The palm was damp. He held her hand a bit too long, and she fought the urge to wipe it on her towel once released. "I'm Ally. It's nice to meet you, but—"

"A pretty girl like you shouldn't be sitting out here alone. No telling who might come along to bother you." He winked at her.

Yeah, no telling. There were plenty of people on the beach. Why had Fred picked her to hit on? *Because you are a loser magnet. First Gerry and now this guy.* At least Gerry had been good-looking, a fact he'd never let her forget.

She had to escape. She should have just stayed in Savannah. Oh, but no, she'd been steamed over the loss of so many other down payments that she wasn't going to let a vacation go to waste, too. It had sounded so practical at the time. She knew better now.

"I was just about to go in, actually. I think I'm getting too much sun." She reached for her bag and slid to the edge of her seat, ready to beat a hasty retreat. Fred placed his hand on her wrist and stroked his thumb over the skin. Ally gently moved away from his hand and out of arm's reach as she stood.

"I'd be happy to rub some lotion on you." Fred's eyes roamed slowly down her body and back up to her cleavage, making her skin crawl. With a slow shake of his head, he said, "That's a crime, Ally. A girl with a body like yours should be showing it off in a bikini." She'd never been so glad to be wearing a one-piece in her entire life, and as he licked his lips in appreciation, Ally felt as if she needed a hot shower.

"Thanks, but no. I'm—"

"Dinner, then. I saw you checking in alone yesterday and figured you'd be looking for some company." *Ugh.* She took another step back. "Um, well, I…"

"I'm staying here, too. Suite sixteen. It must be fate that we're both here on our own…"

It was in her nature to make people happy, but

this crossed the line. There was "nice" and then there was "stupid." She'd made enough stupid decisions—no more.

"Enjoy the beach." She could hear Fred muttering something about her attitude as she left. *Whatever.* What little enjoyment she'd had just relaxing to the sounds of the surf evaporated in the wake of being hit on by some creepy guy old enough to be her father.

Maybe the TV in her room had a movie channel. She could take that shower, order room service for dinner—if they even did room service in this hotel; she hadn't seen a menu when she'd checked in last night—and plan to do some sightseeing on the island tomorrow.

This was the most pathetic vacation ever. Or was she the pathetic one?

The lobby was mostly empty as she waited behind a couple checking in. More honeymooners. The young woman carried a bouquet, and the red-haired man at her side was having a hard time checking in since he couldn't seem to keep his hands off his new bride. They seemed happy, and Ally silently wished them well as they headed for their room.

"I'd like to see about ordering room service to suite twenty-six."

The hotel clerk shook his head. "Sorry. No room service. Just the restaurant."

Lovely. She thought she'd hit her low spot on this vacation with the arrival of Fred, but obviously there was much more awaiting her over the next few days. Like eating every meal alone.

"But I do have a message for you, Mrs. Hogsten."

"Miss Smith," she corrected automatically. Another good reason not to marry Gerry. She'd never liked the sound of his last name.

The clerk's eyebrows shot up in surprise, and he rechecked his computer screen.

Ally sighed. "I know. It says Hogsten, party of two, but it's just me. Miss Smith."

She saw the flash of pity in the man's eyes as the implications of staying alone in a honeymoon suite registered.

No sense trying to explain she wasn't the least bit sorry to still be single. "The message?"

He handed her a folded piece of paper. "Enjoy your evening."

"Thanks." She flipped it open for a quick peek as she walked back to her room. Her mother's number.

Good Lord, what now? She'd hadn't been gone that long, and she'd made sure all of them were squared away before she left.

Kicking the door closed with her foot, she dug in her bag for her cell phone, only to flip it open and remember she didn't have service here.

The minifridge in her room was well stocked

after her trip to the local liquor store last night, and the bottle of Chardonnay called her name. She poured a glass and took a drink before dialing the long string of numbers to call home.

"Oh, honey, it's so good to hear from you!"

Her mom sounded as though the phone call was a nice surprise, which meant nothing was seriously wrong on the home front. That didn't mean she was off the hook, though. Ally drained her glass before she spoke. Instead of refilling it, she took the bottle with her over to the bed and sat down. She might need the whole thing. "You asked me to call. Is everything okay?"

"Oh, we're fine. I guess."

Ally waited.

"Well, other than the fact your sister is going to put me in an early grave with her dramatics…"

Oh, goody. Ring the bell for Mom versus Erin, round 427. Did she really need to be discussing this long-distance?

Breathe in. Breathe out. How typical. Could her family not function for at least a few days without her there? She'd like to think that if she'd really been on her honeymoon, no one would expect her to deal with this. Who was she kidding? If her family tree were any nuttier, squirrels would start showing up at Thanksgiving dinner. She loved them, but not a one had an ounce of sense.

Maybe she'd been adopted. Switched at birth. Or had she been intentionally placed in this family simply to keep them all from spiraling out of control with their dramatics? It sucked to be the grown-up all the time.

When her mom finally paused for a breath, Ally started her peacekeeping duties. "Mom, it is *her* wedding—"

"Maybe so, but you'd think she'd understand how important this is."

It was a wedding, not the trials of Hercules, for goodness' sake. But it took another half hour for Ally to convince her mom of that, albeit temporarily. She banged her head against the headboard gently in frustration.

"And, Ally, honey, the state sent a notice about the property taxes."

"I took care of that before I left."

"So what do I do with the notice?"

"Just set it aside, and I'll get it when I come home. I'll double-check with the state to be sure, but I wrote the check along with your other first-of-the-month bills."

"Oh, then that's good."

The small headache her mother always caused after more than twenty minutes throbbed behind her eyes. "Mom, I'm going to go find some dinner now. I'll see you when I get home, and we'll sort everything out then."

"Of course, honey. Have a wonderful time. We'll talk soon."

With the phone safely back in its cradle, Ally leaned back against the headboard of the king-size bed and hugged the bottle of wine to her chest. *I'm so glad I don't have cell service here.*

Out her bedroom window, she could see the sun setting over the water. Dammit, she was on vacation. Granted, it was the strangest vacation ever, but it was her vacation nonetheless. She was alone in a honeymoon suite, in a place she hadn't wanted to come to, and staying at a low-end hotel because her travel agent was both spiteful and incompetent. And she'd paid top dollar for this disaster. It wasn't fair, and it wasn't right, but there were worse places to be. She should make the most of it.

She'd *earned* a vacation, by God. She'd put up with Gerry for three years longer than she should have in the hopes he'd shape up and be worth the investment of her time and energy. Instead she'd carried him—financially and emotionally—for all that time. Planning and then canceling the wedding had been stressful, and when she added in her family's constant stream of crises, it was no wonder she'd had a headache for as long as she could remember.

She *needed* a vacation. She deserved it. She would take advantage of it.

After one last long drink straight from the bottle,

Ally reached for the phone again. By the time the desk clerk answered, she had a whole new perspective.

"This is Ally Smith in suite twenty-six. No, not Mrs. Hogsten. Miss Smith. I'd like your help in finding a restaurant that delivers and a masseuse who can come to my room tonight for an hour-long massage. And I need to know where the closest spa is. I'd like to get a facial and a manicure tomorrow. Oh, and I'd really love some fresh flowers in here."

"She's a real beauty."

Chris Wells nodded, even if he didn't fully agree. She needed quite a bit of work, but she still held great promise. He'd wanted to have a closer look before he'd know if the problems were just cosmetic or if they ran deeper.

"She's fast, too," the man continued, pride evident in his voice, "but responsive and easy to handle."

"Her reputation certainly precedes her." Chris stepped onto the weathered wooden deck. At just over forty feet, the yacht was compact, yet elegant in design. Sadly, though, she had suffered from too many years of poor maintenance—the cleats were spotted with rust, the leather cover of the tiller was cracked and peeling. Twenty-five years ago, he'd watched his father skipper the *Circe* to her first win, and he'd known then that he'd race one day, too. In a way, he owed much of his career to the boat rocking gently under his feet.

The *Circe* was long retired, her heavy wooden hull no match for the newer, lighter racing yachts made of aluminum or fiberglass. But he wasn't here to buy a new racer—he was here to buy a piece of history and make her into a queen.

His crew had called him crazy when he'd told them he was taking time off to go to Tortola to see *Circe,* but Jack and Derrick would come around eventually. And he wouldn't trust anyone but them to refit her properly.

"Is she seaworthy? Any reason why she wouldn't make it home?"

Ricardo, the boat's current owner, smiled, obviously pleased with Chris's interest. "A few minor things you might want to look at…"

Chris listened to Ricardo's list with half an ear as he fished his cell phone out of his pocket and called home. "Jack. Send Victor and Mickey down here on the next flight. She needs a little work, but I should be ready to start for home by the end of the week."

"So you're going through with it?"

"Definitely." He was handing the check to a bug-eyed Ricardo even as he spoke.

"Why don't you come on home and let the guys bring her back instead?"

Chris took a deep breath as a feeling of rightness

filled him. He was meant to own the *Circe*. "Because she's mine now."

"But we need you here. Paperwork is already piling up on your desk. And, if you're really going to break a record in October, we don't have time for you to putter around the Caribbean."

"I have an assistant to handle the paperwork. Grace can call if she needs anything. October is still a long ways off, and the *Dagny* is ahead of schedule. There's nothing for me to do but admire your handiwork."

Jack sighed and muttered something, but Chris didn't need to hear it. He'd heard it all already. Jack was the world's most compulsive planner—which was great when it came to planning around-the-world trips and designing new boats, but a bit of a pain any other time.

"I'll see you in a few weeks. Have *Dagny*'s sails ready for me when I get home."

"No dawdling in the Bahamas this time, okay?"

Flipping the phone closed, Chris turned back to Ricardo. "I assume you can get me access to the maintenance shed here." He was already making a mental list of what he'd need for the long trip back to Charleston; now he just hoped he could find a good outfitter on the island.

Feeling better than he had in weeks—months, probably—Chris grabbed his duffel bag off the dock and tossed it below. Ricardo was already halfway back to the marina office, presumably to cash the fat check in his hand before Chris changed his mind.

But Chris was already unbuttoning his shirt as he headed below to change. He was looking forward to getting to know his new addition.

Whistling, he got to work.

A massage, a mud bath and a mani-pedi had worked wonders on Ally's outlook. Tortola was definitely growing on her.

After a fabulous morning of being pampered and polished, she returned to her room feeling so relaxed she wasn't sure how much longer her legs would hold her upright. A short nap and a shower later, her attitude adjustment was almost complete. She just needed to find somewhere to eat—napping through lunch was great for the psyche but left her stomach growling.

The nail tech at the spa had recommended she try the little café next to the marina in order to get a true taste of the local cuisine. It was a short walk, and it gave her the opportunity to appreciate the amazing scenery she'd ignored in her foul mood. Until now.

A smiling teenager led her to a small table overlooking the marina. The same breeze that teased her hair out of its braid also gave her background music as it moved though the rigging of the boats. Sunshine warmed her shoulders, and the fish chowder soothed the grumble in her stomach. By the time she'd finished her second mango daiquiri, she knew she was in paradise.

The bustle of the marina fascinated her. Even though Savannah was close to the coast, she herself wasn't all that familiar with boats. Here, though, sailing was obviously a serious pastime, and the marina buzzed with activity. Curious, and with nothing else on her afternoon agenda, she went to explore.

There were no gates blocking access to the docks like the few she'd seen at home, so she wandered aimlessly. Boats of every shape and size and type bobbed gently in the water, and everyone greeted her with a wave as she passed.

Tranquility. Miss Lizzie. Lagniappe. The fanciful names painted on the backs of the boats made her smile. *Tailwinds. Skylark.* The *Nauti-Girl* made her laugh out loud. *Spirit of the Sea.* The *Lorelei.* The *Circe.*

The *Circe* was smaller than the boats around it, and while the others were tidy and gleaming, the *Circe* looked as though she'd seen better days. Planks from her deck were missing and long scrapings marred her paint. A second look, though, showed the scrapes had uniformity to them and a pile of fresh planks was stacked neatly on the dock.

The *Circe* was getting a face-lift.

"I assure you, it's for her own good."

Ally jumped at the voice and the thump of something landing on the dock behind her. She turned and realized Tortola had spectacular scenery indeed.

Holy moly. He couldn't be real. No mortal man had a chest like that. She blinked, but the image didn't change. Muscles rippled under bronze skin as he off-loaded the supplies in his arms. His pecs bunched, then flexed as he moved, and Ally felt a bit dizzy. Struggling to regain her equilibrium, she forced her eyes upward to the man's face.

But it didn't help to steady her. Sunglasses hid his eyes but not the adorable crinkles that formed as he smiled at her. He wiped his hands over the battered khaki cutoffs hanging low on his hips, then slid the sunglasses up and off his face. Eyes the color of the water surrounding them grabbed her, and she found it hard to breathe.

Real or not, she knew he'd be starring in her late-night X-rated fantasies for years to come.

"Her previous owners neglected her a bit, but she's going to be beautiful once I'm done with her."

The slight drawl made her think of home, and something about the pride and determination in his tone tugged at her. "I'm sure she appreciates it."

"I certainly hope so." He reached to her right to grab the faded T-shirt hanging on the piling, bringing that bronze skin so close she could smell the sunshine and the musk of clean, male sweat. As he pulled it over his head, she stamped down her disappointment at the loss of the lovely view of his pecs. "I'm Chris Wells."

"Ally." She shook the hand he offered. It was warm and strong and slightly calloused, indicating he worked with his hands. The thought of those hands on her... She snapped back to the conversation. "I'm sure she's enchanting."

Chris cocked his head, sending a lock of blond-streaked hair over his forehead before he pushed it back. Those highlights were real—he obviously spent a lot of time in the sun.

Ally cleared her throat. "Circe. The enchantress queen from the *Odyssey*."

"Yes, I know. I'm just surprised you do. Not too many people know who she is." He crossed his arms across that unbelievable chest and leaned against the piling.

"I guess I'm a bit of a mythology geek."

Chris's eyes traveled appreciatively down her body, leaving her skin tingling in their wake. "I definitely wouldn't consider you a geek."

The heat of a blush replaced the tingles, and her brain turned mushy. "She so rarely gets the credit she deserves."

"She turned Odysseus's crew into pigs."

Was that a challenge? "Some might say it wasn't exactly a stretch."

"Ouch," Chris said.

"But she also gave Odysseus the information he

needed to find his way home and avoid the Sirens. Odysseus owes Circe one." *Why am I babbling on about this?* She needed to quit while she was ahead. *Find another topic of conversation before he decides you really are a geek.*

But Chris egged her on with another of those smiles. "But they were lovers. *That's* what Circe wanted from him."

Ally laughed and took the opening. Maybe he didn't think she was babbling. "True, but I think that worked out better for Odysseus than for Circe."

"Excuse me?"

She looked at him levelly. "Odysseus and Circe have a fling. After which, Circe gives him much-needed information, and he's gone without a backward glance, leaving her pregnant with triplets. Not so great an ending for Circe." She shook her head sadly.

"What, no romantic sympathies for his desire to get home to Penelope?" Chris teased.

This was fun. She leaned against the opposite piling and mirrored his crossed arms. "Oh, now *Penelope* has my sympathy. Odysseus, the original golden boy of 'all style, no substance,' goes out adventuring, leaving her at home to weave and take care of the kid. She remains faithful while *he* starts the tradition of a girl in every port. Odysseus was a player."

Chris laughed out loud. "You don't sound like you like Odysseus much."

"I won't deny there's something attractive about him, but smart women don't fall for that—at least not more than once."

A blond eyebrow arched upward. "You sound bitter."

She shrugged. "Let's just say I know better. If you ask me, Odysseus got much better than he deserved."

"That's a different take on a classic."

In her primmest voice, she said, "Homer was a man. I don't think he sees it quite the same way a woman would."

"You have a point, Ally."

"Maybe." When he didn't respond, she was disappointed. Were they done now? Should she move on? She didn't want to, but Chris did have a major project underway. He hadn't moved from his lazy pose against the piling, but maybe he was just too polite. She'd wrap it up and let him get back to work. "But you're doing a good thing, bringing *Circe* back to her former glory. I'm sure she'll be lovely."

"She will be. Right now she's just a money pit. I can see now why Odysseus left her. Too needy." He punctuated the statement with a wink.

Feeling better than she had in months, Ally let a giggle escape. "You're terrible."

Chris shrugged. "You started it."

"Well, I stand by my earlier statement, regardless. Your *Circe* deserves the face-lift. I'm sure she'll be a beautiful, *enchanting* ship when you're done."

"Yacht."

"Pardon me?"

"She's a yacht. Not a ship."

"Really? There's a difference?"

"Definitely." Chris levered himself back to his feet. "Ships are those big ones that move cargo and such. These," he indicated the boats around them, "are yachts."

Maybe they weren't done just yet. He didn't seem in a hurry to run her off and get back to work. A little spurt of excitement warmed her blood. This trip was getting better by the second...

"Ally! Ally-girl, I thought that was you."

The voice hit her between the shoulder blades and crawled down her back. *I spoke too soon.* She knew that creepy, gravelly voice. She turned, and, sure enough, Fred was lumbering down the dock toward her like a duck to a June bug. *Why me? Why? I find a hunky guy to talk to and the slimy one has to come and ruin it.* It wasn't fair.

She saw Chris's eyebrows go up in question as Fred lumbered to a stop beside her. "Ally," he puffed, "I saw you headed this way. If you're interested in boats, darlin', I'd be happy to oblige."

At least he's wearing more than he was yesterday. The polo shirt and shorts *were* an improvement, but that didn't mitigate the fact he was *here* ruining her day again.

Fred looked Chris up and down, then glanced

dismissively at the *Circe.* "How about that dinner now? We can let this swabbie get back to work."

Chris stiffened a bit at the insult, but he didn't take the bait. *Just when I thought it couldn't get any worse.* Swabbie? How arrogant could one guy be? And how was she going to gracefully extricate herself this time? Short of jumping off the dock and swimming to shore, she was trapped.

She felt, more than saw, Fred reach for her elbow to lead her away. Desperate, she turned to Chris and mouthed, *Help.*

The corner of Chris's mouth twitched. Dammit, this wasn't funny. She didn't want to be outright rude to Fred, but this needed to be nipped in the bud. *Fine.* Rudeness begat rudeness, and this jerk started it. Her conscience could be salved by that, at least, as she took a deep breath and opened her mouth to be intentionally rude for the first time in her life. "Look—"

"Ally," Chris interrupted smoothly, "I know you're upset I've been spending so much time on the boat, but you don't need to get even by flirting with another man."

She let out her breath in a rush at the save, but then gasped as Chris looked at Fred and shrugged. "You know how women are about these things. They get so jealous over the 'other woman.'"

Her mouth was open to argue with such a sexist statement when she realized Fred was nodding in agreement. She closed it with a snap and accepted the hand Chris held out to her. One quick tug, and she was against his chest with his arms wrapped around her.

And everything else ceased to exist.

The men were talking, but Ally couldn't hear the exchange. The heat from Chris's body and the solid wall of muscle surrounding her had her blood pounding in her ears. Closing her eyes, she inhaled, and the summertime smell of him filled her senses. Every nerve ending sprang to life, and she fought against the urge to rub sensually against him but lost. Her breathing turned shallow and her inner thighs clenched. But when Chris dropped a warm kiss on her bare shoulder, lightning raced through her, causing her to arch into him in response.

His arms tightened around her, and she melted into the pressure...

"Ally?"

The whispered question sent chills over her skin as his breath caressed her ear. Her eyelids felt heavy as she attempted to open them.

"He's gone. You're safe now."

The words hit her like cold water. Reality snapped back into focus, and... Oh, *no*. She felt the hot flush of embarrassment sweep up her chest and neck.

She'd been writhing against him like a stripper

against a pole, and her humiliation was now absolute.

This vacation sucked.

CHAPTER TWO

ALLY WAS A WONDERFUL ARMFUL, but the situation was about to become embarrassing for them both if he didn't release her. The colorful sundress she wore had concealed the lush curves he could now feel as she fitted perfectly into him like a puzzle piece. Curly dark tendrils of hair that smelled like sunshine and citrus caught the breeze and tickled over his skin. When she'd sighed and moved against him, he'd been unable to resist tasting her.

Her plea for help might have spurred him to reach for her, but in reality it had only provided an excuse to act on the need to touch her that he'd felt the moment she'd lifted her chin and started her defense of Circe. A need that had intensified when that Euro-trash wannabe had tried to stake a claim on her.

But now that he was gone, Chris no longer had a reasonable excuse to continue holding her—beyond his own enjoyment, of course. But that enjoyment was beginning to press insistently against her, and in another moment he was going to take advantage of the situation.

As he gave the all clear, Chris felt her stiffen. Ally extricated herself awkwardly, clearing her throat as a red flush colored her chest and neck.

Maybe I'm not the only one who got a thrill from the contact, he thought.

"I, um, ahem, uh—" Ally paused, closed her eyes and took a deep breath. "Thank you for the save. Fred must not have gotten the hint yesterday that I wasn't interested. Maybe now he'll find someone else to stalk."

"My pleasure." *Definitely.* He'd never been one for saving the damsel in distress before, but if this was what it was like, he'd reconsider playing Lancelot.

Ally attempted to smooth the loose hair back from her face, then smiled uncomfortably. But she wasn't beating a fast path off the dock, which was good since he was already hoping he'd have an excuse to touch her again soon.

"Would you like to come aboard? See the *Circe* up close?"

He was treated to a brilliant smile that lit up her deep brown eyes. "I'd like that a lot. I've never been on a boat before. A yacht, I mean."

"You can call her a boat, just not a ship."

"Good, because yacht sounds a bit pretentious."

Her cheeky smile was contagious, and he knew he was grinning like an idiot as he stepped onto the deck and held out a hand to help her board.

"I can't believe you've never been on a boat before."

"Never. Well, unless you want to count a canoe at camp one summer."

He'd spent his entire life on, in or around boats. Sailboats, speedboats, rowboats, tugboats—if it went on the water, he'd built it, raced it or at least crewed it. He'd never met anyone who hadn't even seen one up close before.

Ally seemed to be taking the inspection seriously, as she asked questions about the sails and the cleats and how it all worked. As she trailed a hand along the tiller, his blood stirred, wanting that hand to caress him instead.

He cleared his throat. "She was designed to race, so she's lean. No frills to weigh her down."

"Is that what you're going to do? Fix her up and race her?"

"No, I can't race her. Her hull is too heavy to compete with what's out there now."

Ally looked at him. "But you do race, right? Or you're wanting to?"

Was she serious? A look at Ally's heart-shaped face told him she was. She honestly had no idea. How long had it been since he'd had a conversation with someone who didn't know who he was?

Wells Racing and the OWD Shipyard really had consumed his life—to the extent that it had probably been at least five years since he'd met anyone who wasn't as obsessed as he was. Maybe more like ten. And while part of him wanted to impress Ally with his list of credentials, he held it at bay. It was nice to be incognito for once.

"I race…among other things." It wasn't a lie. Pops still kept his command in the offices of the OWD Shipyard—in name at least—but Chris found more and more of the day-to-day business crossing his desk these days. He juggled a lot, but Wells Racing was still his main focus.

Ally grinned at him. "But do you ever win?"

He laughed before he caught himself. "Occasionally."

"Is it dangerous?" She didn't meet his eyes as she asked that, but the too-casual way she poked at the deck line belied her interest.

"Not really. You *can* get hurt, don't underestimate that, but it's pretty hard to kill yourself."

Her shoulders dropped in relief. "That's good. My brother races dirt bikes for fun. It's pretty easy to kill yourself doing that." Ally poked her head into the hatch. "Not a lot down there."

"Like I said, she's built for racing. Bare necessities only." He liked watching her explore the *Circe*. As the breeze molded her dress to her curves, he realized he liked watching her, period. The erection he'd only recently got back under control stirred to life again.

Ally sat on the edge of the cockpit and ran her hands over the smooth planks of the deck. "This is neat. Thank you for showing me."

Unable to resist, he sat next to her. Possibly a little closer than was called for, but Ally didn't move away. "Neat?"

"Yes, neat. I like to learn new things." She looked sideways at him and shrugged. "In fact, I've decided that this vacation is going to be all about new things. I came by myself, which was definitely a first. I've—"

"You came on a Caribbean vacation by yourself?" Even though she'd been wandering the dock alone, he assumed she had friends or family somewhere on the island.

"It's a long story, but, yes."

He started to ask another question but she cut him off.

"Seriously, it's a long, *boring* story. But I'm here now, and I'm making the most of it. I've tried new foods, let the spa spread mud all over me, and now I've been on a boat for the first time. I'd say I'm off to a good start."

He was still reeling at the mental image of Ally nude while mud was painted sensuously across her breasts. He cleared his throat. "You're quite the adventurer."

She beamed, her brown eyes lighting up. "I wouldn't go that far. But I am taking baby steps." Ally closed her eyes and leaned back to enjoy the sun. It was an artlessly erotic pose—back arched, breasts thrust temptingly toward him, the gentle curve of her neck exposed. "This is wonderful. The wind and the water are very relaxing."

He was anything but relaxed. "Would you like to go out?" he blurted.

Ally sat up and opened her eyes, the shock readily apparent. "I'm sorry, what?"

Well, that hadn't been his smoothest move. He cleared his throat. "Sailing. Would you like to go out sailing tomorrow?"

"Oh, I don't know…"

"Come on. It'll be fun."

"I've never—"

"I thought you were being adventurous on your vacation."

Ally shifted uncomfortably. "There's adventurous and then there's the fact that I'm not a very good swimmer."

"The chances of you going overboard are pretty slim unless you jump."

Ally looked over the mess he'd made of the *Circe,* a wary look in her eye. "But—"

He followed her gaze and laughed. "Not on the *Circe.* She's not up for company yet. I'll borrow a little cat or something. Start slow."

Confusion furrowed Ally's forehead. "A cat?"

"Catamaran. Like the ones you see on the beach down there."

She looked to where he was pointing and nodded. "It's kinda big, don't you think, for my first time? Maybe something smaller, like those over there?" She pointed to some dinghies tied up at the dock.

"Ah, Ally, you don't want to start too small. You want to get the full experience." He dropped his voice and teased, "Bigger really is better, you know. It's not the same sensation at all."

She caught her lip in her teeth, the picture of indecision. "Um…"

"We'll take it really slow and give you some time to get comfortable. We won't go very far until you're sure you're ready. Just nice and easy." He stroked her arm and gooseflesh rose under his fingers. "We won't go too fast, I promise—unless you decide you want to, of course. And I think you will once you get into it. Otherwise, you can relax and let me do all the work while you just enjoy yourself."

Ally's eyes were wide and dark as she exhaled gently. "Are we still talking about sailing?"

Who cares about sailing? He stopped and gave himself a strong mental shake. "Of course. Well? Are you game?" He could see the indecision in her eyes. She wanted to go, but something was holding her back. "Are you afraid? Of the water?"

She hesitated as she looked away. "No. Not afraid, just not any good—I mean, I'm not a good swimmer."

"Do you trust me?"

One eyebrow went up. "I've known you for less than an hour. No, I don't trust you."

Ally was a breath of fresh air—and honest to a fault. "I'm hurt," he teased.

Looking sideways at him, she amended her statement. "But I don't *dis*trust you, either."

That easy smile was really starting to work on him. "It's a start."

"And you did save me from Fred."

"Very true. Surely that merits something."

"If you were a Boy Scout, maybe a badge of some sort." She bit her lip again, sending a jolt through him. "But I don't think you're a Boy Scout."

"You do know how to wound a man. I may not be a Boy Scout, but I am a good sailor. You needn't have any worries about surviving the experience. I'll bet you'll even enjoy it, despite your reservations."

She didn't pick up the gauntlet, but she was coming around. "How about the medium-size one? I can work my way up from there."

"How about dinner instead? If you still want to start small after that, then I'll get the dinghy. But I think you'll come to see the benefits of not setting your sights too low."

Confusion crinkled her forehead, and it took all he had not to reach for her and drag her below, but there was nothing below but a couple of narrow bunks, completely useless for what he had in mind. "Dinner?" she asked.

He feigned shock. "Of course. You don't expect me to go sailing with a woman I barely know, do you?"

Ally laughed and nudged him with an elbow. "I don't know what to expect from you."

"Just a good time, that much I can assure you." *For us both.*

"Then it's a deal." Ally stuck out her hand, but instead of shaking it, he squeezed it gently.

Slightly flustered, she stood and brushed at her dress with her free hand. "Should I, um, go change?"

"You look amazing." She blushed at the simple compliment, and something primal and protective stirred in his stomach. It was an odd feeling. "I, on the other hand, need to shower. You can't be seen in public with an unwashed swabbie."

Ally squeezed his hand back as she apologized. "Fred's a jerk. That comment was uncalled for."

"I've been called worse by better."

"But still…"

She seemed so earnest in her apology and need to console. "Forget it, Ally. You're not responsible for the actions of others."

A shrug was her only response.

"Where are you staying? I'll come get you around seven."

"The Cordova Inn. How about I meet you in the lobby?"

He nodded, and steadied her as she stepped onto the dock. The *Circe* bobbed as she did, and the boat felt a bit empty once she'd left. He was admiring the gentle sway of her hips when she turned and gave a small wave. Another moment and she was around the building and out of sight.

Well, this was an expected turn of events. He'd come to Tortola to get the *Circe* and found the delicious Ally, as well. His father had called the *Circe* a lucky boat, and now he had proof. Not that he was ever one to question his luck—he'd learned early on to take advantage of whatever winds came his way.

He went below to get his shaving kit and wished the repairs were further along. Or that he'd at least gotten a proper bed installed. He didn't mind crashing on the narrow bunks, but the *Circe*'s cabin was low on creature comforts and not exactly conducive to pastimes other than racing.

That would change, just not soon enough.

Of course, the arrival of Mickey and Victor tomorrow would also put a damper on any on-board activities with Ally. Which reminded him—he still had supplies to stow and he needed to call home.

He'd call and check in with Grace, just to be sure

there wasn't anything too pressing, then he'd call Pops and mollify him over the extended absence.

Thanks to the *Circe,* the company, the *Dagny,* and his grandfather were all far away and would remain so for the next few weeks. He stretched, and his fingertips grazed the *Circe*'s bulkheads. He was a free man. *Somewhat free,* he amended as his phone alerted him to an incoming text message.

It could wait a while though. Ally was far more interesting than another discussion of the *Dagny*'s sails or OWD business.

He grabbed his shaving kit and a clean shirt and headed to the marina to shower.

Ally held her composure until she was sure Chris was no longer in sight, then she sagged against the wall of one of the marina buildings. Her legs felt shaky as she let out her breath in a long, unbelieving sigh.

Had that really happened? Had she really just met a real-life Adonis and agreed to…to… She shook herself. *Technically,* she had only agreed to dinner and a sail, but deep down she was pretty sure she'd agreed to something far more. Chris's interest went beyond taking her sailing. She wasn't *that* naive.

She was, however, completely out of her league. Men like Chris just didn't appear in her world every day. Men like Chris were the stuff of fantasies. Or movies. They certainly didn't appear out of nowhere like a dream come true and take an interest in mousy little accountants.

"God, I love this island."

She wrapped her arms around her stomach and enjoyed the thrill. She had an urge to find that fiancé-banging stupid travel agent and give her a big kiss. Checking her watch, she was amazed to realize dinner wasn't that far off. She only had a little over an hour to wait, but at the same time, that hour seemed like an eternity. Not that she was interested in food. That feeling in her stomach definitely wasn't hunger pangs.

Taking a deep breath, she pushed off the wall and found that her legs still weren't completely stable. Which was appropriate, since she wasn't sure she was mentally stable at the moment, either. These things just didn't happen to her. But it had, and she was willing—make that more than willing—to grab this moment and run with it.

She covered the short distance between the marina and the inn in record time and hurried to her room. The light on her phone blinked, indicating she had a message waiting at the front desk, but she ignored it. She wasn't the least bit interested in her fruity family or whatever crisis they'd concocted for themselves today.

Her wardrobe was limited, as she'd never considered *this* possibility while packing, and she grimaced at the selection. All of it plain, boring, un-exciting—rather like her at times. She wished she had time to go shopping, to find something better, but the clock was ticking. When she got home, she'd do some serious shopping to remedy the sad state of her wardrobe. She did find another sundress that was dressier than the one she had on and wasn't shaped like a potato sack. It would have to do.

She showered again and took extra time getting ready, wanting to look as good as possible, but her hair wasn't cooperating. Sighing, she settled for another braid, tucking in the frizzing strands as best she could. At one minute after seven, she took a deep breath and headed for the lobby, half expecting Chris not to show up.

But he *did,* looking like something out of a magazine in loose linen slacks and button-down shirt with his blond-streaked hair brushed back from his face. That fluttery feeling in her stomach bloomed back to life, followed rapidly by the urge to suggest a quiet dinner in her room.

Chris leaned in to kiss her gently on the cheek, an innocent enough greeting under any other cir-cumstances, but in this case, one that melted her insides and made her knees wobble.

"You look fantastic."

"Thanks. So do you." Those blue eyes were going to be the end of her. Seriously. She could stare into them for hours, but when he smiled and they lit…

"Mrs. Hogsten!" The desk clerk approaching her was a wet blanket on her rapidly heating thoughts. She sighed in disgust. Whatever happened to impersonal hotels where none of the employees knew or even cared who you were? She'd *love* that about now.

"Not Hogsten. Smith. Or even Ally is fine."

"Of course, my apologies." At least the pitying look was gone. Instead the desk clerk looked amused as he saw Chris standing so closely beside her. "We have a message for you."

"Thanks." She took the piece of paper and glanced at it quickly as the clerk left. "Call home." Not tonight, she thought, as she stuffed it into her purse. Turning to the far more interesting Chris, she smiled. "Let's go."

"Is everything okay?" The concern she saw in his eyes was kind, but she wanted that other light back. The light that said he was interested in *her,* not what was on a piece of paper in her purse. The one that made her insides turn over and her skin tingle.

"Just my family checking in."

That other look came back into his eyes, and the butterflies in her stomach fluttered to life. "Good." Chris took her hand and led her toward the door. "It's a beautiful evening and the restaurant's not far. Mind if we walk?"

At the moment she'd gladly walk to hell and back if he'd keep looking at her like she was dessert.

Pull yourself together before you jump on him. At least try to act casual about this.

The evening *was* beautiful and warm, and Ally inhaled the hibiscus-scented air deeply as they walked. This was the stuff books were written about, walking at night on a tropical island hand in hand with a gorgeous man who—

"There seems to be some confusion about your name at the hotel."

I will not let reality spoil this moment. "Yeah. Well, it's kind of a—"

"Long story?" Chris finished for her, flashing a smile that made her gooey inside.

"Exactly. And boring to boot. How about you tell me where we're headed instead?"

"Have you ever had pepper-pot soup?"

She stomped down the urge to skip. "Nope, but it sounds great. Remember, I'm all about new experiences this week. I'm game for pretty much anything."

Chris stopped walking and pulled her into the shadow of a huge mango tree. Warm hands settled on her shoulders, and Ally forgot to breathe. "Glad to hear it. In fact…"

It was all the warning she got before his mouth touched hers.

His lips were warm and soft and gentle, but she could feel the restraint, the tension in his hands as they moved up to cup her face and his thumbs stroked over her cheekbones. Rising up on tiptoe, she wrapped her arms around him as his tongue touched hers.

And everything changed.

This. This was the kind of kiss myths were built around. Heat and hunger radiated from Chris's body, warming her blood and making it sing through her veins in answer to the need he stirred in her.

She'd never been kissed like this before, and her world shrank until all that existed was Chris and the feel of him against her and the taste of him on her lips.

A brief jolt of anger moved through her at the thought of all the kisses she'd wasted on Gerry. His lazy, perfunctory, be-happy-you're-getting-anything kisses had never moved her like this.

Like this, she thought, and banished Gerry from her mind as Chris's fingers massaged her scalp, and her knees turned to water. Chris caught her weight as she wobbled, fitting her tightly against him, and what little sanity she had left fled at the sensation: scorching kisses along the tender skin of her neck; the play of muscles under her fingers and the thump of his heart against the chest pressed tightly to hers. The bark of the mango tree bit into her back, but she didn't care.

"Ally," Chris whispered, the sound slowly filtering through the erotic haze around her, and she shivered at hearing her name on his lips.

She opened her eyes to find him staring intently at her, his fingers still tangled in her hair and his thumbs gently stroking her temples. But there was nothing gentle in the way he looked at her, and the fire burning in those blue eyes sent a shiver deep into her stomach.

Chris shuddered, his breath coming in quick pants like her own. She was glad to see she hadn't been the only one to be shaken by the power of that kiss. She didn't have much experience to draw on, but she knew the feeling was mutual. Tightening her fingers on the fabric of his shirt, she pulled him closer, wanting more.

"This isn't exactly the right place."

Belatedly, she realized he was right. While not crowded by any stretch of the imagination, there *were* other people on the street, and several of them were watching the display with interest. She should be mortified, slinking away in embarrassment, but surprisingly she didn't care in the least.

"And, if you plan on actually having dinner tonight, we should probably stop." His fingers slid out of her hair, and she could feel the braid hanging drunkenly to one side as he toyed with the loose strands. A rueful smile played on his lips.

Dinner? She didn't give a tinker's damn about dinner. The only thing she was hungry for was the man plastered against her like some kind of fantasy in the flesh.

Chris sighed and shifted his weight and Ally tightened her grip to keep him from moving away. For a brief moment indecision nibbled at her. She should let him go. She should go on to dinner. She should act nonchalantly about what just happened. A lifetime's experience of responsibility and rationality told her to backtrack to the getting-to-know-you steps they'd leapfrogged over with that kiss.

I don't want to.

The realization shook her to the soles of her plain brown sandals. The sandals were the tipping point. They were practical, boring and suddenly symbolic of her entire existence. She didn't even have sexy, pretty shoes in her life, much less men like Chris.

Chris.

He hadn't moved since she'd tightened her hold on him, but she wasn't sure how long she'd stood there dithering with herself. When she looked up to meet his eyes, she saw the heat and the question there, and her decision became crystal clear.

"I'm not in the least bit hungry, but if you are, I do know a place that delivers to my hotel."

CHAPTER THREE

ALLY SHOULD COME with a warning label attached. Her words came out of nowhere—okay, not exactly nowhere but close enough—to slam into him with a desire that was almost painful. Underneath that artless, wholesome sensuality and cheeky grin was a woman very dangerous to his sanity.

He hadn't meant for the kiss to get out of hand. He just hadn't been able to go another moment without tasting her. The sweetness had been expected, but it was the fire that had caused him to lose control of the situation.

Hell, he'd lost what was left of his mind. Ally deserved better than a mauling against a mango tree in full view of a dozen witnesses. She tensed and he dragged his attention back to her face, only to immediately wish he hadn't. Her eyes were dark and hungry, her lips swollen and moist from his kiss. Public or not, up against a mango tree or not, he didn't care.

He just needed her hands on him again.

"Food can wait."

Her breath caught and she reached for his hand as she turned.

Thank God they hadn't made it very far. Retracing their steps took only a minute, but it seemed like an eternity. Ally's hands shook as she tried to unlock the door, fumbling the keys.

He took a deep breath to calm himself and took over the task, silently agreeing with Ally's muttered "Thank goodness" as they were able to close the door behind them.

One lamp glowed beside the very inviting bed, its sheets already turned down by the hotel staff. The window stood open, allowing the quiet evening sounds of the island to drift in.

Ally seemed slightly uncomfortable once they were alone, her movements stiff as she dropped her bag in a chair and reached up to feel the lopsided braid and try to tuck the haphazard strands back in.

Her hands fell to her sides as he reached for the band securing what was left and freed the curls to riot around her tense shoulders.

"You should wear your hair down more often, Ally." He threaded his hands back through the silkiness, and her shoulders relaxed as his fingers found her scalp.

Eyes closed, Ally's head lolled back, exposing the lovely line of her throat, and his lips took the invitation. She hummed in pleasure, and the vibration moved through his body as he pulled her close once again.

The contact brought her to life once again, the tension leaving her body as she moved against him. He took a moment to just enjoy the sensation, patient this time to savor it as he knew he'd be able to feel all of her in just a few more minutes.

But Ally's hands locked around his shoulders as she moved into him, pressing her lips to his in needy hunger, and all of his good intentions to go slow went up in the flames she fanned in his blood.

Ally felt like she was on fire. She needed to touch him. Needed to prove to herself he was real. Needed to feel him against her, in her. And she wanted all of it *now.*

The buttons on Chris's shirt gave way easily, and the chest she'd admired earlier in the day was hers to explore. Her fingers traced the ridges of muscle, and when she retraced her path with her tongue, Chris sucked in his breath in pleasure as his hands tightened in her hair.

A boldness she didn't know she possessed surfaced and she reached for the waistband of his pants. Chris's stomach contracted at her touch, giving her room to release the button and slide the zipper over the bulge, causing her thighs to clench in anticipation.

"My turn." Chris stopped her hands and lifted

them over her head before he grabbed the cotton sundress and tugged it off in one smooth movement.

For one brief moment, she felt exposed and uncomfortable, but that feeling was soon chased away as Chris tumbled her to the bed. An acre of bronze skin loomed before the hot weight of him covered her and blocked out any thoughts beyond the screaming need his hands were creating as they moved over her skin.

One toe-curling kiss melded into the next as Chris's tongue flicked against hers like a promise. But when his mouth moved lower, trailing moist heat along the swell of her breasts, she nearly arched off the bed in response. The loss of her bra vaguely registered, followed by the whispery slide of her panties down her thighs.

The featherlight kisses across her stomach were driving her mad. She reached for him, but his fingers locked around her wrist and pulled it over her head. Her other wrist soon followed, and Chris wrapped her fingers around the iron rails of the headboard.

His chest pressed against hers, the crisp hairs tickling sensitive skin, as she savored the feel of him against her from breasts to toes. Blue eyes locked into hers as he held her wrists in place.

"I told you I'd do all the work. That all you had to do was lie back and enjoy."

"I thought we were talking about sailing." Lord, was that whispery voice hers?

Even in the shadows of the room, she saw his grin. "No, you didn't." Then his head dropped to capture her nipple between his lips.

Yesss, she thought, and then she wasn't able to think anymore.

"This is amazing. Really wonderful." After an hour of worrying she'd fall off the boat—yacht, catamaran, whatever it was called—she was finally growing used to the feeling and began to understand the attraction sailing held.

"Then could you quit white-knuckling the edge of the tramp? You're doing serious damage to my ego."

"Your ego is in no danger at all." Sure enough, though, she was still gripping the edge of the trampoline suspended between the two hulls as though her life depended on it. With a great show, she let go of the edge and stretched her arms out to catch the wind.

"That's better." He leaned over to give her a quick kiss.

Ah, yes, sailing was becoming more attractive by the minute. Or at least sailing with Chris was. Completely in his element, he controlled the boat with ease as the wind ruffled his hair.

She had vague memories of Chris kissing her goodbye in the small hours of the morning, saying he had some things to do before they set sail. She'd half expected never to see him again and had gone back to sleep with a touch of regret. Not about sleeping with him—oh, no, *that* topped her list of best decisions ever made—but that she didn't have the guts to ask him to stay.

So when he'd shown up around ten that morning with a heart-stopping smile and a picnic basket, Ally had had to fight the urge to pull him straight back into bed and spend the rest of her trip there.

But this was good, too. She had a great view of his gift-from-the-gods body as he pulled on ropes and adjusted sails. Blue shorts rode low on his hips, and now that she no longer needed a death grip on the trampoline, she itched to touch him again.

She still couldn't believe she'd actually...well, not to put too fine a point on it, that she'd had the most amazing sex of her life with this man. He was too good to be true. But, oh, Lord, the things he'd done to her. She hadn't *known*, never even dreamed of the possibilities. Even now, her nipples tightened with need, and a fire burned low in her belly.

The little Beach-Cat, as Chris had called it, had one major flaw: zero privacy. The open design of the boat meant anyone could see what they were doing. Not that there were many folks in sight...

She resigned herself to just putting her hand on his leg instead and looked forward to getting back to shore as soon as possible.

"Are we headed someplace specific?"

Chris adjusted the sails again and the little boat

leaped forward as it caught the wind. "There's a little cove just around the point of the island I thought we could explore. I understand it's pretty secluded."

Her stomach flipped over at the thought. Maybe Chris's thoughts were headed in the same direction as hers.

"But we have a little while before we get there. Why don't you tell me that long story of how you came to be on Tortola alone."

Ugh. Her blissful fantasy was torpedoed by the thought of home. "In a nutshell, I was supposed to come with someone, but that was canceled months ago. The trip was prepaid, and I didn't want it to go to waste, even if none of my friends could come with me."

"Let me guess. That 'someone' is an ex."

Gerry's blond good looks and petulant pout flashed into her mind. Why had she been willing to settle for someone so shallow? "Very much an ex. Thank goodness."

"Agreed. His loss is my gain."

Looking for a way to change the subject before Gerry could spoil her good mood, she went back to sailing. "Does the *Circe* go this fast?"

"We're not going all that fast. Three or four knots, maybe. You could probably get out and run faster than this. And the *Circe* will go a lot faster than four knots."

Pride filled his voice every time he mentioned the *Circe*. "That ship—"

"Yacht."

"Sorry, that 'yacht' means a lot to you, doesn't she?"

"I've been wanting to buy her for a long time, so yeah, I'm pretty pleased she's now mine. But, as you saw, she needs a lot of work. A couple of my friends came by today to work on her, in fact."

A tiny twinge of guilt nagged at her that he'd ditched his repairs of the *Circe* for her. At the same time, she was very glad he had. She stretched out on the trampoline, belatedly realizing she must be getting used to sailing to want to get comfortable. Or maybe it was just the matter-of-fact way Chris handled the cat that put her at ease. The man was born to be on the water, which led her to wonder what he did when he wasn't.

"Where's home for you?"

Chris ran a hand down her side and over the curve of her hip, where his thumb slid under the string of her bikini bottom. "I guess you could now say it's wherever the *Circe* is."

"Really?" She hadn't thought about that possibility. She'd just assumed...well, she wasn't sure what she'd assumed. "But you are American. In fact, with that accent I'd say you grew up somewhere on the southern East Coast."

"South Carolina."

"I'm a Georgia girl myself."

"Let me guess. Savannah."

"You're good."

"At many things." He wagged his eyebrows suggestively at her, and the hand at her hip moved promisingly.

"Oh, I fully agree with that." And she smoothed her hand across his thigh and felt the muscle jump. Chris wanted her. She reveled in the feeling; just a couple of days ago, she had believed she was a boring, plain-Jane loser magnet, but here she was. It couldn't be real: Ally Smith, Femme Fatale. Oh, her ego *definitely* needed this.

Another circle of his thumb reminded her that her ego wasn't the only needy part of her. She couldn't see his eyes behind his sunglasses, but she could *feel* them roam over her body. Even with the heat of the sun on her, she shivered.

A sail flapped and Chris cursed, reaching for the rope and quickly running it through a cleat. Ally was almost glad for the distraction; Chris's undivided attention was a heady thing. She leaned back and closed her eyes, letting the movement of the water lull her as Chris made easy conversation.

But she could still feel his eyes on her.

A bump pulled her out of her languor, and she opened her eyes just in time to see Chris jump off the boat. She sat up quickly. "What the—ouch!"

"I told you to watch out for the boom."

Turning to find his voice, she realized the bump she'd felt had been the cat's hulls reaching the shore. Chris gave a mighty pull, and the boat slid partially out of the water onto the sand.

"Are you okay?" Chris splashed in the shallow water to her side of the boat, his brow wrinkled in concern.

"I'm fine."

"Then come on." He held out a hand and pulled her into the surf with him.

The water was cool, a nice contrast to her sun-toasted skin, and clear enough to see her feet on the bottom. Chris moved into deeper water, pulling her gently along with him. She lifted her feet and held on to his arm, allowing herself to float slightly. The shoreline was empty, and no other boats had moored in the little cove. They were very much alone, an advantage Chris seemed keen to act upon as he pulled her legs around his waist. Strong hands dug into her hips as Chris's mouth found that magic spot on her neck.

"You've been driving me crazy," he growled. "That bikini wouldn't adequately cover a Barbie doll. I nearly ran us aground on the sandbar." His teeth found the string holding her top up, and untied the bow with a simple tug. The grip on her hips loosened, forcing her to grab his shoulders for support as he made quick work of the second string around her back. A second later, her pink top was floating toward shore.

"Um, Chris…"

"There's no one here but us. No one to see you except me. And I want to see all of you."

His lips captured hers for another mind-blowing kiss, but she felt him unhook her legs and quickly slide the bikini bottom off. Chris's trunks bobbed to the surface as he hooked her legs around him again, but this time, no fabric separated them. She moaned at the sensation and he echoed the sound as she moved against him, wanting to feel more.

Although the bathing suit hadn't covered much, being naked in the water was still a shock. She hadn't been skinny-dipping since…well, *ever.* It was decadent and natural and intensely erotic.

Her breasts felt overly sensitized as the water lapped over them, and the position she was in offered him easy access. One arm held her firmly around her waist as his hand captured her breast, caressing it as his thumb grazed across her nipple.

"Ever made love in the ocean, Ally?"

"N-no," she managed to wheeze.

One eyebrow arched up, and the gentle caress became more insistent. "Then I'm glad you're open to new adventures this week."

She hissed as his tongue swirled around her nipple before he pulled it into the heat of his mouth. Oh, *yes.* New adventures. Sign her up for more, as long as Chris would be her trail guide.

While the nips of his teeth drove her insane, one

hand snaked between her legs to find her core. She shuddered as he teased her, his fingers urging her to the edge. How could his skin feel so hot in the cool water? A finger slid inside her, and she rocked her hips into his hand, seeking more. Chris returned the pressure, the heel of his hand hard against her as he urged her on with hot words whispered into her ear.

All she could do was hold on, her fingers digging into his shoulders as she climaxed.

Still thrumming with aftershocks, she opened her eyes to meet Chris's deep blue stare. The intensity there rocked her, causing a rush she couldn't identify, but she couldn't look away.

She kissed him instead, holding his head and pressing her lips to his in an urgent need to share the feeling. Chris's hand moved, withdrawing from her and she ached at the loss.

But it was blessedly short-lived, as Chris cupped his hands under her thighs, lifted her, and slipped easily inside. Gasping, she tightened her legs, squeezing herself against him until their bodies met. Shudders gave way to full-out tremors as he filled her.

Her senses seemed to sharpen, bringing everything into focus—the gentle lapping of the water against their skin, the waves landing on the beach behind her, the warm rays of the sun on her back and shoulders, the throb of Chris inside her, the rapid pounding of her heart, the sounds of their ragged breathing.

Then Chris started to move, holding and guiding her, and her focus narrowed. Nothing existed except this man and the pleasure rapidly peaking inside her. She trusted him to take her all the way, to hold her, please her and not let her drown, so she let herself go, chanting his name in rhythm to his thrusts. As she shattered, she felt Chris pull her close. A moment later, he held her hips tightly against him as powerful shudders moved under her fingers.

"Still feeling adventurous, Ally?"

With a huge effort, she was able to lift her head from his shoulder and open her eyes. One corner of his amazingly kissable mouth curved up in a challenge.

"Definitely."

"Then let's head to shore. I have a surprise for you…"

She felt drunk, more so than the bottle of wine she'd shared with Chris in the cove hours ago could be responsible for. No, she was definitely drunk on sex and sun and the sea—and, of course the man responsible for the best day of her entire life.

Chris helped her off the boat, his hands holding her waist longer than necessary, but she was having trouble keeping her hands off him, as well. The sun had been setting by the time they left their little cove, and a full moon now rode high in the sky, giving her just enough light to see the adorable crinkles around his eyes as he smiled at her.

He brushed his lips gently across hers before pushing the hair back from her face. "I really hate to leave you here, but I need to get the cat back, and there're some things on the *Circe* I really need to check on..."

"It's okay. Go. I'm completely exhausted. I desperately need a shower and some sleep. Lots and lots of sleep. You've worn me out." She rose up on tiptoe for one last kiss. She meant it to be quick, but Chris held her head in his hands and deepened it into a libido-rocking kiss that was both gentle and powerful at the same time. Little flames of desire began to lick at her, and she wondered if she'd ever get enough of him.

"Tomorrow," Chris whispered as he broke the kiss. "Be ready by ten."

"Be ready for what?" Not that it mattered as long as he would kiss her like that.

"It's a surprise. Bring a hat so your nose doesn't get any pinker."

She crinkled her nose experimentally and, sure enough, felt the tightness indicating she'd burned it.

"You're adorable when you do that." Chris pointed her in the direction of her hotel and patted her butt lightly. "Go. Sleep. I'll see you in the morning."

Trekking up the beach to the hotel was difficult

on such wobbly legs, but somehow she made it. A deep sigh at the perfection of the day escaped, followed quickly by a yawn. She glanced back at the beach, and saw the sails of the boat in the moonlight as Chris took it back to the marina. *The best day ever.* And if Chris's promises could be believed, she'd have another—possibly even better, though she couldn't imagine how—tomorrow.

She couldn't wait. She wrapped her arms around her waist and curled into the T-shirt she wore—Chris's shirt. Alone now, she lifted the shirt to her nose and inhaled the scent of him.

Oh, get ahold of yourself. With a shake of her head, she went inside.

Few people were still in the lobby, and she realized that it was later than she had thought. She dug through her bag as she walked, searching for her key.

"Miss Smith! Miss Smith!"

Glad she was no longer Mrs. Hogsten to these people, she turned to see the desk clerk closing in on her fast. Pink message slips fluttered in his hand. "We've been looking for you all day," he said as he thrust the stack at her.

She started to roll her eyes, but caught the anxious look on the clerk's face. All the languor vanished as adrenaline rushed through her veins. "What? What's happened?"

"There's been an accident, Miss Smith. It's very important you call home immediately."

* * *

He was early, he knew that, but Ally didn't seem like the kind of woman who would mind. She was just lucky Victor and Mickey had greeted him with a litany of problems with the *Circe*'s repairs and a Must Call message from his grandfather when he'd returned to the marina last night, because he'd been sorely tempted to turn right back around and join her for that shower. And, of course, sleep would have been out of the question after that.

Instead he'd spent the evening sorting out the *Circe*'s issues and placating his grandfather. But things were back on track and Ally was now foremost in his thoughts.

Sweet, delicious, tempting Ally.

A few phone calls and he'd borrowed the *Siren*, a sixty-foot cruiser with every amenity—most importantly, a plush captain's cabin. The mental picture of Ally stretched across those sheets was enough to quicken his step. *Siren* was stocked with food and wine and ready to sail. They'd moor off Virgin Gorda tonight, maybe go snorkeling in Devil's Bay tomorrow. He knew of a great secluded trail up from the beach...

His attraction to Ally was a bit of a mystery, but that combination of sweetness and sensuality was both intoxicating and refreshing, and had lifted a weight off his shoulders he hadn't realized he'd been carrying. Victor and Mickey had teased him about his uncharacteristically good mood, something they said they hadn't seen since the America's Cup win three years ago.

In response, he'd left them to replace decking and caulk seams today.

The lobby of the Cordova Inn was deserted, and in the light of day, he noticed how shabby the hotel really was. Ally needed to fire her travel agent for booking her into a place like this. Ally's room wasn't far off the lobby—another thing her travel agent should have handled better—and he could see the door standing open.

Good. She's ready to go.

"Pack a toothbrush and a change of clothes, because we won't be back..." Ally's room was empty, the bed stripped of its sheets. A maid came out of the bathroom carrying an armload of towels and started in shock at seeing him there.

"Where's the woman who was in this room?"

"I don't know, sir. I just know to clean the room for the next—"

Chris didn't wait to hear the rest. In a few quick strides, he was back at the front desk, asking the clerk the same question.

"Miss Smith checked out."

"Yes, I can see that," he gritted out. "Where did she go?"

"Home, sir."

"Why?" He really didn't want to play Twenty

Questions with the clerk, but the young man wasn't being very forthcoming with answers.

"There was an accident. Her brother, I think the message said. We helped her arrange emergency flights, and I put her in a taxi to the airport myself this morning at six." He seemed pleased with himself. Apparently Ally could bring out the Lancelot in every man.

"Has her flight left yet?"

"Yes, sir. The first flight to San Juan left at seven-thirty."

He cursed, and the clerk's eyes widened.

"However, if you are Mr. Wells, Miss Smith left a message for you." At Chris's nod, he passed over a folded piece of hotel letterhead.

Chris—

I'm so sorry to leave in such a rush, but there's been an emergency and my family needs me. I wish I could say goodbye in person, but the taxi is waiting and my flight leaves in an hour. Thank you for a wonderful day yesterday—it was possibly the best day of my life. Meeting you was the high point of this trip, and I really wish I could stay longer. Take care. I hope you and the *Circe* have wonderful adventures together. Love, Ally.

That was it? No phone number? No e-mail

address? Not even a "look me up if you ever come to Savannah"? All that was missing was "Have a nice life."

His good mood evaporated. Ally had left without even saying goodbye.

CHAPTER FOUR

WELL, THAT WAS UNPLEASANT. Not the best way to start a Monday, either. Ally leaned on the sink and took a deep breath. Then she grabbed the toothbrush she'd learned to bring to work with her and brushed her teeth. Wiping the moisture from the corners of her eyes, she was glad she'd switched to waterproof mascara last week.

"Look, Kiddo, I'll make you a deal. You let me keep my breakfast and I'll give you a new car when you turn sixteen, okay?" Another wave of nausea had her leaning against the bathroom door taking shallow breaths until it passed. "No deal, huh? Your loss."

Turning off the light, she opened the door to the office she shared with her friend and business partner. Molly stood waiting with a peppermint and a bottle of water.

"Seriously, now. How much longer is this going to go on?"

Ally took both offerings gratefully. The peppermint helped settle her stomach these days. "According to all the books, about six more weeks if I'm really lucky." She sank into her desk chair and rested her head on her hands.

"You're kidding me, right? Six more weeks of listening to you yak up your toenails every morning?" Molly's pixie face wrinkled in an amusing mixture of concern and disgust.

Ally sipped at her water cautiously, but the nausea had gone as quickly as it had come. "So sorry to inconvenience you, Molls."

"It's not that. I'm just worried."

Ally sighed. Snapping at Molly made her feel as if she'd kicked a puppy. "I know, and I'm sorry to be so witchy this morning. Dr. Barton says this is normal. Unpleasant, but still well within the range."

It was Molly's turn to sigh. "'Unpleasant' is an understatement."

"You're not wrong about that." Six weeks to go? Between the sickness in the mornings and the unbelievable fatigue that set in around three o'clock, this first trimester wasn't going well at all.

"Can I get you anything? Crackers? A soda?"

"Just help me find the Miller paperwork. I swear, this baby has stolen all my brain cells."

Molly casually tapped a folder sitting just left of Ally's elbow. "By the way, I talked to the landlord. He said we can have that storeroom for just a little more each month. I thought you could move your desk back there along with the baby's stuff, and we'll put a conference table out here to meet with clients."

Tears gathered in Ally's eyes. After the initial shock of Ally's announcement had passed, Molly had gone into "prep mode," never once questioning her decision to keep the baby, focusing instead on how they'd work out the logistics. Ally sniffed and reached for a tissue. Seemed she could check "overly emotional" on her list of symptoms, as well.

Thank goodness for Molly. She'd be a wreck without her. Her mom had flipped at the news, seemingly shocked that anyone accidentally ended up pregnant in this day and age. Ally had had to bite her tongue not to bring up her brother's pregnant girlfriend, Diane—no one seemed overly surprised about *that* baby. Molly had been the voice of reason then, too. Her family was just too used to Ally being the sensible, smart, reliable one, she'd argued. In a rare moment of snark—showing how truly angry Molly was with the lot of them—she'd postulated that the real reason the family was upset over the news was that Ally's attention would be focused somewhere else in the future. God forbid her family might actually have to take care of their own problems and not be able to run to her to sort them out.

Molly frowned. "You're leaking again."

Ally fanned her face. "No, I'm not. Just something in my eye."

"Hey, I'd cry, too, if I went on my honeymoon alone and still managed to wind up pregnant." Molly tossed the comment over her shoulder as she returned to her own desk.

"Yes, yes, I'm aware of the irony." Right after she'd recovered from the shock of seeing a positive result on the pregnancy test and had realized she'd somehow ended up in the two-percent failure rate of the Pill, *that* irony had hit her right between the eyes.

It would almost be funny if it were someone else.

Molly's keyboard clicked as she went back to work, and Ally tried to focus on the books from Miller's Printing Company. She had to get their payroll data entered and their checks printed before the need for her afternoon nap hit, but she was having trouble concentrating.

From the moment her plane had taken off from San Juan, she'd tried to put Chris out of her mind. She knew she needed to forget him, to just let him and their hours together fade into a dim memory. But it hadn't worked. She'd felt like a different version of herself, as though she'd been on the verge of *something* only to have been jerked back by her family responsibilities.

She'd caught a cab directly from the airport to the hospital, expecting to find her brother barely clinging to life. Instead, Steven was slightly battered from flipping his dirt bike, but awake, lucid and not near death at all—a situation she'd been tempted to remedy when he'd shown no remorse at all for ruining her vacation. After all, as her mother had added, Steven needed someone to deal with the hospital billing department and transfer money from his small trust to pay bills with.

The bitterness of missing out on more delightful days with Chris because of her family…well, she'd almost been over it by the time she'd missed her period, but any hope of forgetting about him had vanished at that point.

She was carrying his baby—a permanent reminder of those two wonderful days. How long would it take for her not to remember him every time she looked at their child? *Her* child, she corrected. This baby was hers alone.

Chris climbed the stairs to his office on OWD's second floor two at a time. His mornings had taken on a pattern these days—an hour at the gym, a few hours on the *Circe*'s renovations, lunch, then into the office. Today, though, he came straight from the yard, bypassed his assistant's desk without stopping for messages and went straight for his computer.

The damage to the *Circe*'s keel was greater than expected, and he'd contacted a friend for suggestions when he and Jack had clashed over the best course of action. He'd snapped a few quick photos with his phone, but couldn't get them to send properly for some reason.

He dug the USB cable out of its drawer and waited for the files to download onto his computer. A few clicks later, and the photos and measurements were off to Pete. Aesthetically, *Circe*'s rehab was going well, but structurally they kept finding new issues to deal with. He'd barely gotten her home—the constant problems had stretched his trip to almost four weeks, much to Victor's and Mickey's amusement and Pops's dismay.

Hopefully, this problem with the keel would be the last.

With the photos sent, Chris closed his e-mail account. The window open on his screen, though, showed another file had been in the download. *That's odd.*

He clicked it open, and Ally filled his screen. Something heavy landed in his stomach at the sight of that cheeky smile. He'd forgotten he'd taken it. They'd been almost ready to sail back when his phone had fallen out of his kit bag. She'd caught it before it went overboard and handed it to him, saying something about…what was it? Boys and their toys, he remembered. In response, he'd snapped a quick photo of her. She'd protested, grabbed the phone away, and distracted him with a kiss.

It had been another hour before they'd set off.

Ally.

He didn't need to look behind him at the bulletin

board on the wall to know that Ally's note with her name and phone number scribbled on the back was still there. A hundred bucks slipped to the desk clerk had gotten her contact info from the computer, but after the initial shock and anger at her abrupt departure had abated—and the struggle to get the *Circe* home in one piece had helped distract him nicely—he'd never followed up on his knee-jerk reaction to want to find her.

He'd put her from his mind, if not his dreams, and gone back to his life, even if the blithe way she'd dismissed him had left a bitter taste in his mouth.

Mickey had taken his life in his hands once to tease him about it—shortly after he'd returned to the *Circe* instead of sailing off with Ally on the *Siren*—telling him it was a fair turnaround considering his own love-'em-and-leave-'em past. That was the closest he'd ever come to hitting a crewmate.

He wasn't sure why he'd even kept her note and number, much less pinned it on the board with the photos of him and his crew in various races over the years.

"Chris?" Marge, Pops's secretary, stuck her head around his office door. "I brought you a sandwich."

After thirty years with the company, Marge was more family than employee, and she'd mothered Chris shamelessly since day one. She was well past retirement age, but had said the place would fall apart without her and claimed they'd have to carry her out of there in a box. He and Pops certainly weren't arguing with her or forcing her out of the door.

Crossing to Chris's desk, she laid the sandwich on the blotter and ruffled his hair. "Jack said you two had a disagreement about the *Circe*."

The sandwich smelled delicious, and his stomach growled at the reminder he'd skipped lunch when the keel had distracted him. "Jack always comes running to you, the tattletale. She's not his boat."

"And I'm sure you're right about the keel. Just don't forget to eat. Who's she?" Marge was peering at the picture of Ally, still open on his desktop.

"Just someone I met on Tortola." He closed the picture.

"And you took her sailing? You never take anyone sailing. She must've been some girl." With a confidence not every employee would have, Marge clicked the photo open again and studied it carefully. "She's pretty, but not what I'd call your usual type."

He closed it again and unwrapped the sandwich. His favorite. Marge was too good to him. "Well, Ally was an aberration."

One of Marge's penciled eyebrows went up. "Ally is it? Ally of the mystery phone number, perhaps?"

He nearly choked on the large bite of roast beef but managed to swallow it painfully instead. "Is there anything you don't know?"

"It's right *there.*" Marge pointed. "It's not like I had to go looking or anything. Eat."

Dutifully, he took another bite.

"That's a Savannah area code. Have you called her?"

Oh, good Lord. "No. And I doubt I will. Too much going on."

"Piffle." Marge waved the excuse away. "You just don't want to. I hope the poor girl isn't pining away waiting for your call."

"I doubt it." *She would have had to have left a phone number.*

With a shrug, Marge walked back to the door. "That's a pity. Oh, and your grandfather wants an update on *Dagny* when you have a minute."

No, Pops wanted to try to talk him out of it again. Finding fault with the *Dagny*'s progress was only his newest tactic.

Once Marge left, Chris ate and debated with himself as he stared at the icon on the desktop that would open Ally's picture if he clicked on it again. *What the hell.* He probably should have called her already, just to be sure that her brother was okay. It would have been the right thing to do, after all.

He closed his office door, then dialed.

"AMI Accounting Services. This is Molly."

A business? Did he even have the right number? "I'm looking for Ally Smith."

"She's, um, away from her desk at the moment. Can I take a message?"

This was actually good. He'd salve his conscience *and* avoid further meddling from Marge by putting the ball in Ally's court. He'd called. Done his part. "Sure. This is Chris—"

"The contractor?" Molly interrupted, but didn't give him a chance to answer. "*Great.* Ally said you'd be calling. Actually, I can give you the information since she's busy."

"I'll just—" he started again, only to be interrupted with another torrent of words.

"We just need an estimate right now, but we don't need to start work right away. We've got until March to get it ready, after all." Molly laughed, but then hurried on before he could say anything. "We need to finish out the storeroom into an office for Ally—did she mention the lighting? She'll need to be able to darken the back half of the room where the crib will go. She doesn't think it will be a problem, but I think we should go ahead and have the electrics for that done while y'all are finishing out the walls. Don't you agree?"

One word out of the flood stopped him cold. "Excuse me, did you say crib?"

"Oh, it won't be a huge crib—I don't want you

to think the space is *that* big." There was that laugh again, but he was still stuck on *crib*. "It's really just a cubbyhole for Ally and the baby."

Ally and the baby. And Molly said they had until March. A quick count backward meant that if Ally was pregnant, she'd conceived the baby in June. They were on Tortola in June. She'd told him she'd broken up with her ex months before, which meant she'd gotten pregnant on Tortola.

Adrenaline surged through his system.

"What time do you close today?"

"Oh, we'll be here until at least five-thirty or so. Can you come this afternoon?"

Without a doubt. "And your address?"

"Four seventeen West Jefferson, suite C. We'll—" Chris hung up.

Ally was pregnant. There was a strong possibility the baby was his. Not only had she fled Tortola without saying goodbye, she hadn't bothered to try to find him and let him know she was carrying his child? Maybe she'd tried to, but...no, he wasn't that hard to find. Chris Wells might be a common enough name, but between knowing he was from Charleston and the sailing, she'd have found him quickly enough with one search on Google.

She had no intention of telling him. Unexpected anger coiled in his chest.

Keys. Phone. That was all he needed. He opened

his office door to find Marge and his assistant in the outer office.

Without slowing his pace, he talked as he passed them. "Good. You're both here. That saves me time. Marge, tell Pops I'll talk to him about the *Dagny* tomorrow. Grace, I'm gone for the rest of the day."

Marge recovered first. "Where are you going?" she called after him.

"Savannah, damn it."

Okay, this was getting ridiculous. Morning sickness was for mornings. If she was going to start losing both her breakfast *and* her lunch every day, she and the baby were going to starve to death long before they made it out of this phase.

She brushed her teeth for the third time that day and went back to her desk where the rest of her lunch awaited her. One look at the guacamole on her taco salad caused her stomach to heave in protest.

"What now?" Molly asked around a mouthful of burrito.

"Can you get that off my desk? Just get it away from me, please. The guacamole is—ugh."

Molly, bless her heart, moved quickly, closing the box and carrying it outside without question. Once the offensive condiment was out of sight, her stomach felt much better.

Molly brought her the peppermints once she

returned. "That's so sad. You love guacamole and it's so good for you."

"But the baby doesn't love it, obviously, and I'm willing to give in on this."

"Since you're the color of guacamole right now, that's probably a wise choice. Tortilla chip?"

That seemed safe enough. It was the craving for something salty and spicy that had led her to suggest they order Mexican for lunch in the first place. She would just omit the guacamole for the foreseeable future.

"By the way, one of the Kriss brothers called while you were indisposed."

The peppermint actually tasted quite nice with the salsa. "Really? That was fast. Their office manager said they were out of town until tomorrow."

Molly shrugged. "I think they're going to come by this afternoon and give us the estimate." Her brow wrinkled. "He was kinda rude on the phone, though. Are you sure this is the company you want to go with?"

"Michael Kriss did that work for my mom last year. She raves about him."

"Your mom raves about a lot of things."

"Yes, but when it comes to updating or decorating the Dingbat Cave, she is remarkably focused."

"Then I'll withhold judgment until we meet them and get the estimate."

Ally nibbled on another chip. "Speaking of judgment, Erin kicked me out of the wedding last night."

"She didn't! *Why?*"

"Because I'll be seven months pregnant and she doesn't want my big belly drawing attention away from her on her 'special day.'"

The picture of outrage, Molly nearly sputtered. "That's insane. What did your mother say?"

"Oh, she's on board, but it all kind of got lost in the melee after Steven made *his* big announcement."

"Do I even want to know?"

It was a good thing Molly understood her family. "My brother is now a Scientologist."

Molly spat her water across the desk. "Just like that? He woke up one morning and decided he was converting?"

"Pretty much. My grandmother swears she's seconds from a heart attack at the news, Mom is convinced she'll never make it into the Junior League now, and Erin claims Steven is just seeking attention since he's recovered from the accident." Leaning back in her chair, Ally propped her feet on her desk and crunched another chip.

"And your dad?"

"Dad went fishing, so he hasn't weighed in yet."

"Erin just wants all the attention on her and the wedding."

"You got it."

"I'm so glad you passed the edict they were no longer allowed to call here unless someone was bleeding."

"Me, too. I finally took the phone off the hook last night and went to sleep around eight. I was just too exhausted to deal with any of them."

"Good for you. Can I slap Erin next time I see her?"

Bless Molly and her loyalty. "At least I don't have to wear that ugly green dress now."

"Small favors." Molly trailed off into her usual mutterings about Ally's clan, but was thankfully distracted by the phone before she worked up too big a head of steam on Ally's behalf. Once Molly got wound up it was hard to calm her back down.

Ally entered the last few numbers into the computer file, waited for the screen to update, then hit Print. Payroll for other companies was AMI's bread and butter, and she normally found the process boring. Today, though, the monotony of folding and stuffing checks was just what her mind needed. Between her own problems, her family, and the brain-numbness the baby caused, the simple, repetitive action felt soothing.

Two hours later she had all the checks for all four of their biggest clients ready. She took a few minutes to log on to her mother's bank account and pay the bills before she logged on to her e-mail account. Four e-mails from her sister. Ugh. She did not want to deal with that right now.

She eyeballed the stack of checks. Molly normally took care of delivery, but the prospect of getting out of the office for a little while was tempting. Two businesses were within walking distance, and a walk in the August sunshine would be good for the baby. And she could stop for a smoothie on the way back.

The sunshine helped clear the cobwebs from her head and being out in the neighborhood improved her mood. She loved the entire City Market district with its variety of restaurants, interesting stores and true community feel. The rent on the office was high, but worth every penny. Ally dropped off both sets of checks, then dawdled in Franklin Square for a little while to enjoy the afternoon. Next year she could bring the baby here when they needed a break from the office.

She shouldn't delay getting back any longer. After a quick stop at the vegan deli for a banana smoothie for herself and a mango one for Molly, she rounded the last corner.

A very sleek red sports car like the kind James Bond would probably drive was parked in front of their building. As she approached, the driver's side door opened and a tall blond man got out. There was something vaguely familiar about the man…

Recognition hit a split second before he turned

around. Her pulse jumped briefly in excitement before reality hit and her heart dropped like a stone into her stomach.

Casually, as though he had every reason in the world to be right outside her office, Chris leaned against the car and crossed his arms across his chest, eerily reminiscent of that first day on the dock weeks ago. Only last time he'd seemed relaxed, open and approachable. Today he looked like he'd been carved from stone, and his jaw was tight. In a tone that could easily cut glass he simply said, "How are you, Ally?"

CHAPTER FIVE

HOLY HELL. Ally tightened her numb fingers around the cup she held as her heart jumped back into her chest and pounded erratically. She leaned against a mailbox for a moment as she tried to gather herself. *Breathe. Be calm.*

"This is certainly a surprise." Pleased her voice didn't shake too much, Ally punctuated it with a small smile.

Chris didn't return it. "Seems we're both having surprising days, then."

She didn't know what to make of that statement. In fact, she didn't know what to make of *anything*—not why he was here, not what she should say in response. "I thought you were still on Tortola with the *Circe*. What brings you to Savannah?"

His voice was clipped, succinct, the lazy drawl disappearing. "I brought the *Circe* home to Charleston. I came to Savannah to find you."

She'd dreamed once that Chris had come to her, and he'd said almost those exact same words. But the reality version wasn't at all like the dream. No, in her dream, Chris had smiled as he said the words, causing those adorable crinkles around his blue, blue eyes. Those eyes were cold now, and one eyebrow arched up in a mocking challenge. What *kind* of challenge, she wasn't sure.

She nearly blurted out, "Why?" but caught the question in time. From the look on his face, she didn't think she'd like the answer. Instead she went to her next pressing question. "How'd you find me?"

"You mean since you didn't leave a number on your brief goodbye note?" he mocked. "Seriously, Ally, in this day and age it's not all that difficult to find someone when you want to."

Something nasty lurked behind his words, sending a cold shiver through her insides. Her hand went protectively to her stomach, but she caught herself at the last second.

The instinctive movement didn't pass unnoticed, though, and she winced as Chris's eyes narrowed. "My question is, why didn't you find me?"

There's no way he could know. Bluff your way out of this and leave gracefully. "I enjoyed our time together—honestly, I did—but it was over and done with. I had no idea you'd leave Tortola. Or that you'd be so close to Savannah." That was the truth. *Why* did he have to be from Charleston, for goodness' sake? Why couldn't he be from Florida or someplace far, *far* from here? "It seemed best just to let it go."

Chris levered himself off the car and took a step toward her, his voice dropping dangerously. "That's not what I'm talking about, and you damn well know it. It would have taken you approximately five minutes to find me if you'd tried. And you should have tried as soon as you found out."

He knew. Oh, God, he knew. How? Paniclike flutters in her chest made it hard to breathe. No, there was no way he could know. "When I found out what?"

"Don't play dumb, Ally. It doesn't suit you. You're pregnant. About six weeks if I understand correctly. And six weeks ago you were with me."

There was the nausea again. She swayed on her feet as it washed over her. Chris grabbed her elbow. "Are you all right?"

She took a deep breath—inhaling the scent of him and letting it coil through her—and blew it out slowly, trying to will the nausea away. Game over, time to just face it. "How did you find out?"

He tilted his head in the direction of the office. "Your business partner—Molly, right?—she told me today when I called."

She needed to sit down, but there was nothing on the sidewalk to use as a seat. This was too much to process at once. The happy thought of Chris calling her *before* he knew about the baby was quickly stomped down by the need to wring Molly's neck. She took deep breaths to calm herself. It didn't work.

"I take it from your reaction that it is my baby."

All she could do was nod. The swimming feeling in her head was too much for anything else.

"And you had no intention of telling me?" Each word was clipped and sharp. This wasn't the Chris who'd taken her sailing and made her laugh. And made her cry out with his touch. This Chris was livid. Cold.

"I just—"

"There's no 'just,' Ally. Yes or no."

"No! I mean yes. I mean—" Over Chris's shoulder, she could see that Sarah, the owner of the bookshop across the street, watching her carefully, a worried crease on her forehead. A quick glance around showed Sarah wasn't the only one paying attention. No one was headed in this direction—*yet*—but they had an audience. At least her office didn't have street-front windows, or else Molly would be out here wanting to know what was going on. This public display had to stop.

She lowered her voice. "Look, I can't talk about this. Not now. And certainly not *here*."

The muscle in his jaw twitched. Chris looked around, noted the interest they'd garnered and nodded sharply. "Agreed."

Relief swept through her. She set the smoothies on the mailbox and rummaged though her bag for a pen and piece of paper. "I'll call yo—"

"Where do you live?"

Her head jerked up so quickly a neck muscle spasmed. "What?"

"We need to talk. Privately. Your place seems like the obvious choice."

She'd hoped for a reprieve. A chance to plan strategy. A chance to at least get her heartbeat under control. "But…"

"Right here, right now, or your place. Take your pick."

How dare he sweep in here and start ordering her about? She didn't have to "take her pick" about anything. She didn't need this kind of upset. She should just walk away. But guilt nagged at her. To be fair, he did have cause to be angry.

As she argued with herself, the tension in Chris's jaw seemed to increase. She wasn't going to get out of this, so she needed to pull herself together and deal with it as gracefully as possible. Better to get it over with now.

Yeah, keep telling yourself that.

"My apartment is about ten minutes from here. I'll need to get my stuff and tell Molly I'm leaving for the day. I'll be a couple of minutes."

Another nod, this one so small it was barely perceptible. The man was so tense, the cords in his neck were visible.

She managed to open the office door calmly enough and made it inside. Once out of Chris's eyesight, though, her knees began to wobble again as the magnitude of the situation hit her.

Zombielike, Ally placed the mango smoothie on Molly's desk before collapsing in the adjacent chair.

Molly brightened as she reached for her drink. "Thanks. Yum." She took a sip before looking closely at Ally, and the corners of her mouth turned down in concern. "Are you okay? You look pale. Are you going to barf again?"

Possibly. "I'm fine." The emotional toil of the last ten minutes—not to mention the thought of what was still to come—washed over her and she rubbed her eyes tiredly.

Molly took her answer at face value. "Some guy came in looking for you about twenty minutes ago."

A hysterical giggle tried to escape. "Oh, he found me."

"He was *all* shades of cute. Who is he? Is he single?"

Fatigue—probably not all due to the baby this time—washed over her, and she rested her head in her hands. "Molls, *please* tell me what possessed you to tell a stranger over the phone that I was pregnant."

Indignant, Molly nearly choked on her smoothie. "I did no such thing."

"Really? Chris says he called here today and you told him I was pregnant."

"Chris? Who's Chr— Oh." Molly's lips puckered.

"Someone did call, and when he said Chris, I thought it was the Kriss Brothers. I mentioned why we were fixing up that room. Are you telling me he was… That the guy who came in here… That he's—" Ally watched as all the pieces fell into place for Molly. "Oh, Ally, I'm *so* sorry. No wonder you look so pale."

There was that hysterical laughter again. Ally went to her desk and turned off her computer. "I'm taking the rest of the afternoon off. I'll see you tomorrow."

"Of course. Go home and lie down. We'll sort this all out tomorrow. I have to say, though— hummina, hummina. No wonder you…"

"Molly…" she warned.

"Okay, okay. What did he say?"

"Let's just say he's a bit angry I didn't find him when I found out."

"I told you that you should. He has a right to know."

"I know." Overwhelmed again, she swung her chair around and sat. "But being pregnant was complicated enough, I didn't need anything else. I thought he lived on his boat in the Caribbean, for goodness' sake. How was I to know he really lived in Charleston and wasn't just 'free spirit sailor boy'? Like I needed *another*…"

"Another Gerry?"

"Exactly. I have enough folks—not to mention

the baby—relying on me as it is. I just got one un-employed pretty boy off my hands, I didn't want to get another one to support. For all I knew, Chris Wells was just another Gerry waiting to happen."

"Wait a minute." Molly's eyes widened. "Chris Wells? And he's from Charleston? He's *the* Chris Wells?"

"Maybe. Why? Who's *the* Chris Wells?"

"I thought he looked familiar. Good Lord… Ally, I know you didn't want to contact him, but are you really telling me you didn't at least look the man up on Google out of curiosity?" Molly was already at her computer, fingers flying across the keyboard.

"I didn't want to know. It was just easier if I didn't. Look, he's waiting for me, and he's not in the most patient of moods right now."

"He can wait one more minute. Come here." Molly swiveled her computer screen around as Ally sat in the chair across from her. "You need to see this."

Chris on a sailboat, grinning at the camera. Her heart did a quick double beat as that was the Chris she remembered—not the very angry man waiting for her outside. "And?"

Molly sighed deeply. "Listen carefully. Ever heard of the OWD Shipyard outside Charleston? The *W* stands for Wells. OWD is the primary sponsor of Wells Racing, and the owner's grandson, *Chris,* captains their boats. Team Wells has won every major race in the last five years—including the America's Cup. They're considered unbeatable. My God, Ally, you certainly know how to pick them. Chris Wells is the Tiger Woods of sailing."

Slowly, Molly's words started to sink in, and the information on the screen in front of her corroborated her story. "How do you know this?"

Molly waved a hand dismissively. "Back when I was dating Ray, he was really into ships and racing. It was all he talked about."

"Yachts." She couldn't believe what she was seeing. Chris was a celebrity. And the heir to the OWD Shipyard to boot.

Molly looked at her blankly.

"Those are yachts, not ships." He'd lied to her. Said he raced some and occasionally won. Yeah, right. He was the freakin' god of the sailing world and he'd led her to believe... Well, he hadn't really led her anywhere, but he certainly hadn't been totally honest, either. Chris wasn't the only one angry now.

Not caring much anymore that Chris was waiting for her, she continued to click through the links, and each Web page brought a new emotion. She welcomed them. By the time she heard the chimes over the door, announcing that he'd gotten impatient and had come to get her, she no longer felt quite so shaky or defensive.

"Are you ready yet, Ally?" Anger still radiated from him, but she no longer cared how mad he was.

Molly, bless her heart, tried to defuse the situation. Extending her hand to Chris, she introduced herself. "We didn't meet properly earlier. I'm Molly, Ally's business partner."

Chris nodded, but his eyes never left Ally. He seemed to be trying to stare her into the ground, but she felt steady and refused to give him the satisfaction of cowering this time.

Grabbing her things, she stood. Time to get this over with. "Yes, I am. You drive. I'll see you tomorrow, Molls."

Chris watched as Ally led the way to his car and climbed in without waiting for him to assist. Something had changed in the last few minutes, and he now felt anger radiating from her.

Other than the terse directions she provided, she sat in silence as they drove. What did she have to be so irritated about? He was the wronged party here. When he'd seen her come around the corner, his body had leaped to life, his blood heating and his hands itching to touch her again. But the look on her face when she'd recognized him had killed that feeling as it answered almost every question he'd asked himself on the drive down from Charleston. She was pregnant. The baby was his. And she hadn't planned on ever telling him.

When he'd realized it was all true, the anger had boiled over and he'd blasted her with it. He hadn't handled the situation as well as he'd planned, and now guilt nibbled at the edge of his ire.

The only important answer he didn't have yet was *why,* but he planned to rectify that soon enough. With Ally practically vibrating with hostility as she sat next to him, though, he doubted he'd get a satisfactory answer at the moment.

In an attempt to both appease his guilt and ease the tension between them, he backtracked to less volatile territory—at least while they were in a small, enclosed space. "How are you feeling?"

Ally's eyebrows went up and she seemed poised to attack. Instead she closed her eyes and took a deep breath. "The mornings are pretty rough, and I'm tired a lot."

"And that's normal?"

She nodded. "Unfortunately." Her lips twitched in amusement, and, for a brief moment, he flashed back to Tortola, back to when her inability to hide her reactions had charmed him. But the moment passed quickly, and her amusement faded as rapidly as it had come. "Turn left. That's me on the corner."

The two-story Victorian sat gracefully among its historic neighbors, beautiful and well cared for despite its age. He'd been so occupied on the short drive, he hadn't noticed she was directing him to the heart of Savannah's historic district. "*This* is your place?"

Ally didn't break stride as she climbed the steps to the spacious verandah and slid her key into the lock. "The first floor is. I may not be the heir to a shipyard or have zillion-dollar endorsement agreements, but I do all right."

So she did know who he was. She may not have known when they met, but at some point she'd done her homework. Which meant she could have contacted him if she'd wanted to. His ire flared up again.

Ally's sandals slapped against hardwood floors, and the sound echoed off the high ceilings as she moved around the room before settling on an overstuffed red sofa. The apartment suited her—or at least the little he knew about her—old-fashioned around the edges but still modern. The absurdity of the situation hit him at that moment. A woman he barely knew was carrying his child.

"You wanted to talk. Let's talk."

The challenge was there; he no longer had the element of surprise on his side, and Ally must feel as though she had the home court advantage now. "How long have you known?"

"That I was pregnant? About three weeks."

"And in all that time, it never occurred to you that you should tell *me?*" Agitated, he paced in front of the sofa she sat on, hoping the extra expense of energy would keep him from lashing out again as his temper built.

"To what end? As far as I knew, you lived on a boat somewhere in the Caribbean and hooked up with a different girl every night of the week."

"And you assumed the swabbie wasn't worth telling? He was good enough to sleep with on vacation, but not good enough to help you raise a child?"

"Be reasonable, Chris. It's not a matter of 'good enough.' I was just trying to be rational about this."

"When you found out differently, you didn't call me because…"

"I only found out about the great Chris Wells twenty minutes ago, so it didn't affect my assessment of the situation."

"You expect me to believe that when you found out you were pregnant, you never once tried to find out more about me?"

For the first time in this ridiculous conversation, Ally's temper seemed to flare. "To be brutally honest, I had enough on my plate to figure out. I wasn't all that worried about *you*."

"Oh, no. I can't see why the *father* of the baby would have any impact whatsoever on your plans."

As fast as it had come, the heat fled from her voice and her tone became conciliatory. "Don't take it personally. I loved every minute we spent together, but it was just a summer fling. It was over, as far as everything was concerned."

He gestured at her stomach. "I beg to differ."

Ally sighed and rubbed her face. "Look. My hormones are a mess right now, I cry at the drop of a hat, I'm so exhausted I can barely keep my eyes open, and I haven't been able to eat all day. I can't deal with this level of hostility, and I don't see much sense in continuing to shout at each other. Let's just cut to the chase, okay?"

Personally, he felt there was a lot of ground still to cover, but only a true jerk would continue to upset a pregnant woman. It wasn't good for the baby.

His baby.

While anger had been driving him since Molly unwittingly dropped the news, the magnitude of the situation finally slammed into him. He was going to be a father. Hard on the heels of *that* realization was the even more shocking understanding that he wanted this baby.

Now he needed to sit down. He chose a chair across from Ally and nodded for her to continue.

Ally took a deep breath before she spoke. "I didn't try to find you because I didn't think it would matter. You didn't strike me as the kind of guy who was looking to be tied down, so telling you about the baby—even if I'd been able to locate you—didn't seem like a winning situation." He started to interrupt, but she hurried ahead. "*Obviously,* I was mistaken with that assumption, and for that I apologize. I didn't set out to get pregnant, but I know I want her. Or him. You don't have to worry, though. I have a good job, plenty of friends and family, and I can handle this. I don't expect anything from you."

Wringing Ally's neck sounded very tempting at the moment. "What if I expect something? This is my child, too, remember."

Genuine shock at his statement sent Ally's eyebrows up-ward. Had she never once considered that possibility while she was "handling" things?

"Well, um, I'm sure we can work something out. Visitation arrangements or…"

"That's not good enough."

"Then what *do* you want?" There was a beat of silence before Ally laughed. "It's not like we can get married or anything."

Actually, that was a possibility he hadn't considered yet. He hadn't had three weeks to make decisions. Hell, he'd barely had three *hours*. "Why not?"

"Be serious."

"Maybe I am."

"I'm not looking to get married at the moment." A shadow crossed her face but disappeared a second later.

"Neither was I, now that you mention it, but the circumstances have changed."

That seemed to spark something, and her calm facade dropped. She stood and paced, and her hands moved agitatedly as she talked. "But the century hasn't. We don't have to get married because I'm pregnant. There are other—"

"I'm not going to be delegated to the occasional

weekend." He'd had enough of that with his own parents in the early days after their divorce. Until his mother had decided not to bother anymore, at least.

"Then what do you want?"

Before he even realized what he was doing, he was on his feet and his hands were gripping her arms. "To be a part of my child's life. To be his father!"

Ally shook off his grip. "I'm offering you that. We'll just have to figure something out that works for both of us. Charleston is only a couple of hours away…"

As unbelievable as it sounded, Ally seemed to think he was really going to settle for whatever little plan she had turning in her head. Not likely. "Damn it, Ally—"

She spun on him in a fury. "Don't even look at me like that. How dare you come storming down here and start making demands? This is *my* baby, and *I'll* be the one making the decisions."

He moved toward her, and she took a step backward. "*Your* baby? Hel-lo, you didn't get pregnant by yourself. That baby is just as much mine as it is yours."

She lifted her chin and tossed down the gauntlet. "Maybe not. Maybe I lied and it's not yours after all."

So much for cutting to the chase and discussing this like adults. "Don't try me, Ally. You won't like the results."

Brown eyes narrowed and a flush rose on her chest. "Is that some kind of threat?"

"I don't make threats. Just promises."

The flush continued to rise up her neck, and Ally's lips compressed into a thin line. "Get out," she snapped. "Now."

He stood his ground. "This conversation is not over—"

"Oh, yes, it is. Leave." Stalking across the room, she picked up the phone. "Leave or I'll call the police."

"Now who's making threats?"

"You're not the only one who doesn't make empty threats. Get out of my house."

He'd never had anyone try his temper the way Ally did, and he was moments from saying or doing something he might regret later. Maybe it was best he leave before then. As he opened the door, he warned her one last time. "This doesn't end here. This is far from over."

"Oh, no. It's over. I assure you of that. Goodbye, Chris." She slammed the door behind him and he heard the lock click into place.

She thought it was that easy? That it was over just because she said so? She might have gotten away with it on Tortola, but the circumstances had changed dramatically.

He had his phone out of his pocket and his assistant on the line before he even had the car started.

Ally was in for a rude awakening.

* * *

Ally's anger carried her as far as the kitchen for a glass of water before it deflated in a rush that had her knees buckling. Ice rattled in the glass as she filled it from the tap with a shaky hand. Easing onto a bar stool gratefully, she sipped carefully and cursed Chris for making her lose her temper.

She *never* lost her temper. She was the calm one while everyone else spun out of control. Molly had always praised her flair for diplomacy, a skill she'd honed over years of dealing with her family and their constant dramatics. Why had it failed her now? Instead of calmly—rationally—coming to a workable agreement and smoothing ruffled feathers, she'd managed to make the situation worse. Where was her famed calm and diplomacy today? It had to be the hormones. This pregnancy was really messing with her head.

But now that she could see something other than a red haze... Ugh. She may not know Chris very well, but she had a sinking feeling she'd made a huge tactical mistake in firing up his anger.

Her five minutes with Google earlier today had told her a lot about the great Chris Wells. A true golden boy, he came from old Charleston money and had the whole sailing world worshipping at his feet. Maybe she should have given in to her curiosity sooner; then she wouldn't have been at such a disadvantage today.

"You sure know how to pick them," Molly had said

it with a kind of begrudging awe, but Ally knew that wasn't the case at all. Molly saw his good looks, his charm and his money, and therefore branded him a good catch. Ally, though, knew better. Looks, charm and money didn't equal squat in her book. Gerry had looks and charm to spare, yet he'd been an emotional black hole. She'd invested far too much in his dreams, only to get nothing in return except four years of doing his laundry. Golden boys had a tendency to expect the world to revolve around them, and she had learned her lesson the hard way. Hell, her own brother was a shining example—handsome and full of charm, he'd been dazzling girls since junior high. But he was self-centered and expected everyone to dance to his tune just for the privilege of basking in the reflected glow. His girlfriend, Diane, would have been history by now if she hadn't turned up pregnant, and even impending fatherhood hadn't tamed Steven.

If she'd found all this out about Chris and hadn't been carrying his child, she probably wouldn't have contacted him. Once bitten, twice shy. Between her brother and Gerry, she had enough experience to know that Chris would be a very bad idea.

And now she had someone else to think about, someone she *had* to put first. How long would Chris want to play Daddy before he got bored and went back to his far-more-exciting world? No way she'd put her son or daughter through that.

Most likely Chris was just reacting out of shock,

anger and guilt. It would pass now that he knew she didn't expect anything from him, and his sense of responsibility would fade. She just needed to wait it out. After all, even as mad as he was at the moment, what could he do?

Glad she hadn't completely lost her ability to be rational, she sent a quick text message to Molly to let her know everything was okay and that she was now going to take a much-needed nap. The usual afternoon fatigue was even worse in the aftermath of such emotional upheaval.

She pulled the shades to darken the bedroom and didn't bother to do any more than kick off her shoes before stretching out across the comforter. As she closed her eyes, the image of Chris climbing out of that car—that one second when she'd recognized him, before he had turned around and she'd seen the anger on his face—was waiting for her. And now that she was alone and sleep was crowding in from all sides, she couldn't ignore the fact her heart had skipped a beat in excitement, and for a fraction of a second her whole body had screamed to life.

If only things were different....

Don't go there. Ally rolled over and punched the pillow into shape. This was not the time to play If Only. She knew better than that. Things were what they were, and the sooner she got that through her head the better.

But it didn't stop her mind from toying with the might-have-beens until sleep dragged her under a few minutes later.

CHAPTER SIX

THE WORST PART of Chris's job had to be the paperwork. He had no patience for the pages of numbers and reports that cluttered his desk on a daily basis. He'd rather be down in the yard doing something—*any*thing, even welding, which he hated—rather than be stuck inside buried under a pile of paperwork. But, as Pops reminded him daily, OWD was still a family business, and as the only direct family Pops had left, Chris had to do his part.

That was soon to change, though. Chris being the only Wells left in line, that is. The news of Ally's pregnancy had thrilled the old man and put a new spring in his step. A great-grandchild—security for keeping OWD in the family—had shifted Pops's focus. He'd been a little disappointed Chris hadn't chosen to go about procreating in the old-fashioned way and that more children wouldn't be forthcoming anytime soon, of course, but he'd been more than just a little pleased, anyway. In the past few years, Pops's encouragement to get married had crossed the line into harping, so Chris knew Pops would see this as hope Chris did intend to settle down and have many more children—if not with Ally, then with someone else.

But it had shifted—at least temporarily—focus off the *Dagny* and the solo attempt.

He understood all too well where Pops's concerns stemmed from, but sailing had come a long way in the last twenty years, and his father's boat, the *Fleece,* had lacked many of the technological and safety features currently being installed on the *Dagny.* Yes, any attempt to sail solo around the world was dangerous, but the chances of him ending up like his father were considerably less.

Nope, no matter what Pops's hopes and plans were, he'd still be making his announcement at the club's annual gala on September tenth. That would be just enough time to get a buzz going before he set sail in October, but not so long that it lost its newsworthiness before it happened.

In the meanwhile, though, he still had to go over the shareholders' reports. Resigned, but determined to get it done in the least amount of time possible, he dug into the stack of papers. Engrossed and concentrating, he didn't know Marge had even entered his office until the large manila envelope landed on his desk.

"The courier from Dennison and Bradley

dropped this by for you. Can I ask why that shark has been circling the office recently?"

Marge always referred to his grandfather's attorney as "that shark." Where the animosity came from, Chris didn't know. Marge seemed to like everyone else in the world, but she always absented herself whenever Dennison came around and spoke disparagingly of him afterward.

"He's taking care of a few things for me." Opening the envelope, his copies of the papers served to Ally this morning slid out in a satisfying bulk of legalese.

"That's what worries me." Marge's brows drew together in a concerned frown. Marge, too, had received the news of the baby with a mixture of joy and shock, and had tossed in an "Aren't you glad you called her?" as well. But in the three days since he'd returned from Savannah and shared the news, Marge had hovered about, watching with great interest and asking vague, random questions about his plans. As she closed the office door and settled in the chair across from his desk, he assumed he was about to find out why.

Marge squared her shoulders and took a deep breath. "Your grandfather is going to either kill me or fire me but, either way, I'm not just going to stand by quietly again."

He knew his grandfather would do no such thing, and he knew Marge knew it, as well. "Again?"

"It wasn't my place to get involved before. I was still new here and figured there was a lot more going on than I knew about. But after seeing how it's turned out…" Marge stopped and shook her head. "Porter talks to me, and he's simply bubbling over with the idea of a great-grandchild. And if he's called in that shark Dennison, he's falling back on the same dirty tricks he and your father—God rest his soul—used years ago on your poor mother."

"My poor mother?" It was all he could do not to laugh at the turn of phrase. "My mother got exactly what she wanted in the divorce—freedom."

"And I'm telling you that wasn't what Elise wanted at all. You were too young to understand at the time, but I'd hoped that over the years you would learn the truth. Maybe if Paul had lived, you would have found out, but after he died, Porter closed ranks around you even tighter than before. He's basically a good man, so I always assumed his behavior was fueled by Paul's anger and then later his own grief over Paul's death. But now, I'm not so sure."

He'd never heard Marge speak a single ill word about Pops, so the clipped words and barely concealed distaste in her voice came as a surprise. Her hesitancy to just spit out whatever was bothering her was also odd. Marge had practically raised him, and she'd never once held back. Obviously, whatever she was stewing about was important.

Marge wasn't making a lot of sense, but she had his attention nonetheless. "Start at the beginning."

"Your parents started off with a bang—all fireworks and excitement. Elise was sweet and shy and very sheltered, and she never stood a chance against Paul's looks and charm and money—something I'm sure you're familiar with, seeing as you're him made over." Marge's stony facade cracked a little as she smiled at him with pride.

"But that's neither here nor there." She waved away the comment. "Unlike you, Paul never could be convinced to take an interest in the business, and Porter indulged his obsession with racing. Paul was always gone—another race, another title, other women—and your mother simply couldn't continue to put up with it. All she wanted was a simple, amicable divorce."

"Which my father gave her."

Marge's brows went up at the interruption. "At first, yes. Then a couple of years later she met that nice man and wanted to marry him. It wasn't a problem until she told your father she'd be moving to California after the wedding and they'd need to work out a new custody agreement. I think that was the day your grandfather finally went gray-headed from the news. Your mother left here in tears. I'll never forget it. Next thing I knew, that shark Dennison was in the mix and he buried your mother in restraining orders, custody papers and competency hearings. Money buys a lot of legal experts, and Elise wasn't able to fight back."

A vague memory stirred of his mother on the phone, holding papers in her hand and crying. He glanced at the stack of papers Dennison had drawn up, and guilt nibbled at him.

"I think you're beginning to get my point. They just wore her down until she couldn't fight them anymore. Then, to compound the issue, they let you think she'd willingly walked out of your life."

No wonder Marge had been the one to comfort him after his mother had left. She'd known the reason why. He felt the slow burn of anger in his stomach, but there was nowhere to direct it. His father was dead. His mother was dead. Marge had done the best she could in the situation. And Pops…well, it was tough to stir up too much anger towards a seventy-year-old man who was all the family he really had left.

"All I'm saying, Chris, is that if those papers are what I think they are—and the look on your face tells me they are—then *don't*. Don't do to Ally and your child what was done to you. You can work this out. She doesn't deserve it and your child deserves to have its mother."

Marge sat back in the chair and folded her hands in her lap—the signal that she'd said her piece and was done. Now he was faced with a dilemma. He'd let his temper carry him to this point—Ally had been served with these same papers first thing this morning. At least he had Marge's information before he had to talk to Ally about them and made the situation worse. In fact, he was surprised he hadn't had an angry phone call already. It was a lot to think about, and he needed to plan his next move carefully.

The intercom on his desk buzzed, and Grace cut in. "Mr. Chris, there's a— Hey! Wait!" At the same moment, his office door burst open and Ally stood there, chest heaving and curls rioting around her head. She held a familiar manila envelope in one white-knuckled hand.

"You bastard! How dare you. You—" Anger choked off her words.

Grace was right behind her. "I'm sorry. I tried to stop her."

Three women looked at him. Grace in apology, Marge in question and Ally… Well, he was just lucky looks couldn't kill.

So much for time to think and plan.

It was a good thing she didn't own a gun. It had taken a little while to figure out the legalese, but once the meaning of those papers had sunk in, fury consumed her. Even the unflappable Molly had been taken aback at the extent of the lawsuits.

That fury had only grown during the drive to Charleston, and she'd broken every speed limit in two states in her rush to confront Chris. Now that she was here, she was itching to do him physical harm, especially since he had the gall to look surprised to see her.

She couldn't form words. Every phrase she'd practiced on the drive was trapped behind the anger choking her.

While the blond-haired assistant sputtered behind her, a matronly woman rose from the chair in front of Chris's desk. As she turned, Ally saw both concern and, oddly, affection in her eyes.

"You must be Ally. You're even lovelier in person." The woman's kind smile and gentle pat to Ally's arm as she passed seemed surreal. "Let's go, Grace."

The older woman ushered the younger one out and closed the door behind her, leaving Ally alone with Chris, who looked remarkably calm and unperturbed for someone who'd just served enough legal papers on her to put that lawyer's child through college with the expense.

"Would you like to sit?" Chris came around from behind his desk and gestured toward the chair the woman had just vacated.

Had she crossed into the freaking *Twilight Zone?* "I don't know if I should. You'd probably use my decision to sit against me later."

She couldn't tell if the slight inclination of Chris's head was meant to be mocking or conciliatory as he perched on the edge of the desk. *The jerk.*

"I expected I'd hear from you today. I kind of assumed you'd call, though."

Molly had suggested the same thing, claiming distance would make it easier to deal with Chris and his outrageous demands. She'd been too mad to listen. "You questioned my competency, my fitness to be a parent. You're demanding my medical records and serving me with an order to keep me from traveling outside Georgia or South Carolina, and you wonder why I came to confront you in person? Maybe we should be questioning *your* mental stability."

"Actually, my attorney did all of that. I just told him I wanted my child and that you were unwilling to come to an agreement."

How dare he try to blame *her* for this? "So you decided to serve all this—" she tossed the envelope onto the desk "—on me? It won't work. I'm not going to let you take custody of this baby. I'll fight you."

"But you won't win."

A red haze clouded her vision, and she curled her hands into fists, her nails digging into her palms. "This is the twenty-first century. I have rights, and no judge in the universe would rule in your favor. I'm not incompetent." She lifted her chin in defiance. That much she was sure of. She was the poster child of competency.

"Maybe not, but it'll still cost you buckets of money to prove it."

All the air left her lungs at his matter-of-fact pronouncement, but Chris just shrugged. "I hate to be the one to break this to you, but it doesn't really matter if I can do half of what's in that envelope. My lawyers will serve you with motion after motion, and you'll be forced to respond to each one."

The possibility of a long, legal battle sobered her. It wouldn't matter if she was in the right; the repercussions would be horrific—not only on her, but on her family, on Molly, on the baby. *Especially* on the baby.

"Zillion-dollar endorsement deals will buy a lot of legal expertise, Ally."

Dear God, he was right. She didn't have the money to fight. She'd be bankrupt just responding to a *fraction* of the motions in that envelope. And if she couldn't fight him, would he win simply by default? Her stomach dropped. She'd made a horrific mistake in angering him, and she'd walked straight into this mess with her pride and anger. But what could she do now?

Chris seemed to realize when that last thought crystallized for her. He indicated for her to sit again, and took the other chair. "Maybe now you'll be more open to negotiation."

Negotiation? Just the two of them? She looked carefully for the trap, but Chris's face was the picture of friendliness and conciliation. Oh, she'd love to kill him. "You mean to tell me... You did this to... This was all just scare tactics?" Hesitant relief now mingled with her earlier anger, and the emotional toll left her drained as her head spun. As much as she'd like to turn on her heel and march out of there, she needed to sit.

"No, not just scare tactics. If we can't come to a workable solution, I will do whatever it takes. Hopefully, it won't come to that."

She tried to sort her scrambled thoughts, but those blue eyes locked on hers didn't help the process. She'd spent the past three days trying to figure out what to do, and she wasn't any closer to a solution than she was when Chris had stormed off her front porch. Trying to balance what was right for the baby with what would be good for them both in the long run... Chris's arrival had thrown all of her carefully made plans into the wind.

Then those papers had arrived and she hadn't been able to think at all. Chris's sudden willingness to be reasonable just brought back all of her earlier problems—this time coupled with the suspicion she wasn't going to like these negotiations.

Anger had kept her not-just-in-the-morning sickness at bay so far today, but as it ebbed, nausea swept back in. She fumbled in her purse for the bag of saltine crackers stashed there. She nibbled slowly on one, grateful for the stalling tactic, as Chris frowned. Then he left, returning a minute later with a paper cup.

"Ginger ale. It should help."

She nodded her thanks and sipped carefully. A few deep breaths later, her stomach settled some and the queasiness waned.

"I'm guessing discussing this over lunch is out of the question?"

Looking up, she saw a hint of laughter in those blue eyes, and the corner of his mouth twitched. He found her nausea amusing, did he? Next time, she'd just let fly on his shoes. See how funny he thought *that* was. "I'll stick with the crackers."

Of course, sitting in Chris's office with those horrible papers still on his desk waiting for him to tell her what he wanted from her wasn't helping her stomach much, either. Chris certainly had the upper hand in this "negotiation," and she knew it. *You have no one to blame but yourself,* her conscience nagged. *You fired the opening shot.* She needed to forget about her stomach and focus on keeping Chris reasonable—

"How's your brother?"

The change in topic jarred her, and she looked at him blankly.

"Your brother got hurt. That's why you left Tortola so suddenly, right?"

How'd he know that? "He's fine now. He flipped a dirt bike in a race and it landed on him. He was banged up a bit, but Mom just did her usual freak-out and I had to come sort everything…" *Don't give him more ammunition to use against you later.* Her batty family was a liability now. Great. She tried to shrug off the statement. "You know how moms are."

Chris didn't answer. Instead, he leaned back in the chair and crossed his legs at the ankles, looking far more relaxed than was at all fair, considering the emotional mess *she* was at the moment. "And you're in business with your best friend. That's interesting. You're a bookkeeper, correct?"

These questions she could answer properly. Nothing about AMI could possibly be used against her later. "Bookkeeping and general accounting, payroll, taxes—we do it all. My degrees are in accounting and finance, and Molly is also a CPA." She couldn't keep the pride out of her voice. "We've been in business for six years now and we operate totally in the black. Our clientele continues to grow, and we've won several small business awards…" At Chris's amused smile, she stopped. "What's so funny?"

"This isn't an interview. You don't need to read me your résumé."

Confusion reigned. "Then why did you ask?"

Chris sighed. "I'm trying to get to know you a bit better. We're about to have a baby together, and we hardly know each other." His eyebrow quirked up suggestively. "We didn't spend much time talking before."

In a flash, the memories of how they did spend their time hit her, and the muscles in her thighs tightened as the images caused a physical response. She hadn't allowed her thoughts to go there since Chris had shown up so unexpectedly and turned her life upside down. But now they were alone, he was within arm's reach, and he was smiling at her knowingly.

Argh. She tamped the memories down and focused on the moment. Chris wanted to play get-to-know-you games, but she wanted to get this over with so she could figure out what her next move should be. The suspense was killing her.

Just don't antagonize him again. Be calm. Be diplomatic. "Can we get back to the matter at hand? I apologize for the other day, and obviously you do have a right to be a part of your baby's life. I want to work this out amicably, but you have to tell me specifically what you're after." Proud of herself, she sat back in the chair.

Chris steepled his fingers and looked thoughtful. "You're sure you don't want to get married?"

Oh, God. "Positive," she managed to choke out.

"It's a simple, obvious solution."

"And one that's guaranteed to put us right back in this situation in a few years—only then, we'd be fighting out the divorce as well as custody arrangements." She wasn't ready to think about marriage to anyone—not now. She'd already had one narrow escape—a lucky one—but it had taken its toll. Plus, she wouldn't be able to resist his golden-boy looks and charm forever, and then she'd be in real trouble when it all went to hell. "Like you just said, we barely know each other. Great sex is hardly a foundation for a good marriage." *Did I actually just bring up sex again? Damn.*

Chris leaned forward in his chair, and now only inches separated them. Her pulse kicked up a notch and her skin grew warm. "Great sex? Try amazing, Ally." One finger trailed down her arm, causing the hairs to rise. "And there are worse places to start. At least we know we're compatible in that aspect."

Compatible didn't even begin to describe it. Her entire body was screaming for him now. She swallowed hard. "Chris, stop." To her utter amazement and relief, he did, leaning back to put space between them. She took big gulping breaths of air to clear her mind, but his scent still hung in the air between them, and inhaling only made the sex-charged cloud worse.

Stay angry. Don't let hormones confuse this issue.

But maybe she wasn't the only one having a hard time pulling it together. Chris dragged a hand through his hair and shook his head as if to clear it. Then, blowing out his breath in a loud rush, he stood and extended a hand to her. "Come on. I'll take you down to see the work on the *Circe.*"

Now what? She needed a map to keep up with him. "Why? We still need to ta—"

"We're not going to find any solutions today, Ally, because we're on opposite sides of the table. You've agreed that we barely know each other, so it seems the next logical step would be for us to get to know each other. We have some time before any decisions have to be set in stone, and it will make the whole process easier if we're friends. So I'm going to take you to the yard and show you how the *Circe* is coming along."

Chris stood there with his hand out to her, but she hesitated. After the roller-coaster ride she'd been on this morning, she didn't trust herself to see clearly. She didn't understand the mercurial changes of Chris's attitudes, and she had a hard time keeping up. She wanted to believe he was sincere, but from the corner of her eye, she could still see the hateful envelopes on his desk. Of course, her traitorous body was on board for "friendliness" and anything else that might come from it, and her hormonally confused brain kept going back to that If Only game where everything had turned out differently. The tiny part of her mind that was still able to think rationally tried hard to tamp down the other emotions and feelings confusing her. It was enough to give her a pounding headache as she tried to figure out what to do.

Then Chris smiled at her, and the crinkles nearly did her in. He had a point—regardless of how they worked out the details, they were going to be attached to each other for the rest of their lives through this child.

Six weeks ago, she'd made a decision that had changed her life forever by sleeping with him. Now she had to decide how she wanted to go forward, and animosity wouldn't be a good choice—for her or the baby. "You want this baby, don't you?"

"Very much."

Options. Decisions. She had to choose quickly. She was caught between Scylla and Charybdis, and ironically, the *Circe* was offering her a possible safe navigation through with minimal losses. She was slowly gaining a new—albeit grudging— respect for Odysseus.

But that didn't mean she was going to just roll over. "Are you willing to phone your lawyer right now and call him off?"

"Yes. I'm willing to be reasonable as long as you are."

"Do that first," she said, putting her hand in his as she let him help her to her feet. "*Then* you can show me the *Circe*."

"You've done an amazing job. She looks much better than she did." Ally ran her hand over the new seats in the *Circe*'s cockpit. "And the cabin is going to be positively decadent—I guess her racing days really are over."

The cavernous OWD workshop was usually alive with people and noise, but with most of the men gone to lunch at the moment, it echoed instead. Glad for the lack of an audience, Chris watched Ally carefully as she explored the dry-docked *Circe*. While she seemed to accept his offer of a truce, she was still wary.

Ally's arrival, so hard on the heels of Marge's revelations, had thrown him. But he was used to thinking fast on his feet, making the most of whatever opportunity came his way, and he was secretly quite pleased with how quickly he'd managed to adapt the situation to suit him.

Dennison hadn't been pleased to get the phone call and had tried to convince him to reconsider, but Chris was now hopeful he and Ally could work this out. Therefore, he concentrated on repairing what little relationship he had with Ally.

As she sat back in the cockpit and gave the tiller an experimental push, Chris assessed his options. While he'd originally floated the idea of marriage halfheartedly, it had oddly taken on new appeal. Marriage had never been on his radar before, and it would certainly solve a lot of problems. Ally was smart and beautiful, and she was already carrying their child. They got along well enough—especially in bed. Successful marriages had been built on a lot less.

The thought of Ally in bed led to the thought of

Ally in the ocean, Ally on the beach, Ally on the trampoline of the catamaran...his entire body grew hard at the memories. Oh, yes, they were certainly more than compatible there.

"What's that one called?"

Ally's question brought him back to the matter at hand. He looked where she pointed at the yacht dwarfing the *Circe*. "That's the *Dagny*. It means 'new day.'"

"And it's a racing yacht? It's awfully big."

"Ninety-six feet, but designed to go long distances very quickly with only a one-man crew. I'd offer to take you aboard, but Jack is a little possessive of the *Dagny* at the moment."

"Jack?"

"A cousin who designs all of Team Wells's racers. The *Dagny* is his latest pride and joy."

"And how far is a 'long distance'? I mean, I would have considered Tortola to Charleston a pretty long distance but the *Circe* made it, and she's tiny in comparison."

He laughed. "I said the *Dagny* would cover long distances *quickly*. The *Circe* might make it around the world, but not in any reasonable amount of time."

Ally looked at him strangely. "That's what you're planning to do? Sail the *Dagny* around the world? Alone?"

"And break the record at the same time."

"Wow." She sat quietly, her brow furrowed as she thought. "How long does that take?"

"If I'm going to break the record, less than sixty days."

The furrows got deeper. "Oh."

"Ally? Is everything okay?"

The frown lines disappeared as she brightened and plastered a smile across her face that didn't quite reach her eyes. "I'm just trying to reconcile this Chris with the one I met on Tortola."

"Same guy." He grinned at her.

"Not exactly."

"But close enough."

"Maybe."

She fell silent, tracing the pattern on the seat cushions with a finger, and he wondered what she was thinking about. In the silence, Ally's stomach growled. Loudly.

She blushed, placing a hand over her stomach. "Excuse me. I haven't eaten much today— between the morning sickness and, well, everything else that happened."

He stood. "Then I get the chance to feed you, after all. Let's go."

Ally hesitated. "Um, I should probably head home…."

He'd almost forgotten Ally's overly cautious nature, but even coupled with what she euphemistically called "everything else," he didn't realize he'd have to coerce her just to get her to have a meal with him. Of course, she was probably still a bit distrustful of his motives, but they had to get past that if they were going to work anything out. And if he'd learned anything as the captain of Team Wells, it was how to build a crew. Food helped.

"I never did get to take you out for a meal before, so I think I'm due. You need to eat, the baby needs to eat, and I haven't had lunch, either."

Her brow started to furrow again, but she seemed to catch it in time and shrugged instead. "You're right. Food would be good. Just not Mexican."

He jumped to the ground as Ally carefully descended the ladder propped against the *Circe*'s hull. Reaching up, he grasped her waist to guide her down the rungs and felt a tremor run through her. Like an electrical current, it vibrated through his fingers and shot through his veins, and he was loath to let her go when her feet finally touched ground.

Ally didn't turn around, and his fingers tightened on her as the heat of her skin seeped through the thin cotton of her dress. He remembered the feeling. Obviously so did she.

With her back to him, those wild curls tickled his face, the fresh citrus smell of her filling his nose and warming his blood. Experimentally, he moved his thumbs in small circles and another shiver shook her. Only inches separated them. If she'd just lean back a little…

Voices filled the room, chasing the silence away as the men returned from lunch, and Ally stepped away.

As she faced him, he noted the flags of color on her cheeks and the way her teeth worried her lower lip. Ally might be angry with him or wary of him or any other number of things, but she wasn't immune to him.

Satisfied with that knowledge for the moment, he allowed her the space she seemed to need to get herself back under control.

"I think— I mean we… Um, I, uh, guess…" She blew out a deep breath and brushed her hair away from her face. "Let's just go, okay?"

She turned on her heel and took two steps in the direction of the door before she stopped. The *Dagny* was right in front of her, and she looked at it carefully, her eyes tracing over the rigging before returning to the three hulls of the trimaran. Her mouth twisted briefly and she nodded, almost imperceptibly, before she set her shoulders and turned back to him.

Her smile—a real one, this time—snared him. "Are you coming? I'm hungry."

CHAPTER SEVEN

"AND AFTER THAT, everything went fine. We had a nice lunch, and I came home." She'd been too tired to do much more than send a quick text to Molly last night, so Ally brought her up to speed on the revelations of yesterday while they tackled the much overdue and mindless chore of filing.

"You certainly seem in better spirits this morning."

"My breakfast stayed down, so that was a nice way to start the day."

"That's not what I mean."

"I know." Ally grinned. "But it's still good news, right?"

"You just seem to be in a really good mood for someone who still has the threat of a massive, ugly legal battle looming over her."

"You don't get it, do you?"

"Obviously not."

"Dagny."

"It's a boat. It's what the man does for a living. I don't see the connection."

"Okay, pay attention. Chris got all upset over the news of the baby, then I escalate that by handling the situation badly, too. Like any man, he had to fight back."

"And he used the big guns."

"The biggest. *But* right now, this is still fresh news for Chris. That will fade. At this very moment, even with impending fatherhood on the horizon, he's still planning on going off on this around-the-world race thing. We talked about it a lot yesterday, and he's bordering on obsessed with it. That, and rehabbing the *Circe*. After that, there'll be another race and another boat vying for his attention. He'll lose interest in me and the baby soon enough— between the distance and everything he has to do for this race, we're not going to be high on his radar—and by the time the baby gets here, Chris will have figured out that he doesn't want to be tied down with a child." Ally closed the file drawer with a satisfying bang. "He'll have moved on. Maybe we'll work out some kind of settlement to salve his conscience or some visitation plans or something, but I guarantee he'll tire of this baby stuff soon enough."

"You sound pretty sure of that."

"Molls, racing is everything to him. He only works in the shipyard to make his grandfather happy. Wandering feet and an adventurous soul don't exactly equal Father of the Year. Look at my brother. Diane's been slow coming around to this simple fact, but even she's starting to realize that Steven will never marry her and settle down." Hungry again, she dug in her desk drawer and found an apple. Biting into it, she savored the taste and the lack of roiling nausea. "Nope, all I have to do is just bide my time and ride this out and Kiddo and I will be fine."

Molly's shoulders relaxed. "I'm glad to hear that. Oh, and by the way, the Kriss brothers are coming by Monday to work up an estimate on your new office."

"Excellent." And she meant it. After the upheaval of this week, she was finally feeling as if she had things back under control. TGIF indeed. She had about a thousand things she needed to do today. She'd been next to worthless most of the week, and poor Molls hadn't been able to pick up all of the slack, but her to-do list was manageable, if long, and without continual distractions she'd be able to get caught up and still enjoy the weekend.

But she found it hard to concentrate. The radio played softly, Molly's keyboard clicked away in the background, and the phones were silent, yet she couldn't seem to make the columns of numbers on her screen add up properly. After two hours of working on the same account, she'd made little headway, and she closed the file in disgust. She did mundane things instead—balanced her brother's checkbook, renewed her father's fishing license—but those simple chores didn't require much of her attention.

Her e-mail inbox was empty—since Erin had kicked her out of the wedding, she was no longer forced to referee the ongoing battles between her mom and her sister over caterers and flowers—and the lack of family drama felt odd. Maybe that was why she was unable to focus; she wasn't used to working *without* constant interruptions.

She'd certainly have plenty of interruptions once Kiddo arrived. The thought made her smile. She should enjoy the peace while it lasted—Erin couldn't stay mad at her forever, Steven would do something else stupid soon enough, and she'd be back in the mix. Plus, with two new babies in the family...

She shook her head to clear it and reopened the file from earlier. *Focus.* It took her another hour to find the mistake, and she was relieved to see it was the client's error, not one caused by her inattention.

When the phone rang, she jumped on the distraction eagerly.

"Hi, Ally." Her heartbeat accelerated at the sound of that now-familiar baritone, before she reminded herself she didn't need to panic. She only needed to humor him.

She tried for an upbeat, noncommittal tone. "Hi, Chris. What's up?"

"I'm done for the day and should be headed that way in another hour or so. Can you be ready by six?"

"Six?" She nearly choked on the word. "Ready for what?"

"Dinner."

"You want to go to dinner?" Her voice sounded strangled and Molly looked over, eyebrows raised in question.

Chris chuckled, and the sound did strange things to her already confused insides. "I'd heard forgetfulness was a side effect of pregnancy, but really, Ally. I told you I'd call and we'd go to dinner."

"I didn't know you meant tonight." *Every other male on the planet waits at least a week before they call—if they call at all.*

"Do you have other plans or something?"

Lie. Tell him you're busy. "Um, well..."

"Good. I'll pick you up at your place at six. Bye, Ally."

She was still sputtering her refusal when the line went dead. She placed the phone in its cradle and buried her head in her hands.

"What was that about?"

Ally didn't bother to look up. "He's taking me to dinner tonight."

She heard something that sounded suspiciously like a snort from Molly. "So much for staying below the radar."

"Molls…" Lifting her head, she saw a smirk playing at the corners of Molly's mouth. "This is not good."

This is not good was rapidly becoming her mantra. She left work a little early and took a nap, waking up still groggy an hour later. Cold water splashed on her face helped wake her up a bit, but the fatigue still grabbed at the edges of her mind.

Molly's lecture about the importance of appearing keen on Chris's ideas—for the time being, at least—echoed in her head as she pulled on a simple skirt and a sleeveless silk shirt. After clipping her unruly hair at the nape of her neck, she tried to add some color to her pale face. Deciding it wasn't going to get much better, she took one last critical look in the mirror before turning off the bathroom light.

She still had a few minutes before Chris was due to arrive, so she booted up her laptop and took it to the couch. She typed Chris's name into the search engine, but hesitated over the enter key.

Part of her still didn't want to know. She'd convinced herself weeks ago that the less she knew about Chris the better off she'd be. But that had backfired in her face. Molly had been more than willing to play research assistant, but Ally had held her off, still undecided about how much she did want to know. Even last night, after she'd returned from

Charleston, she'd purposefully left the computer turned off, willing to just ride this out. But now, with Chris headed to her door, seemingly serious about this get-to-know-you game, she had no choice but to learn everything she could about him.

Taking a deep breath she hit Enter, and seconds later Google returned its list.

The impressiveness of Chris's accomplishments floored her. From his earliest races when he was still in his teens to his most recent win, Chris had racked up an impressive résumé around the world. It didn't seem to matter where or what kind of boat he raced, he rarely lost, and never finished lower than third place. It seemed Wells Racing had several teams, and while Chris captained their most successful one, he also oversaw the entire racing operation.

OWD Shipyard built a variety of yachts—not just the ones Chris sailed—and their designs were popular all over the world. From what she could find, Chris had his hands in that aspect of the business, as well.

Oh, and here was a mention of Chris meeting with the OWD stockholders in his grandfather's place. And look, he ran summer camps for inner-city kids to learn sailing, and donated huge chunks of cash to environmental causes.

Good God, when did the man sleep? How on earth had he found the time to go to Tortola and sail the *Circe* home? Of all the men in the world she could have hooked up with, how had she, of all people, found the one who just happened to be the world's only zillionaire business-man/champion racer/philanthropist paragon? It boggled the mind.

Remembering their discussion yesterday, she added "world solo record" to her search terms to narrow the results. Google returned very few this time. While several sites speculated Chris would one day attempt to do it—and most likely break the record in the process—none seemed to know that plans were in the works to do just that.

The last link on the page had a very odd headline, and Ally clicked through. The Charleston *Gazette* must have put all of their archives online because the date on the article was close to twenty years ago. She scanned the first few lines quickly and almost closed the window before the impact of the words sunk in. Carefully, she started over again.

After an intensive nine-day search, rescuers have located the boat of missing sailor Paul Wells floating abandoned ten miles off the coast of Darwin, Australia. Based on the heavy damage to the hull, rescuers believe Wells, who was attempting to break the solo circum-navigation world record, perished in recent storms in the Timor Sea. Wells was a native of

Charleston and is survived by his father, Porter
Wells, and his eleven-year-old son, Chris.

A rock landed in her stomach. Chris wanted to
attempt the same stunt that had killed his father?
Was the man insane?

Wait, hadn't Chris told her before that sailboat
racing wasn't all that dangerous? "It's hard to kill
yourself," he'd said. She changed her search terms
to give her more information about solo circum-
navigation, and from the results it seemed it wasn't
all that hard to die after all.

Great. The father of her child had a death wish.
Maybe that's why he was so keen on claiming this
baby—he'd have a piece of immortality in case his
boat sank in the middle of the Pacific Ocean.

That thought made her a little sick.

The doorbell rang and she quickly shut down the
laptop before she went to answer it. Taking a deep
breath to prepare herself, she opened the door to Chris.

Who looked so good the air in her lungs came
out in a painful rush.

With the sun behind him, he seemed surrounded
in a golden glow. A black T-shirt hugged those
strong shoulders and skimmed over the planes of
his chest before disappearing into the waistband of
low-slung faded jeans. He grinned, and her heart
melted a little as her senses sprang to life. *This* was
the Chris she'd flipped for, and her body definitely

remembered him. He leaned in to give her an innocent peck on the cheek in greeting, but even that brief touch of his mouth burned her.

"Come on in." Ally stepped back to allow him to pass as she tried to compose herself. How different this time was from Monday when he'd been here, so angry the air around him had nearly burned from the heat. Today he seemed comfortable, almost relaxed.

Well, at least one of them should be, and it wasn't shaping up to be her. With a sigh, she closed the door behind him.

"You look great, Ally. Are you hungry?"

"Starved." Amazingly enough, she was, but she would've lied if necessary. Her living room usually seemed open and spacious, but Chris seemed to fill it completely, making her overly aware of him and creating an uncomfortable feeling of intimacy.

"Then let's go." Chris reached for her hand, and the touch of his hand sent a shiver through her. Yesterday she'd chalked up her immediate physical reaction to his touch as a simple aberration—something to do with all of those pregnancy hormones sweeping through her—but the repeat of the sensation today underscored her need to keep him at arm's length.

Literally.

But he made that extremely difficult to accomplish. He kept *touching* her—to help her out of the car, to guide her as they walked, to tuck a wayward strand of hair behind her ear—and her nerves were a complete jangle by the time they reached the restaurant on the riverfront.

Chris made small talk, and although her mind kept wandering to deeper places, she managed to keep up her end of the conversation. At the restaurant Chris sat opposite her, and finally she had enough distance to begin to incrementally relax.

A drink would have helped, but when Chris waved away the wine list, she remembered it would be a long while before alcohol touched her lips again. She'd have to find her courage outside of a bottle.

"I brought you a present." Chris slid a small black box across the table.

Jewelry. Jewelry came in boxes like that. "That's really not necessary." She scooted the box back to his side of the table.

"Yes, it is. It's what men do when they're trying to impress a lady."

She thought about Gerry and muttered, "Not the men that I know."

"Then you know a sorry class of men. No wonder you dumped your ex."

She looked up sharply to see if he was teasing. The look on his face didn't help her any there. "The fact he was sleeping with someone else had a lot to do with it."

Chris nodded sagely. "Then he wasn't only sorry,

he was stupid, as well. I don't know what you ever saw in him."

That comment brought a laugh and suddenly the wariness lifted. "Me, neither."

He pushed the box back to her. "Then open your present."

Sliding off the red and white ribbon, Ally pulled the lid off carefully. Inside, nestled against black velvet, she found a circular gold disk attached to a delicate chain. Holding the disk to the light, she could see the design: two lions rampant, flanking a pillar.

"It's beautiful." From the twitch of his lips, she realized she was missing something. "Okay then, tell me what it means."

"I thought you said you were a mythology geek. It's the symbol of Rhea."

Rhea, mother of the Titans, the goddess of female fertility and motherhood. Rather appropriate, considering. "Of course. Those are the lions that pull her chariot." She ran her thumb over the design. "I've never seen anything like it before. It's lovely. Thank you."

Before she realized it, Chris was behind her, seemingly uncaring of the curious stares of the other patrons as he took the necklace from her fingers and placed it around her neck. The disk settled perfectly in the hollow between her breasts. His fingers brushed lightly against her nape as he fastened the clasp. The touch was gone as quickly as it had come, and Chris returned to his seat.

His eyes moved over her like a caress. "It suits you."

The words and appreciative stare caused her face to heat, and she was very thankful for the dim lighting in the restaurant and the well-timed arrival of their server with their food.

As they ate, the conversation moved easily through current events, how she was feeling, and the book she was reading before Chris casually mentioned something about the *Dagny* that gave her the opening she needed.

She tried to keep her tone light. "It's a really ambitious goal, but isn't sailing around the world by yourself a bit dangerous?"

Chris set his drink down slowly and looked at her strangely. A moment later he nodded in understanding. "You've been doing some research. It was an accident. It's not likely to happen again."

"But that doesn't change the fact…" She trailed off, unable to finish the sentence.

"That my father died doing the same thing?" he provided for her.

"Exactly." She pushed her plate away, suddenly not hungry any longer.

"Things have changed a lot in the last twenty years, Ally. We've come long way. GPS systems, automatic emergency beacons, satellite communication, improved ship design—it's very unlikely anything catastrophic will happen."

He sounded so calm and sure about it. She wanted to smack some sense into him. "But from what I've read, there's at least a thousand easy ways to die out there."

"Concerned, Ally? I'm flattered. Just yesterday you would've been pleased to hear of my possible imminent demise."

"That's not funny." *Maybe a little bit true, but still not funny.*

Chris shrugged. "Don't worry, though. Should I be lost at sea or eaten by sharks, you and the baby will still be well taken care of."

For the first time that day, nausea rolled through her stomach. It must have shown on her face, because Chris leaned forward to take her hand, concern pulling down the corners of his mouth. "Hey, I'm just kidding about the eaten-by-sharks bit. I didn't mean to upset you."

"I don't see how you can treat this so lightly."

"I'm not. Trust me when I tell you the *Dagny* is the safest, most well-built ship on the planet, and I don't plan to take unnecessary risks." His thumb brushed over her knuckles, soothing her. "I need to do this—not only for me, but for my dad and the company, too. But you don't need to worry about it. I fully intend to make it home in one piece."

I'm sure your father had the same intention. She

didn't say the thought aloud. After all, she really didn't have any business getting involved in his plans. She shouldn't have brought it up in the first place.

The light brush of his thumb increased in pressure until he was practically massaging her fingers. The mood was getting too tense and his touch too familiar. To break it, she mimicked his earlier tone. "Then I'll just cross my fingers you *don't* end up as shark bait."

"I appreciate that," he said wryly.

At that tentative understanding, Chris signaled for the check. As he paid, Ally nibbled on her thumbnail and wondered why she cared so much all of a sudden.

Ally had to be the most incomprehensible woman he'd ever met. It could be downright frustrating at times to try to figure her out. The upside, of course, was that she was utterly fascinating. Her moods changed rapidly and without warning, like a squall rising from nowhere, but that unpredictability was part of her allure.

And that allure was becoming increasingly impossible to resist.

He wanted her. Intensely. It didn't seem to matter whether she was spitting fire in his direction or trying to freeze him out, his body burned for her. From the moment he'd met her on Tortola, she'd been a craving he couldn't seem to satisfy.

Wanting her had gotten him into this situation, and eventually—in spite of her objections—he and Ally would have to come to a workable solution, even if right now they were in complete disagreement as to what that solution would entail. The idea of marriage had grown on him, but Ally still seemed dead set against that. He'd have to convince her differently. Sex might work in his favor there—after all, he knew she wanted him, too, and it might be just the right angle to work. Logic argued he should take this slow, win her over the old-fashioned way, but logic wasn't controlling him at the moment.

He wanted her. Pure and simple.

Now, preferably.

Ally kept a careful distance as she walked beside him to the parking lot. If she only knew what was running through his mind…

She seemed lost in thought on the short drive back to her place, occasionally biting a fingernail as she stared out of the window at the darkness. He was still easing the car into a space in front of her house when she had her seat belt unbuckled and her hand on the door.

"Thank you for dinner. And the lovely necklace. I'll see you—"

Nice try. "I'll walk you up."

Ally seemed poised to argue, but she did wait for him to come around and assist her from the car. At the front door, she put her key in the lock and tried again.

"Good night."

"Aren't you going to invite me in?"

"I don't think that's a good idea, Chris. Let's just take this one step at a time. No need to rush things."

He stepped closer, close enough to feel the heat radiating off her and see her eyes darken. "Who's rushing?"

Ally stepped back a pace, the door blocking a further retreat. "I'm not stupid, Chris."

Her hair had escaped its clip again, and he caught the lock that trailed over her shoulder, winding it around his finger. "I never claimed you were."

Ally stammered as her breathing picked up pace. "We...we...we can't just pick back up where we left off. Everything is diff-different now." Even as she spoke, her hand slid gently over his forearm, belying her words. "There're so many complications..."

"It's not that complicated at all." He shivered as her hand worked its way over his chest, coming to rest over his pounding heart. He traced a finger along the stubborn curve of her jaw, and she lifted her chin, putting her mouth only inches from his. "This is pretty simple."

Ally lifted her eyes from his mouth and met his gaze. The hunger there rocked him. A second later she rose on tiptoe, and the hand on his chest slid to his nape. "I'm probably going to regret this."

Her lips landing on his blocked his response, and

as she fitted her body against him his argument died in the flames that stroked him.

This he remembered all too well. The inferno Ally stoked in him. The feel of her mouth moving hotly under his. The taste of her as his tongue swept inside her mouth to explore. The little moan that vibrated through her as his hands slid over her back and pulled her tightly against him.

The sound of a car passing penetrated the sensual haze Ally wove around him, bringing his attention back to the fact that they were on her porch, providing a show for the neighborhood. He reached behind her, found the key still hanging in the lock and pushed the door open. Ally stumbled backward, pulling him over the threshold, and he was able to kick the door closed with a foot.

In the half-light and privacy of her living room, Ally's kiss deepened, turning carnal with need. Her hands tugged at his shirt, pulling it free from his jeans and over his head, and her hands slid over his skin, causing his muscles to contract at her touch. He worked the buttons of her shirt quickly, and it slithered to the floor.

Ally broke the kiss and stepped back. Even in the dim light, he could see the flush on her chest and the rise and fall of her breasts with each shallow breath. With a long look that scorched him, she reached for his hand and led him down the hall.

CHAPTER EIGHT

YOU'RE CRAZY. SEND HIM HOME. Don't do this. Her conscience hammered the words at her as she led Chris the short distance down the hallway. Her whole body was alive, though, for the first time since she'd left Tortola, and the electric hum thrumming through her easily outweighed any arguments her brain might want to put forth.

Chris had a pull on her she didn't quite understand, but now wasn't the time to try to work it out. The light in his eyes and the promise in his kiss were irresistible, and she really didn't care about tomorrow's complications tonight.

It wasn't as if she could end up pregnant or anything.

Chris traced a finger gently down the line of her spine as she walked, and goose bumps rose on her skin. His hand splayed across her back. Two more steps and they were in her room, the bed beckoning.

He caught her shoulders and pulled her against

him. The skin of her back met the hard planes of his chest as he nipped the sensitive skin of her neck. Warm hands smoothed around her waist to massage circles on her stomach before moving up to allow his thumbs to graze tantalizingly over the flesh spilling over the cups of her bra.

Her breasts were more sensitive these days, and the exquisite sensation had her grasping at his thighs for support. Her fingers dug into the denim as he increased the pressure and circled a finger around the hard point of her nipple. Her head fell back against his shoulder, allowing him greater access, and the heat of his breath tickled her ear.

She moaned as he slid her straps off her shoulders, and her breasts were released into his hands. Chris murmured in appreciation as he teased her aching nipples, causing her to writhe against him.

One hand on her stomach held her in place as he moved his hips against her, his erection pressing insistently against the curve of her bottom. The other hand inched her cotton skirt upward to the tops of her thighs, and she hissed as Chris's fingers slipped beneath the lace edge of her panties and found her.

She exploded almost immediately at his touch, bucking hard against his hand as the orgasm moved endlessly through her. Chris whispered words of erotic encouragement in her ear, fanning the flames, until she sagged against him, her trembling legs no longer able to support her weight.

He turned her then, his mouth moving over hers hungrily, stealing her breath, as he made quick work of her remaining clothes. Ally cursed her numb fingers as she fumbled with his straining zipper, the need to touch him overwhelming. When it finally released, she hooked her hands in his waistband, drawing his clothes downward as she sank to her knees.

Chris's hands threaded through her hair, massaging her scalp as she took him into her mouth. She heard his sharp hiss of pleasure as she ran her tongue over his hard length, and his fingers tightened.

In two quick moves, Ally found herself between the soft bed and Chris's hard body, and every erotic dream she'd had in the past six weeks came true as he slid into her and sighed her name.

The husky sound of her name on his lips caused her to open her eyes. While the shadows of the room cast hollows around his features, she could see the intensity in his eyes as he moved against her, pushing her to another release.

Her fingers dug into his shoulders as she held on, greedy for what he could give her, and when the tremors began, he redoubled his efforts, holding her hips firmly and picking up the pace. She arched as the pleasure turned too intense, only vaguely aware that the sounds she heard came from her as she went over the edge. From a distance, she heard Chris groan as he gathered her close and stiffened, and time seemed to freeze as he held her while the after-shocks moved through them.

Chris's breathing was harsh in her ears and his heart thumped heavily against her chest. Ally chased after her scattered thoughts, refusing to listen to the small voice in her head saying, *This is where you belong.*

She'd given in to the sensual pull of Chris, knowing full well it would only complicate their situation further. The intimacy of Chris, in her bed holding her while her heartbeat slowed to normal, unnerved her, but even as she worried, her fingers toyed with the fine hairs at his nape, loving the feel of him against her again.

After one last deep, shuddering sigh, Chris rolled to his back, pulling her with him to pillow her head on his chest. His fingers combed through her tangled curls as she listened to the even thump of his heart.

The silence wasn't quite a comfortable one, and the longer it stretched out, the more tense Ally became, the wonderful afterglow evaporating as quickly as the moisture on her skin.

Fatigue was catching up with her, fuzzing her brain as she tried to think. Was he planning to stay the night? He certainly didn't seem in any rush to move. Should she let him stay or usher him to the door? If she let him stay, it would only make things much more difficult later.

Yeah, because I don't want to get too used to having him around.

"Chris," she whispered, only to be interrupted by her own jaw-cracking yawn.

Chris's hand circled on her back until she completed the yawn and tried again. "Shh. Just sleep now. We'll talk later."

We should talk now, she told herself, even as her brain latched onto the idea of sleep and the weight pulled on her. But the soothing caress of Chris's hands was too much to resist, and she started to slip away. *But this is really nice, too,* her body told her, already relaxing against him.

Just don't get used to it, she reminded herself.

Ally's breathing deepened, evening out as she slept, each exhale sliding across his bare chest like a caress. She talked in her sleep, mumbles he couldn't understand. He tried to pick up a word here and there, but nothing she said made sense.

It would be too easy if, like in a movie, she'd tell me everything I needed to know while she was asleep. Insight into her thought process would help. A lot.

He knew Ally was humoring him, to a certain extent, simply because of the leverage his legal team gave him. He could tell by the wary look she couldn't quite hide completely. But her response to him tonight hadn't just been an attempt to play along. Passion had brought down that wall, revealing the Ally he remembered, and at least while she slept, she couldn't argue with him.

Ally turned over and snuggled her back up against his side. Pushing up onto his elbow, he curved around her, spooning her to his chest. She sighed deeply in response.

Chris smoothed a hand down her arm and over her stomach, stopping at the flat plane beneath her navel.

Their child was right under his hand.

Something primal swept through him—a feeling of possessiveness, a need to protect. Slowly, an inkling of what had driven his father to battle his mother so ferociously dawned on him. It didn't make what he had done right—far from it—but Chris was starting to understand the sentiment.

He didn't want to fight Ally. To drag her and their child through the courts until one or all of them were destroyed by the process.

Ally mumbled in her sleep, and it brought a smile to his face. He was making the right decision; he knew that for certain now.

He closed his eyes, his hand still in place, rising and falling slightly with Ally's breath. As he drifted toward sleep, he realized that, unlike for his father, that primal feeling extended to his child's mother, too.

Ally woke to the smell of bacon. It didn't make sense to her groggy brain. Her mom knew better than to drop by early in the morning or without warning, so it must be the neighbors upstairs. Why did they have to be so loud on a Saturday morning…

She rolled over, intending to put a pillow over her head and go back to sleep, but the mess of covers on the other side of the bed reminded her she hadn't slept alone last night.

That memory caused her to sit up as the details fought for notice: a pair of men's shoes on the floor by the door; her bra hanging drunkenly off the back of a chair; the noise and aroma coming from her kitchen…

Chris was still here. And he was now cooking breakfast.

She nibbled her thumbnail, unsure how she felt about that. One thing was for sure—she wasn't going to take the risk of facing him naked with bedhead. She padded quickly to the bathroom, grabbed a robe and did her best to make herself presentable. She came out, still knotting the robe, just as Chris stuck his head around the corner.

"I thought I heard you." His shirt was a bit wrinkled from a night on the floor, and a dark shadow traced his jaw, but he still looked too good for her equilibrium to handle. Especially when he grinned like that. "Are you hungry?"

After so many weeks of morning sickness, the absence of nausea felt strange. Maybe she was finally getting past it. Thank goodness. She nodded and let Chris lead her into the sunshine-lit kitchen.

She loved her kitchen. She loved to cook. But never in the three years she'd lived here had anyone cooked for her, so the neatly set table for two caught her off guard. It was a very simple breakfast, just bacon, toast and fruit with a cup of tea steaming invitingly on the side.

A lump rose in her throat. Chris had made her breakfast.

She tried to clear the lump. "It smells wonderful. Thank you."

Chris just grinned at her again as he moved through her kitchen with ease, bringing milk and jam to the table. "I tried to keep it simple, as I wasn't sure how the whole morning-sickness thing was going."

"I think I'm getting over it. I'm certainly starving today."

"Then eat." He slid several strips of bacon onto her plate before sitting back to sip his coffee. The bacon was extra crispy without being burnt—just the way she liked it.

"You're a good cook."

Chris accepted the compliment with a nod of his head. Ally didn't know what to say next. On the rare mornings Gerry had gotten up anywhere close to breakfast time, he'd read the paper while eating, claiming mornings were too early for civilized conversation. Since he'd moved out, she'd taken up the newspaper habit herself for lack of anyone to talk to. What did people talk about at breakfast?

Chris picked up the conversational ball, but as he asked, "When's your next doctor's appointment?" she wished for a different topic.

"End of this month. They'll do the first ultrasound then."

"I'll be there. Just e-mail me the time and place."

"You don't have to—"

"But I *want* to, Ally."

She nodded as she buttered her toast. "So when are you heading back to Charleston?"

One eyebrow went up. "Eager to get rid of me?"

Not at all. Where had that come from? Even with the slight awkwardness she felt, she kind of liked having him here, doing something simple and homey like eating breakfast. *Don't get used to it,* she reminded herself. "You're welcome to stay, but surely you have other things to do."

"I do have to leave in a little bit. I have a club meeting this afternoon." Much to her surprise, it wasn't relief she felt at his words. If she was going to be honest with herself, she'd have to call that sinking feeling disappointment.

Chris leaned forward, his eyes lighting up. "There's a race next Saturday—a short one just for fun and bragging rights. Would you like to come?"

Ally chewed her bite of bacon slowly, stalling for time. Chris was trying to include her in his life, and she got the feeling that inviting her to a race was a milestone of sorts. Maybe he really did want this to work out between them. Her chest expanded at the thought, and that raised an even bigger question.

Did *she?*

She could be her normal, cautious, rational self, or she could be the adventurous Ally she'd discovered on Tortola. Normal Ally said to keep her distance and stay safe; adventurous Ally wanted to take the chance, enjoy whatever came her way for as long as she could.

Good Lord, she was becoming as crazy as her family.

Chris reached over casually to refill her mug, and the simple gesture warmed her, making her feel she was making the right decision. "I'd love to see you race."

His grin confirmed it.

Her phone rang, disturbing the coziness of the moment. Chris handed her the cordless handset from the counter, and she glanced at the caller ID. She set the phone down and picked up her tea instead. At Chris's questioning look, she shrugged. "It's my mom. I knew the silence was too good to last. Let the machine get it."

A chuckle was his only response, but it was soon drowned out by her mom's voice.

"Ally, honey, where are you? You haven't called in days. You can't still be upset at Erin. I know she hurt your feelings, but it is her wedding, you know."

Ally rolled her eyes.

"Just be thankful your sister is nothing like mine. Now, lunch has been pushed back to one-thirty tomorrow, and I need you to stop by the store and get the wine. With everything going on today, I just don't have the time. I swear, your grandmother is going to put me in an early grave…"

Ally walked across the room and turned the volume down on the machine. Chris did not need to hear her mother carrying on about the crisis of the day. "That could take a while. I'll listen to the rest later."

"I take it Erin is your sister, but why would you be upset with her?"

Ally tried to think of a tactful way to put it, but came up empty-handed. "She kicked me out of her wedding."

"Why?"

"Because I'll be seven months pregnant at the time."

Chris frowned. "I know this is your family we're talking about, but isn't that…"

"Selfish? Self-centered? Slightly sanctimonious?"

Chris leaned back in his chair and spread his hands. "Well, I wasn't going to say it."

"Erin's turned into a Bridezilla over this wedding. I'm kinda glad to have an excuse to be out of the fray."

"And you're expected to have lunch with her tomorrow?"

Ally returned to her chair and poked at her fruit. "The Sunday family lunch. Isn't it a time-honored tradition for every family?" She sighed.

"You don't sound too keen on that tradition."

"As I'm sure you've gathered by now, my family is a little bit nutty. They're not happy unless they're driving me insane." Ally wanted to take the words back the moment they left her mouth. She'd gotten so cozy with Chris this morning, she'd forgotten her need to keep her crazy family under wraps.

"I understand the feeling."

That got her attention. "Seriously?"

"I can't sympathize completely because I don't have siblings, but I do have several cousins. And Pops can be over-the-top sometimes." The corner of his mouth curved upward. "Families drive everyone insane. It's just part of the package."

"Well, my family has a jumbo-size package of crazy going on. It's almost like they try to outdo each other."

"Is your mom a good cook?"

Ally nearly choked. "Are you angling for an invite to lunch?"

"I should probably meet them at some point—we are about to be related, after all. Plus, you shouldn't have to bring the wine since you can't drink it."

Related. Chris said it so offhandedly, like it was a foregone conclusion. Technically he was right, but it still sounded like something else entirely. But showing up to a family event with Chris... "I don't know."

Chris looked at her oddly. "I take it you haven't discussed me with them yet."

"Not exactly. I mean, they know I'm pregnant, but I made it clear the topic of the father was off-limits."

"That was before. Now that you know I'm going to be around, they should probably get used to the idea." At her skeptical look, he added, "What, you don't think they'll like me?"

"Oh, they'll like you." *And then I'll never hear the end of it if this doesn't work out.* On the other hand, she'd never hear the end of it, anyway. She'd held her family at bay for the time being, but eventually... Of course, once Chris met the Bat Crew, he'd probably beat feet back to Charleston, solving a number of her problems right there.

She just wasn't sure if that's what she really wanted anymore.

"Then it's a date." Chris drained the last of his coffee, and Ally watched in amazement as he grabbed empty plates off the table and efficiently put everything in the dishwasher. She didn't know people with a Y chromosome could load a dishwasher.

She stood to help, only to be waved away with an "I've got it." The surprises just kept coming from Chris. Domesticity was not something she expected from a golden boy like him.

Chris closed the dishwasher with a snap and

came to kneel next to her. "As much as I hate it, I have to go. I'm going to be late as it is." He kissed her gently on the forehead. "I'll see you tomorrow."

Ally followed him to the door. "That's an awful lot of driving for one weekend. You don't have to come tomorrow. It's okay."

He was threading his belt through the loops of his jeans and didn't look up. "The driving is a pain, but it's not an issue anymore."

"Oh." Had he changed his mind in the last two seconds?

"Victor had the tail rotor taken apart this week, but he promised to have the helicopter back in working order sometime today."

Her mouth dropped open. "Helicopter? You own a helicopter?"

Chris smirked, then hooked a finger under her chin, closing her mouth and turning it up to his at the same time. "Not personally, but the company does. It saves a lot of time." He brushed his lips across hers. "Bye."

Ally closed the door and leaned against it. She could hear the powerful motor of his car roar to life, then fade into the distance as he drove away.

Like she didn't have enough to process. He owned a freaking helicopter, as well. And he'd be flying down tomorrow just to have lunch with her family. Suddenly, the hundred miles between Savannah and Charleston didn't seem like such a stumbling block.

Just when she'd begun to think she had her feet

under her and a plan in place, Chris had pulled the rug out. Bit by bit, he was slowly chipping away at her entire wall of defense.

How this vapid family produced someone like Ally baffled him.

She'd picked him up at the helipad, then spent the entire drive to her mother's house "preparing" him, saying her family was a bit crazy but generally harmless. He hadn't said anything in response to her anecdotes, because everyone thought their families were a bit insane or embarrassing.

Instead, he'd been introduced to the most selfish, narcissistic, self-centered people on earth. They were quick to put two and two together and realize he was the father of Ally's child, but that hadn't stopped the snide remarks made to Ally about her unwed, pregnant state. Yet no one seemed to make the same comments to Steven or his obviously pregnant girlfriend, Diane.

Ally favored her mother, Hannah, who didn't look old enough to have three adult children, but the similarities ended there.

Hannah vapidly bounced from topic to topic, complaining about everything from wedding plans to the way Ally wore her hair. Erin, whom he mentally dubbed "princess," treated Ally to conde-scension while simultaneously expecting Ally to manage everything. Ally's brother was a real piece of work, a man-child who was obviously used to the women of his family waiting on him hand and foot. It extended to his girlfriend, as well, who even in an advanced state of pregnancy perched on the edge of her chair waiting to care for his next need. Through it all, Ally's father wore the look of a man who'd learned it was easier not to interfere while his family swirled around him.

The entire lot disgusted him. Was Ally sure she wasn't adopted?

After half an hour, he'd been hard-pressed not to drag Ally out of that toxic atmosphere, but she'd given him a pleading look and a whispered "It's okay. They'll get it out of their system soon."

No wonder Ally approached the world with such caution. Her entire family had the emotional maturity of fifteen-year-olds, and no matter what happened, it was Ally's job to fix it or else take the blame and to soothe ruffled feathers. When her brother handed Ally a checkbook for her to balance, it was almost the last straw. Couldn't these people handle anything without Ally?

An hour later it hadn't gotten any better, and Chris's appetite and patience were long gone. When his phone rang, he went onto the porch to take the call and stayed out there to cool off before facing her family again.

"They're usually much better behaved in front of com-pany." Ally spoke from behind him. "I'm sorry."

Her heart-shaped face was earnest and concerned, and all the light had gone out of her eyes.

He bit back the disparaging remarks. This was Ally's family, after all, and she obviously cared for them. He wouldn't score any points with Ally by insulting her family—however well-deserved and correct the observations were. "They're certainly..." He searched for an adjective.

"Crazy?" Ally provided. "I told you that," she added with a sigh.

It wasn't the word he would have chosen, but it would do. "They're nothing like you, that's for sure." He touched a finger to her chin.

"Somebody has to be the grown-up. Can you imagine how they'd function if I weren't around?" The corner of her mouth tipped up like she thought it was amusing.

"They're adults," he said, although it was a loose interpretation of the word. "They can take care of themselves."

"You'd think." Ally seemed to ponder that statement as she leaned against the porch railing. "It's just easier to humor them than it is to deal with the fallout."

"Let me guess. The reason you left Tortola so unexpectedly wasn't simply because Steven had been in an accident, but because someone had to come deal with the grown-up stuff."

Ally inclined her head slightly. "Of course I was worried about Steven, but, yeah, they needed me

to deal with the hospital and the insurance companies and such. They don't deal well with actual emergencies."

He tried to keep his voice light. "What are they going to do when you're busy with the baby and not able to drop everything when they call?"

She paused, seeming to think about something, so he let the silence stretch out. "Molly asked me the same thing."

"Maybe it's worth thinking about."

Ally kicked off the railing and started to pace. "Sometimes I get really fed up with them. They're flighty, they can't hold down jobs or be responsible about *anything*. They loved my ex, and looking back, I can totally see why. He was just like them. Happy to just sit back and let me take care of everything."

Bitterness tinged her voice, and she seemed to be talking to herself now. "Calling me home from my vacation was par for the course. And at the time, I actually thought they'd done me a favor."

"A favor?"

"After I got over the anger at having my vacation interrupted, I realized that given a few more days, I probably would have latched onto you. Tried to bring you home with me."

Understanding dawned. "And I'd be just someone else for you to take care of. A beach bum with no job."

She nodded. "No offense intended. I still toyed

with the idea of trying to find you for a little while, but then I turned up pregnant."

"And you figured the baby would be enough responsibility."

"God, yes. I just didn't have any more to give."

"So doing it alone was your solution?"

"It was easier than trying to figure out how *you'd* fit into the picture." She snorted. "Of course, that's before you showed up and proved you didn't need me to take care of you, too."

"That's because I'm an actual adult—not like them." He jerked his head in the direction of the house. She winced, then nodded in agreement. "I don't need a keeper."

"I know that now. I misjudged you, and I'm sorry."

He stepped forward and smoothed his hands over her crossed arms. She'd provided him with an opening. "I'd like to help take care of you, you know. You and the baby."

Ally's eyes met his, and he could see the confusion there. She really had been flying blind through this. And while the front porch of her parents' house wasn't exactly a good place to be having this conversation, he forged ahead.

"We kind of went about this all backward and out of order, but that doesn't mean we can't make it work."

Ally inhaled sharply. "You're talking about getting married, aren't you?"

He took a deep breath and asked for patience. "Yes, Ally, I'm talking about getting married. But not immediately."

Her shoulders dropped and she sighed audibly in relief. That irked him a little. "But this game we're playing—dancing around like there's a better solution—is crazier than your family." His voice turned husky. "There's a lot to build on." This time when she inhaled, he watched her eyes darken and knew she was also thinking about the night before last. His body hardened in response.

"Chris, I—"

"Shh." He pressed a finger over her lips. "You brought me home to meet your family. You're carrying my baby. We get along fine—when we're not antagonizing each other, that is." Her mouth twisted into a small smile. "I think that's a good start."

From inside he heard the noise level increase, then the sound of Erin's voice. "Ally! We need you in here!"

Ally's eyes flicked in the direction of the door. He moved closer, until he could feel the warmth that always radiated off her body.

"Forget them for a minute. Hell, forget them altogether. Think about yourself. About the baby." He pressed a kiss against her lips. "About us."

"Al-*ly!*" Erin's voice took on an impatient whine.

Ally seemed lost in thought for a moment. When

her eyes met his again, the spark was back. Her lips curved into a conspiratorial smile. "Can you get me out of here?"

Relief—followed quickly by desire—flowed through him. "My pleasure."

"Get the car. I'll grab my purse." Ally raised up on tiptoe to kiss him—a lighthearted, happy kiss like he hadn't felt since Tortola. She was out of his arms and in the house in a flash.

Whatever she told her family, they weren't happy to hear it, and she burst back through the screen door to a litany of loud complaints. She grabbed his hand and pulled him down the steps and to the car.

He opened the door and she slid in, giving the openmouthed assembled crowd on the porch a wave as he started the engine.

As the wind picked up speed through her open window, Ally's hair came loose, flowing around her face as she leaned against the seat back with a happy smile and closed her eyes.

"Where to?"

"My place."

He floored the pedal.

CHAPTER NINE

LIFE WAS JUST TOO GOOD to be true. Ally wanted to pinch herself, but she'd be black-and-blue by now if she acted on the impulse every time she thought about it.

After their escape from her mom's house on Sunday afternoon, she'd spent an unbelievable afternoon in Chris's arms, taking him back to catch his ride long after sundown. Victor, Chris's crewmate and pilot, had worn a knowing grin as Chris had given her a goodbye kiss that thrilled her to her toenails, reigniting a spark that should have been sated by then. If Victor hadn't been waiting, she'd have dragged Chris back to the car for a quickie in the backseat.

The look on Chris's face said he wouldn't have objected.

Molly had taken one look at the dopey grin on *her* face Monday morning, and not a lot of work had been accomplished as she'd insisted on a play-by-play recount of the weekend. When Ally got to the part about Chris and her family, Molly had merely snorted and said, "I like him more and more."

Her family, on the other hand, wasn't speaking to her—other than one message from her mother on the answering machine, chiding her for her behavior. The four days of silence had been...well, not quite bliss, but a least a welcome break from the norm.

The scent of stargazer lilies filled the air in her and Molly's office, and Ally knew she still wore the same dopey smile for the fifth day in a row. It was hard not to; Chris had only managed one quick trip down to see her on Wednesday night for pizza, but he called and sent e-mails—not so many or so often that she felt smothered, but enough to make her feel, well, *special*. The flowers arriving this morning just intensified that feeling.

She still worried a bit that she wasn't making the smartest of decisions right now—that the hormones shaking up her normal equilibrium and the heady rush of Chris's attentions were affecting her judgment—but she wanted to believe she was. Even Molly encouraged it and joked about expanding the business to an office in Charleston.

That was a little further ahead than Ally liked to plan at the moment. Being caught between a dream-like possibility and a contingency plan wasn't good for her higher brain functions, but she was hopeful—even if she didn't say it out loud too often.

"Why don't you just go ahead and call it quits for the day. Head on up to Charleston and get the weekend started early." Molly grinned. "You're not doing me much good here, you know. All that smiling and sighing is getting on my nerves."

"Can't. Chris has meetings tonight with sponsors and he has to be at the yacht club early in the morning to prep for the race. I'd just be in the way."

"I doubt that."

"Anyway, there's work to be done here." She scooted her chair up to the desk, determined to actually work now. "I'll try to keep the mooning to a minimum."

"Yes, please do try." Molly shot her a mocking smile before turning her attention back to her own keyboard.

The concentration lasted for only a few minutes before her cell phone rang. Chris's ringtone—he'd downloaded it himself on Wednesday night while they'd eaten pizza on the floor of her living room. She glanced up at Molly as she answered and saw her eyes roll.

"Hey."

"Hey, yourself. Any chance you can sneak out early today and come on up?"

"Molly just asked me the same thing. I thought you were busy tonight."

"Technically, I am. But I'll make time for you."

A warm glow settled in her stomach, followed

quickly by that need to pinch herself again. Molly waved for her attention from her desk, and when Ally made eye contact, Molly mouthed the word, "*Go.*"

"I guess I can get away."

"I'll send Victor down to get you. What time?"

The thought of flying in that tiny helicopter made her feel queasy—as if the morning sickness was coming back. "I'll just drive, if that's okay."

Chris made an exasperated sound.

"One step at a time. We're not all daredevils like you."

"It'd be easier my way, though. Faster, too. Plus, you don't know where you're going."

"I'll get a map."

Thankfully, Chris didn't push and instead agreed to e-mail directions to her. She told him she'd call when she was on the road, hung up and started shutting down her computer.

"I'll make this up to you, Molls," she promised as she headed toward the door, mentally reviewing her packing list as she walked.

"Like you'll ever have the time." Molly waved goodbye. "Drive carefully and I'll see you Monday."

Molly's parting words bothered her as she threw her clothes and toiletries in a bag, but she couldn't put her finger on why.

She finally shrugged it off as yet another side

effect of pregnancy brain—right up there with her new case of forgetfulness—and simply enjoyed the drive up to Charleston, singing along with the radio.

It wasn't until late that night, as Chris curled around her in bed, his hand absently stroking across her stomach as he dozed, that she realized what Molly's words meant.

No matter what happened with Chris, things would never go back to "normal."

The man was an absolute god. Neptune, Poseidon and Chris Wells. *Mercy.*

Ally's eye hurt from peering through the telescope for so long, but she couldn't pull away from the sight of Chris, two miles out at sea and rounding the second buoy.

She'd known the water was his element, but a simple day sail on a borrowed catamaran hadn't prepared her for *this*. Watching Chris skipper his seven-man crew…damn.

Although the water was choppy, sending up spray as the boats moved through the waves, Chris stood sure-footed at the helm, moving in perfect harmony with the boat—as though it was an extension of his body instead of an inanimate object. The wind whipped through his hair and fluttered the sails. When he shouted an order across the decks, men scrambled. Then Chris was working the winch, drawing her attention to the movement of back and arm muscles outlined under the shirt the wind nicely plastered to his skin. Her mouth went dry.

"Taylor's hoisted a flag." The words came from beside her, and Ally snapped her attention to the man who'd been her tutor for the day. Carl Michman held the impressive title of vice-commodore of the racing association, but as far as Ally could tell, his main job today seemed to be to keep an eye on her and explain what was going on.

She hadn't heard Chris get up this morning, but she did have fuzzy memories of him kissing her goodbye as he went early to prepare for the race. He'd left keys to his apartment and car on the table for her, along with a note giving her directions to the club and the instruction to find Carl when she arrived.

Ally's heart thudded in her chest. "What does that mean? Has something gone wrong?" Her confidence in Chris's assurances that sailing was perfectly safe had been shot down after only a few hours listening to the stories being passed around the observation deck. Near drownings from falling overboard, horrific head injuries from being hit by the boom—the people surrounding her had plenty of war stories that had her hair standing on end long before the gunshot started the race.

One boat had already dropped out when a crew member got caught in a rope and dislocated his shoulder. Hell, even her new friend, Carl, a spry man in his late sixties who embodied every stereo-typical image she had of an old sailor, had his own stories to tell—including one where something called a jammer had left him with only nine fingers.

These people obviously had no sense of self-preservation.

Carl chuckled and patted her arm kindly. "It's just a protest flag. It got tight around that buoy there, so I'd bet it's a right-of-way argument."

"Oh." Carl had tried to explain the rules, but she still didn't understand much of what was going on. And to be honest, she wasn't that interested in the race itself—watching Chris in action was enough to hold her full attention, and she focused the telescope back on her only object of interest at the moment.

The boat was easy to find, thanks to the colorful spinnaker with the Wells Racing logo. From there, she could focus on the cockpit.

Although Chris said the race was only for fun, he was obviously intent on winning. Even through the scope, she could tell he was loving every minute of it. Forget golden boy; Chris was a golden *god* out there. It was what he was born to do.

Would the baby take after him? Was the love of water and wind genetic? The multigenerational makeup of the members of the yacht club seemed to imply it was. At what age would Chris expect to have their son or daughter—there *were* mixed gender crews out there, after all—on the water, risking loss of fingers and brain damage? The thought made her a bit sick.

She gasped as Chris artfully ducked the powerful swing of the boom and the boat shot forward as the wind filled the sails, increasing the distance between Chris and the other boats as they raced hell-for-leather to the last buoy. But there was no way the other boats would catch up. The familiar ear-to-ear grin spread across Chris's face as he savored the moment.

"And that pretty much seals it." Carl rubbed his hands together.

Ally heard movement behind her and she turned to see a mass exodus off the platform.

It took a while for the boats to make it in, and she hung back from the crowd, unsure what she should do and not wanting to be in the way as they helped tie up boats. Sure-footed, Chris jumped to the dock, and the throng converged on him with much back-slapping and high-fiving. It didn't take long, though, for Chris to make his way through the crowd and catch her up in an embrace that lifted her off her feet. Then, in front of everyone, he kissed her.

She could almost taste the adrenaline and endorphins pumping through his blood, and the powerful arms that held her radiated energy and excitement from the thrill of the race. The rush made her light-headed. Only when her toes touched the dock again, bringing her back to reality, did the catcalls and wolf whistles intrude. She felt her face flush, but Chris was unrepentant at the public display.

Chris kept hold of her hand as the crowd swept inside, but as the glow of his kiss faded, the hollow feeling inside her chest grew, getting worse with each round of drinks as the party stretched into the evening.

Ally sat on a picnic table on the verandah of the clubhouse, just outside the sphere of activity. She didn't want to intrude on something she obviously wasn't a part of, but she didn't want anyone to think she was being antisocial, either. It was just easier to watch the waves and think.

Easier didn't mean less painful, though. She had a lot to think about, and none of it felt good.

Chris was different today—not the Chris she was used to, the one who made her insides do all kinds of funny things when he smiled at her; the Chris she'd met on Tortola; the Chris who downloaded silly ringtones onto her cell phone; the Chris that had almost made her believe they'd be able to pull this strange relationship off.

Here, he was "the Chris Wells," and she was seeing a part of his life she hadn't been able to imagine before.

She couldn't compete with this. Racing wasn't just part of Chris's life—it *was* his life, a major piece of who he was, and she'd never stand a chance at equaling it. And since it wasn't in her blood, she'd never fully be a part of it, either.

Until today "Chris Wells" had been an abstract idea; she'd kind of seen racing as simply Chris's job, much like bookkeeping was hers. Something easily compartmentalized—a nine-to-five job that was put aside at the end of the day.

But it wasn't, and the knowledge was forming a painful lump in her chest. Her job wasn't a lifestyle—a dangerous lifestyle at that. She thought of the hollow look in Diane's eyes as she'd sat beside Steven's hospital bed, bandages swathed around his head and arms, and realized that Steven's daredevil hobby took an emotional toll on her. Could *she* handle that?

"Are you okay?" Chris's voice shook her out of her mental wanderings, and she found him staring at her with concern.

She forced a smile. "Just a little tired. Long day." It wasn't a complete lie. It had been a long day, and she was worn-out.

Belatedly she realized the sun had fully set. How long had she been sitting here lost in thought? The breeze off the water kicked up, and she rubbed her arms to ward off the chill bumps.

Chris shrugged out of his team jacket and wrapped it around her shoulders, cocooning her in warmth and the smell of him. "Then let's head out. I just need to say goodbye to a couple of people first."

"You don't need to leave because of me. I'm fine."

He shook his head. "I just forgot you get worn-out easily right now. I'll be right back, and we'll go."

And so it begins, she thought as he disappeared inside. Chris would eventually come to resent her and the baby for infringing on this part of his life. The pain in her chest intensified. She should have thought this through more carefully, *before* she'd jumped in with both feet.

She was still making excuses as Chris opened the car door for her. "Seriously. We don't have to leave."

"You're practically swaying with fatigue. Let's get you home."

His casual mention of "home" rattled her and warmed her at the same time. "Then just drop me off at ho—your place, and you come back here. Enjoy your party."

He chuckled as he shifted gears. "It's not really *a* party, Ally, much less *my* party. Just people hanging out."

"That would be a party," she grumbled.

"We probably should have left hours ago. You must be bored to tears by all that talk of boats."

"Actually, it was pretty eye-opening." *Understatement of the year.* "And if you want to go back, I'll be fine."

"And miss the possibility you might get a second wind later?" He cocked his head and winked at her. "Not likely."

She opened her mouth to argue, but Chris cut her off. "Ally, it's no big deal. I see these people all the time." He laced his fingers through hers and squeezed. "I'd rather be with you."

The knot in her chest finally loosened as warmth spread through her at his words. Maybe she was worrying for nothing.

"Anyway, you'll see them all again in a couple of weeks."

"What?"

"The end-of-the-summer gala." He stretched out *gala,* giving it a formal sound. "Now, *that* is an actual party. Did the baby borrow your brain again?" he laughed. "You said you would come."

"Oh, yeah." She'd marked it on her calendar in pencil, not sure she'd still be around by then. "Sure. Black tie. I remember." He'd said he wanted her to be there when he made his big announcement about the *Dagny* and the solo attempt. *That* whole idea still put a knot in her stomach when she thought about it. When had her thinking changed from "Oh, goody, he'll forget about us because of the race," to "Oh, no, what if he kills himself?" It made her head hurt.

Ally closed her eyes and dozed, the hum of the motor and the background music from the radio lulling her as Chris stroked his fingers over her knuckles. Next thing she knew, the bright lights of the parking deck under Chris's building were blinding her as she tried to pry her eyelids open. Chris guided her to the elevator, and when the mirrored doors closed, she cringed at the sight.

A day in the wind hadn't done her hair any favors. Her braid hung drunkenly to one side, while the curls that escaped frizzed randomly around her face. Her cheeks were pink from either the wind or the sun, only emphasizing the dark circles under her eyes. The fluorescent lights weren't helping any, either.

Chris just laughed as she tried to smooth the loose hairs back from her face. *Easy for him.* Being outdoors all day was a good look for him. His tanned skin glowed—even under the harsh lighting—and the blond streaks in his windblown hair looked artfully arranged.

Hell, who was she kidding? *Everything* was a good look for him. The man looked godlike even while he slept. It was enough to give a girl a complex.

"Go to bed before you fall over," Chris said as he opened the door to the loft and dropped his keys on the table.

She wanted to argue, but the exhaustion dogging her heels kept her from even making a token protest. Ally slipped out of her shoes and headed toward the bedroom, turning back questioningly when he didn't move to follow her.

"But if you wake up feeling better, let me know." The suggestive grin sent a bolt of desire through her—a surprise since she felt half-dead. She nearly retraced her steps.

Chris shook his head. "Sleep, Ally."

She did. But when Chris slid carefully under the covers later, the movement woke her up. Still groggy, she turned into his arms anyway.

Her blood sang as his hands moved over her. As always, she couldn't think straight when Chris kissed her, but in her slightly fuzzy state, she didn't mind. And with her brain not working overtime, the realization that she was in love with this man slipped into her consciousness.

Adrenaline slammed into her veins, heightening the already exquisite sensation of Chris's mouth on her skin. Blue eyes locked with hers as he slid inside her, nearly pushing her over the edge with one thrust.

For her, at least, this was making love—not just sex anymore. The connection of her emotions to the act caused a strange ache in her chest and at the same time brought a pleasure to her body that had her seeing stars. She shouted Chris's name as her orgasm rocked her.

Chris held her in the aftershocks, his fingers brushing the hair out of her eyes until she could see the small smirk of male satisfaction he wore. The strange ache increased as he kissed her gently, and Ally finally put her finger on why.

He now had the power to break her heart.

CHAPTER TEN

"SHE LOOKS GOOD, son." Pops backed up his assessment of the *Circe* with a low whistle. "I'll admit I had my doubts when she limped into port."

"I didn't." He never would have brought the *Circe* home if he had, but the results of her rehab *were* even better than Chris had hoped. Jack had outfitted her with the most cutting-edge advancements in sail design and navigational equipment, but he'd managed to integrate it without detracting from her original style. The *Circe* was sleek and beautiful, and he had no doubts she'd be fast in the water. Right now she was still in dry dock, but she'd be where she belonged by the end of the week and he'd find out for sure.

But her interior was the true marvel. Turning a racer into a luxury cruiser provided a challenge, but the results were better than expected. The galley was tiny but had all the necessary comforts. Most importantly, though, the *Circe* now had a small, private cabin tucked neatly under the bow, fitted with a custom-designed, very decadent bed. Ally would look spectacular tangled in those sheets.

Pops opened the door to the head and laughed. "Interesting choice."

Chris merely shrugged. Yes, the design had taken up space most people would have reserved for a larger main salon area, but he wasn't planning on much shipboard entertaining. Using the space to install a proper shower just big enough for two suited his purposes much better.

"Makes me wish I was twenty years younger." Pops sat on the portside couch and extended his arms along the back. "Quite the bachelor pad."

Only Pops could still use the phrase "bachelor pad" in this century without any trace of irony. "I think you could still find use for one—age notwithstanding. You're pretty spry for an old guy." He sat on the opposite couch and stretched out his legs while Pops chuckled. But amusement aside, the comment gave him the opening he needed.

"But I prefer to think of the *Circe* as a private retreat. I don't need a bachelor pad anymore."

White eyebrows went up. "Really? You're planning to marry Ally after all?"

"Just as soon as I can talk her into it. She's a little gun-shy when it comes to weddings."

"Then, congratulations. And let me say how glad I am to hear it. All these young people today having babies out of wedlock…" He shook his head sadly.

"In my day, if you got a girl in the family way, you took responsibility and married her. It's the right thing to do." A pause, then he added, "It's how I got your grandmother to marry me."

That got Chris's attention. "Really?" In the few memories he had of his grandmother, she seemed so proper and circumspect. He never would have dreamed Gram would have needed a shotgun wedding. He chuckled. "I guess it runs in the family, then."

"Back then, it was worse on the girl. More of a stigma—not at all like now. But if you ask me, you make a baby, you get married. Kids deserve to have both a mother and a father around."

"I think my mother would be shocked to hear you say that." Pops pulled back like he'd been hit, and Chris regretted not easing into the subject differently. The opening had been there, and he'd taken it without thinking.

"Your mother is a different situation entirely."

"Not really. From what I understand, when I set Dennison on Ally a couple of weeks ago—" had it really been less than two weeks? "—all he had to do was copy over the paperwork from twenty-five years ago. That was just a replay."

"We did what we had to do to protect you."

"From what? My own mother?"

Pops leaned forward, his face pulling downward into a frown. "I don't know what you think you know, but I assure you that removing you from your mother's custody was the best—the *only*—choice at the time. That man she wanted to marry…"

Talking about this was only poking at scars that were long healed—uncomfortable and nonproductive. He never should have brought it up. But he had. "Well, she's not around to refute your claims, is she?"

"You don't understand." Pops tried to wave the discussion away.

"You can't justify what you did. And you nearly let me do the exact same thing." He snorted. "Hell, you practically *encouraged* it."

"I don't need to justify it. One day, when your own child is here, you'll understand what the prospect of losing that child will drive you to do. Am I proud of what we did to Elise? No." Pops shook his head ruefully. "Would I do it again? In a heartbeat, if it meant the difference between keeping my grandchild close or losing him."

The thought of not being a part of his child's life was a physical pain. He knew how the idea felt now; it would only be a thousand times worse once the child was here, a part of his life. But, still… "There had to have been other choices."

"Your mother wanted Paul to sign away his parental rights so her new husband could adopt you. Wanted to move you to the West Coast while you were still young enough to forget everything here. There was no way in hell I was going to allow that to happen."

"So, you deprived me of a mother instead. Let me think she'd walked out on her own. And I never bothered to follow up once I got old enough to do so. I guess that's my loss, and I'll just have to deal with it."

"Have you ever considered that *she* could have tried to get in touch with *you?* Your father was awarded custody, but your mother had visitation rights. She just chose not to exercise them."

That was news. And it put a different perspective on things. "Marge said—"

Pops nodded in understanding. "So *Marge* is who got you all riled up. Figures. Marge was still new then. Her take would be skewed by the fact she wasn't privy to all the facts. Like she is now, it seems," he grumbled.

Chris understood that grumble all too well.

"The fight didn't turn ugly until the end. There was no middle ground as far as your mother was concerned. Your Ally seems more reasonable."

"Only because Dennison hit her with the full package straight out of the gate. She didn't have a choice."

"So why are you complaining? It's all working out quite well, I'd say."

Only Pops would see it that way—without noticing the absurdity of the situation. Arguing with

Pops had the same effect as railing at a storm, only with less satisfying results. Maybe stubbornness was a prerogative of old age. The choice was with him, though, whether to let this go or continue to carry the grudge.

If he was going to move forward with Ally, he'd have to let the past go. But just in case... "Let me be very clear *now,* though—Ally and the baby are my business, not yours. I'm taking care of it, and no matter what might happen, you aren't to try that trick again."

Pops's eyebrows rose, and Chris could see the wheels turning in his head. He knew the old man too well: Pops was trying to decide if that was a threat or a challenge. Chris raised one of his own eyebrows in return, and Pops laughed.

"You're a Wells, through and through, that's for sure." Sobering, he added, "I just hope that when you kill yourself on the *Dagny,* you'll rest easy knowing your child is being raised by strangers."

He'd won the round, even if Pops refused to admit it. "Ally hardly counts as a stranger, and again, I have no intention of killing myself. You're just shopping for another reason for me to call the whole thing off."

"You're damn right I am. I'd pull your sponsorship if I thought it would help."

"I'd only find another sponsor."

"And I know that, which is why I haven't." Pops took a deep breath, and as he released it, he suddenly looked every one of his seventy years. "Your father was uncontrollable. A risk taker. He thrived on the adrenaline. And you're like him in a lot of ways. But unlike Paul, you have a good head on your shoulders, so think about this. You have a child on the way. A woman you want to marry. A whole future ahead of you. Why would you want to risk all of that, risk destroying the people you care about most, just for *another* title? You have plenty of those. You're glorymongering *and* making the same mistake Paul did—putting his own dreams ahead of the well-being of others. If it was just me and the business, that would be one thing, but now you have a whole new set of responsibilities that you're not even considering."

It was the longest, most impassioned speech he'd heard Pops give on the subject. In the past, Pops had just called it a "damn fool stunt" and left it at that, his own bad memories clouding the issue.

"Pops, this is much more than just 'glorymongering.' Do you know how many people are depending on me for this? What it would mean for the business? You've seen the economy—you *know* the importance of diversifying so that if the bottom falls out again, OWD will stay afloat. Jack's designs for the *Dagny* will bring us a ton of new business. Every piece of equipment on the *Dagny* will be in high demand after this—*those* businesses need this to happen. Our stockholders need this to happen.

There's a lot more going on here than just my quest for another title."

"Don't deny this is personal, son."

Chris pushed to his feet, nearly banging his head against the top of the cabin. "Of course it's personal. But it's business, too."

Pops shook his head. "It doesn't mean I have to like it."

"You'll like it when I break the record, I promise you that much." His attempt at humor didn't erase the worry lines on Pops's face. "I'll make you a deal. One attempt, then back to normal. Even if I don't break the record, I won't try it a second time."

Pops's mouth twitched into a small smile. "Normal for you is on the edge anyway, you know."

He returned the smile. "True. But the solo is still over a month away, and since I don't have anything edgier on the cards than taking the *Circe* out, you can scale back on the worry."

"Good. You do know every one of these gray hairs is your fault."

Pops had finally relaxed some. Good. "But they look good on you. Very distinguished."

"I'll remind you of that when your son—"

"Or daughter."

"God help you if you have a daughter." He gestured at the interior of the *Circe.* "Of course, if Ally's impressed with this, you may end up with more than one."

That was a sobering thought. He hadn't thought about more children.

Pops didn't seem to notice. "When will she be in the water?"

"Later this week. If all goes well, I'll be able to take Ally out for a sail this we—"

They heard the shouts first, Pops's head snapping up. Chris bolted to the stairs, Pops close on his heels. A second later a crash shook the *Circe,* causing Pops to stumble slightly on the stairs. Chris reached to steady him, holding his arm as his head cleared the cabin opening.

Smoke rolled in through one of the open bay doors. Men rushed in that direction carrying fire extinguishers. Chris swore loudly, and he heard an identical curse from his grandfather.

"Go. Find out what's going on. I'll call 9-1-1."

Leaving his grandfather in the *Circe*'s cockpit, Chris bypassed the ladder, jumping to the ground and running to the accident.

"Problem at shipyard. Must cancel tonight. Will call tomorrow. Sorry."

Ally read the short message for the fortieth time, hoping more words might have appeared since the last time she'd checked. None had. Her heart sank as she flipped her cell phone closed and leaned back against the headboard.

She'd been disappointed, yes, when the message

had arrived yesterday afternoon, but as today wore on with no call or additional messages from Chris, the vultures of doubt had begun circling. At sundown, they'd perched on her shoulders, the disappointment and doom palpable.

It's exactly what you expected.

Yes, but being right didn't make her feel any better.

Maybe it's not what you think. Things do come up, you know.

Another truism, but also unhelpful. That only made her feel worse, because it meant she was mooning so much over Chris that she was unable to handle the simple fact that he might have more important things on his plate than her.

When had she regressed back to her teen years? Adults didn't act like this. An adult would remember her earlier decision to take one step at a time. Adults didn't pout or stare at the phone willing it to ring.

Obviously, she wasn't an adult where Chris was concerned.

She grimaced at the phone and tossed it to the foot of the bed in childlike disgust.

It rang immediately and she scrambled to find it in the folds of the duvet, cursing herself the entire time.

"Allison Renee, enough is enough."

Ugh. She should have checked the number. "Hi,

Mom." Leaning against the headboard again, she closed her eyes and fought back the disappointment.

"I've stayed out of this spat between you and your sister—"

No you haven't.

"But whatever is going on with you has gone on long enough."

"Mom, I'm pregnant. If Erin is too immature or selfish to appreciate that it isn't always about her, there's nothing I can do about it."

"You could try to be more understanding of the stress she's under."

"It's a wedding, for God's sake. Sorry, but I can't stir up a lot of sympathy for her stress levels."

"Allison..."

Maybe it was the disappointment of Chris canceling dinner, maybe it was the extra hormonal edge from the baby, maybe it was the memory of the look on Chris's face when her family had acted so abysmally, but this time, her mother's patented warning whine grated across her the wrong way. Instead of feeling guilty or just relenting because it was easier, she felt angry at her mother—and her family in general.

Her family wasn't crazy. Or eccentric. Or even flighty. They were just selfish and immature. Why hadn't she realized this earlier? And why had she let it get this bad?

"Mom, here's the thing. Erin is *your* daughter. I've gone above and beyond sisterly duty, and I'm tired of it. She's a spoiled brat and I'm tired of mollycoddling her. You want to do it? Fine. But I'm over it."

"Ally—"

She cut her mom off. She was just getting warmed up now, and everything she'd been holding back just seemed to flow out of her. "And Steven is just as bad. If he can convince everyone else to cater to him, that's great. But I'm out of that, too. He's a big boy. He can handle his own life.

"Not a one of you has asked me how *I'm* doing. How *I'm* feeling. How *I'm* handling things. It's like y'all don't even care."

"That's not true at all."

"Mom, stop. I love you and Daddy both, but somehow we all got flipped around and I turned into the grown-up. I'm about to have a family of my own, and that's where my attention needs to be. I can't parent the whole clan. I shouldn't have to, and I certainly don't want to."

With the words out there, Ally felt better than she had in months—*years, possibly.*

"What has brought this on, Ally? Why are you acting like this?" Her mother's voice broke.

What did I expect? Sympathy? Understanding? An apology? She'd brought a lot of this on herself—she knew that—but it also meant it was her prerogative to change the game. "Mom, this is way overdue. I'm sorry your feelings are hurt, but things have to change. When y'all are ready to act like a family—a family that I'm a part of, not in charge of—then we'll talk again."

Her mother sputtered, and Ally had a suspicion she'd made her mother cry. Her outburst didn't feel so great *now*. But she couldn't back down; this was long overdue. "I'm sorry, Mom. I do love you, though. Call me back after you've had a chance to think about everything I've said."

This time she placed the phone on her nightstand. Just in case.

She slid down under the covers and hugged her pillow to her chest. One good thing about being pregnant was the fact she could always nap. It was a good way to pass the time. But her dreams were scattered and wild. She was alone on a boat in the ocean with wind and rain pelting her. She could see the shore, but couldn't figure out how to set the sails properly, and the boat just rocked helplessly on the waves, being pulled farther out with the current. She could see people on the shore, but no one heard her calls for help, and they went on with their business, unaware or uncaring she was out there.

She woke when she heard her phone beep, indicating a new message.

She pried her eyes open, but the room was now totally dark—her nap had lasted a good three hours and the display on her bedside clock now read eleven-fifteen. She couldn't shake the lingering unease from her dream, and she fumbled for the phone.

Her heart jumped when she saw the message was from Chris: "Didn't want to wake you. Will call soon. Sleep well."

He hadn't forgotten her after all. That put a smile on her face, and she rolled over and went back to sleep.

Chris let the wind catch the *Circe*'s sails as he cleared the entrance to the bay and headed into open water. He was right—she handled like a dream. He had about three hours to put the *Circe* through her paces before he had to be back. He had plenty of time to make his lunch meeting and then meet Victor for his ride to Savannah for Ally's doctor's appointment.

After the mess of this week, just thinking of seeing Ally was a balm to his brain. Although the explosion was a stupid, careless accident—and the workers responsible for creating it had been disciplined appropriately—no one had been seriously hurt and the clean-up, while slow, was progressing. That hadn't kept everyone from OSHA to the union reps from crawling all over his shipyard and creating a nightmare, though.

Even worse, the ensuing mess had kept him close to home all week, cooped up in his office from dawn till dusk. He hadn't been anywhere—much less Savannah—for days.

The sea air worked wonders, clearing the debris from his mind, and he turned the *Circe* away from the wind. Maybe he could get Marge to stock her with provisions while he was gone this afternoon. He'd be able to bring Ally straight back to the dock tonight and they could anchor for the night a couple of miles up the coast. He was eager to christen the *Circe* properly.

They could head out by six, maybe seven, depending on how long it took at the doctor's office. Granted, he didn't have a clue how long that would take—he didn't frequent obstetricians' offices as a rule—but they'd have something to celebrate tonight. He'd like to have that celebration on the *Circe,* even if they stayed tied up at the dock. It seemed fitting somehow.

He thought about the ring, locked up in the safe at the office. He'd save *that* for tomorrow, giving them a different reason to celebrate. He wanted Ally to marry him—soon. Enough dancing around the subject. Enough splitting his time between two cities and going home to an empty apartment every night. He wanted Ally here, and the only way to work that would be to get her to marry him sooner instead of later.

The wind was slightly erratic, but the strong breeze soon caused the boat to heel. He let the sheet out, letting the sail go wide, and the boat leveled off.

He hoped Ally would choose a small ceremony—something they could pull together before he left on the *Dagny*—but he'd settle for her moving into his place. If she wanted a big wedding—one to rival her sister's—then she'd have two months to plan it. That, plus supervising any work she wanted done converting the spare bedroom into a nursery, should keep her occupied for fifty-some-odd days.

Maybe it wasn't ideal timing, what with the solo coming up, but they'd make do. Nothing in their relationship had been normal to date, so why start now? He smiled at the thought.

Now to convince Ally of his plan.

After weeks of fighting with seemingly everyone—from Ally and Pops to his lawyers and now the union—and having both his professional and personal life turned upside down, the contentment he felt now seemed odd and out of place. He inhaled deeply, sure life would be on an even keel from here.

The snap of the mainsail caught his attention, and his head jerked up in time to see the sail sag. A second later the wind was in his face, changing direction completely and filling the mainsail from the other side. Cursing his inattention, he turned, only to see the boom swing violently toward him.

Everything went black.

CHAPTER ELEVEN

ALLY SAT IN HER CAR in front of Dr. Barton's office staring at the ultrasound image the tech had given her. To her, the baby looked a bit like an alien peanut, but the tech had assured her everything was perfect and as it should be. She'd heard the baby's heartbeat; she had a DVD of the session tucked in her purse, showing the baby doing slow somersaults. It had been the most amazing, awe-inspiring thing she'd ever seen, and it brought tears to her eyes.

And Chris had missed the whole damn thing, the jerk. That brought tears to her eyes as well, and she swiped at them angrily.

"I want to be there," he'd said, and she'd believed him. When he hadn't shown up at her office to pick her up at the agreed-upon time, she'd started calling his cell. Nothing but voice mail. She'd waited as long as possible, finally heading to the doctor's on her own so as not to miss the appointment. She left messages, including the address of the office, telling him to meet her there if he was running late. She'd held out hope until the tech had dimmed the lights to start the procedure, but the disappointment had tainted the excitement of seeing their baby for the first time.

Their baby. Ha. So much for that.

"Sorry, Kiddo," she told her stomach. "Sorry if I got your hopes up. I was pretty hopeful there, too." She put the car into gear. "It won't happen again."

The bitter taste stayed in her mouth as she called Chris every name in the book on the way back to her house. She saved a couple of choice insults for herself—naive, foolish, harebrained, besotted, blind, lovesick…she had plenty to choose from.

Somehow she wasn't surprised to find Molly waiting on her porch when she got home. Molly had been livid when Chris didn't show, and she'd even offered to go in his place. At the time, Ally had still been holding out hope he was just late and would still show, so she'd gone alone.

Molly's pixie features twisted when Ally got out of the car alone. She even looked down the street as if to see if Chris was following in his own car. Ally shook her head.

"The bastard."

While the show of support warmed her, it also caused tears to gather again. "We knew it was coming, right? Better sooner than later."

"He's still a bastard."

Ally unlocked the door and Molly followed her

in, still muttering epithets. "So we're back to plan A. It's a good plan. A sound plan." Her voice broke a little and she swallowed hard. "You want to see the video of the ultrasound? Kiddo looks like a little alien peanut."

"Later. Right now I want you to call Chris's office and find out where the hell he is."

"Molls…"

"Here," Molly handed her a piece of paper. "He may not be answering his cell, but someone at the shipyard will answer the phone and they'll know how to find him."

Ally eyeballed the note, recognized the number of the shipyard and looked at Molly suspiciously. "Did you…?"

"No. I didn't call. I wanted to, but I decided to give him the benefit of the doubt. Which he obviously doesn't deserve. The rat."

She stalled. "Molls, it's not—"

"Fine, I'll go start the popcorn and warm up the DVD player. You call and find out. It's one phone call. Then you'll know."

"Fine." Ally sank onto the sofa and dialed. The phone rang and rang—more times than most offices would allow—before a woman answered breathlessly.

"Um, hi. This is Ally Smith and I'm trying to find Chris—"

"Oh my God." She heard a scraping sound like

the woman was covering the phone with her hand, then she heard a muffled, "It's Ally. She's looking for Chris."

What in the world was going on there? Another muffled scrape as the phone was handed to someone else, and another woman came on the line, the voice cautious and placating. "Ally? This is Marge Lindley. We met when you came to the office."

Okay. "Hi, Marge. I'm looking for Chris. He was—"

"Honey, I'm so sorry we didn't call you sooner."

Something in Marge's voice set off alarm bells in her head. Ally took a deep breath.

"Chris took the new boat out this morning, and… Well, he said he was only going to be gone for a couple of hours, so we didn't know until he didn't meet Victor as planned…"

Her lungs froze, and the alarm bells rang louder.

"We've called out the Coast Guard, and Victor's still out looking for him in the helicopter—"

The subject the woman was dancing around finally crystallized. They didn't know where Chris was either. If Victor was out looking for him…and, oh, God, the Coast Guard?

This was bad.

Chills ran over her skin, and her stomach fisted painfully. Marge was still talking, but it barely registered as background noise.

"Ally? Ally?"

It was hard to breathe around the knot in her chest. "I'm here."

"They're pinging his GPS. They have coordinates for the boat. They'll find him."

Pinging his GPS only meant they'd find the *boat*. If Chris wasn't answering hails or his phone... She felt light-headed and dizzy.

Molly pushed open the kitchen door. "Popcorn and orange jui— What's wrong?"

"Chris." It was all she could manage. Oh, God.

"You. Head between your knees before you pass out." Molly took the phone from her hand and put pressure on her shoulder blades, forcing her head down. Ally could hear Molly take over the conversation, asking questions while rubbing comforting circles over her shoulders.

She'd been cursing him, and all the time he'd been... The horror stories she'd heard just last weekend provided more than enough fodder for her imagination.

She tried to breathe slowly. Deeply. Tried to remember that Chris was half water god and therefore whatever was going on didn't necessarily mean the worst. Tried to calm herself because worry and panic weren't good for the baby.

"Are you okay?"

Ally sat up slowly as Molly placed the phone on the side table. She hadn't heard the end of the conversation. "What did Marge say?"

"The harbormaster saw him leave the docks a little after seven. From what I understand, that's not unusual—him going out by himself early in the morning. His assistant knew he had a lunch meeting, so they assumed he'd gone straight from the dock to the meeting." Molly moved purposefully around the house as she talked, taking the food back to the kitchen, bringing Ally a pair of jeans and indicating she should put them on. "His lunch date just assumed something had come up, so he didn't bother calling the office when he didn't show. When he didn't show up at the helipad to come here, Victor sounded the alarm."

Molly handed Ally her purse, folded a sweater over her arm and picked up two paperback books from the shelf. "Let's go."

When Molly was in full Managing Mode, it wasn't wise to argue. Anyway, Ally wasn't in much of a state to argue. Between her overactive imagination, anger at herself for not realizing something might have gone wrong and anger at Chris for putting himself in this situation to begin with...well, there wasn't much room for higher cognitive functions. "Where are we going?"

"Charleston. Victor can't come get you, because he's assisting with the search, but I know you'll want to be there when they find him. I'm driving."

* * *

Chris looked terrible. Well, as terrible as it was possible for a man like him to look. He was pale beneath a bad sunburn, caused by lying unconscious in the cockpit of the *Circe* for several hours, and a huge white bandage swathed his head. According to his grandfather, a white-haired man everyone called Pops, Chris had a nice-size gash under there.

But he would recover. Ally sat in semidarkness, the late-afternoon sun still peeking through the hospital window shades next to his hospital bed while Chris slept. Although he'd been unconscious when the Coast Guard boarded the boat, they'd been able to wake him and do tests that showed the injury, while scary, wasn't going to cause long-term problems. Other than the laceration and the concussion, he'd suffered dehydration from the blood loss and being in the sun, but the IV drip in his arm would fix that up, as well.

Marge had called her cell to let her know Chris had been found and was en route to the hospital, but by the time she'd arrived, he was already stable, sedated and in his hospital room to rest. Ally had agreed to stay while the others went home to rest, promising to call with an update as soon as she could. Molly had gone back to Savannah, and with Chris asleep, Ally had plenty of time to think.

He'd been gone for over eight hours before anyone even knew he was missing. Stupid men and their testosterone-driven need to do crazy, stupid, reckless things. Although she'd only known he was missing for an hour or so, she'd aged ten years in the interim. Chris's grandfather looked as if he'd been pulled through the wringer, poor man.

She couldn't handle this kind of stress. What was more important, she didn't want to. She wanted a nice, normal life. To think, a couple of months ago she had been bemoaning her boring, uneventful existence, and had jumped on the chance to shake things up when Chris had arrived like a gift from the gods.

She'd shaken things up, all right. Let's see, she was now pregnant and in love with someone who seemed to eat adrenaline and risk for breakfast every morning. Boring and uneventful had never sounded so good.

"Ally?" Chris's voice was raspy, and her head snapped up.

She moved to the side of the bed and carefully touched his arm above the IV tube. His blue eyes stood out sharply under the white bandage. "You're awake. How do you feel?"

"My head hurts like hell."

"No doubt. You took a good crack there."

Chris's warm hand caught hers. "Good thing I'm hardheaded." A small smile crossed his face, then faded. "Sorry I missed the doctor's appointment. How'd it go?"

Although she knew it was far too early, she could

swear she felt the baby flip over. "Kiddo's fine. Perfectly healthy. I've got pictures to show you."

"Good." His eyes slid closed. "Wish I'd been there, though."

Yeah, me, too. "I'll let you rest."

"No, I'm okay. The lights just make the headache worse." His fingers stroked over her knuckles. "I'd planned to take you sailing tonight. Guess we'll have to reschedule."

"Pops said the *Circe* didn't suffer any damage, so they towed her back in and put her in her berth—whatever that is."

That brought another small smile. "So you met Pops."

"Yeah. Sweet man. By the way, I didn't know your middle name was 'The Damn Fool Idiot.'"

Chris chuckled, then grimaced as he put a hand up to his head. "I shouldn't laugh. It makes my head hurt."

"I think a better idea would be to not get in the way of the boom if you don't want your head to hurt." She hooked a foot around the chair leg and pulled it closer so she could sit. "Or at the very least, maybe you should tell people what time to expect you back."

"Duly noted."

Ally sighed and leaned her head against the bed rail. "You certainly had everyone worried."

The hand holding hers squeezed slightly. "Sorry about that." His words slowed as his body gave in to the need to rest. "Remind me to have Jack check the GPS systems on the *Dagny*…" The sentence trailed off as his breathing deepened and evened out in sleep.

But Ally's head jerked up at his words. The *Dagny?* The solo attempt? The man was lying in a hospital bed from his most recent solo sail and he was thinking about the next one? One that was far more dangerous than just being a couple of miles off the coast? Did he have no sense of self-preservation? If *this* could happen on a simple day sail, the possibilities of what might happen in the middle of the freaking ocean… Oh, dear God. She wanted to pull her hair out.

She untwined her fingers and eased her hand from under his. The man was insane. Twisted. Cracked. Not firing on all cylinders. That boom must have hit him pretty damn hard to knock *all* the sense out of his head.

Anger flared. She'd been so caught up in everything else, she'd lost sight of the one thing she'd known from the very beginning: Chris was a golden boy, expecting the world to dance to his tune, regardless of the costs to others. Just like Gerry. Just like her brother. Hell, just like her whole damn family—selfish and self-serving to the core. Chris needed the thrill, needed the adrenaline rush, the glory, and the adulation like he needed air to breathe. Let someone else pick up the pieces.

God, she had to be some kind of masochist—how else could she explain her compulsion to love people like that?

After he raced the *Dagny,* then what? What would be the next rush he'd chase? Obviously she and the baby wouldn't be able to compete with that need for very long. They'd never be enough. A bitter laugh escaped. Last week she'd convinced herself it was silly to be jealous of a boat, of a hobby—hell, of a lifestyle—but now she realized it wasn't jealousy talking. It had been the rational part of her brain trying to get through the rainbow-hued gauze her hormones had wrapped around her mind and body.

But now she was thinking clearly. Finally.

If only she'd realized this before she'd fallen in love with him. Before she spent the last few weeks tying herself in knots over him. Before she'd taken years off her life worrying about him.

At least she wouldn't be sitting home biting her nails and pacing the floor while he took off on the *Dagny* or whatever other harebrained scheme he came up with to court death.

What about the baby?

Well, plan A had been shot down, and now plan B was in pieces at her feet. She'd move on to plan C. That's what lawyers were for, after all. She'd just hope Chris could be reasonable and wouldn't let his lawyers bury her the way he'd threatened before.

Chris shifted, drawing her attention back to him. Her heart cracked and tears sprang to her eyes. Getting over him would be tough—especially since he'd always be a part of her life, however tangentially. But she had to do what was best for her and for the baby, and keeping herself as distant as possible seemed the wisest course.

Even if it did hurt like hell.

She slipped into the hallway, closing the door silently behind her so as not to wake him. She was dialing Marge's number when one of Chris's crewmates came down the hall. Jack, maybe? Derrick? She'd met so many people so quickly.

"How is he?"

"Sleeping," she answered. "He woke up for a few minutes and was lucid, so concussionwise, I think he's okay."

The man nodded. "Do you need anything?"

"Actually, something important has come up and I need to get back to Savannah. Chris is resting comfortably, but could you stay with him until Pops or Marge comes back?"

"Sure."

"Thanks." She tiptoed back into Chris's room and grabbed her belongings. Leaning over to kiss

208 MAGNATE'S MISTRESS…ACCIDENTALLY PREGNANT!

his sunburned cheek, she whispered, "Thank you for the fun times. I'm sorry, though."

Tears burned in her eyes, drawing strange looks from Chris's friend as she hurried past him. She was in the hospital parking lot before she realized she didn't have a ride home. Molly had figured she'd want to stay the night, and Ally hated to call and make her drive the round trip for the second time in one day.

Victor. Victor could have her home in no time, and he'd volunteered his services anytime she needed him. Her mouth twisted. She doubted Victor or Chris extended the offer for a situation like *this*. But she didn't have a lot of other options, plus Molly would only have to drive to the helipad.

She couldn't do that. Instead, she went to the reception desk and asked for a phone book. In no time, she had a rental car lined up and a taxi on its way to get her.

See, she reminded herself. *There's always a plan C.*

This time when he opened his eyes, the room was dark, the only light coming from somewhere to his left. The pain in his head was receding a bit, but his skin felt tight and dry. What time was it? How long had he been sleeping?

It must have been a while, since he remembered nurses waking him up several times to ask him silly questions about his phone number and the president of the U.S. The grogginess he remembered from earlier had passed, though, and he was clearheaded now.

Chris turned and saw Jack dozing in a chair next to the bed, a book resting on his chest. "Hey."

Jack started, then rubbed his eyes. "You're awake."

"Where'd Ally go?"

Closing the book, Jack shook his head. "Good to see you, too. You look like hell."

"I've been worse."

Jack shrugged. "True. But to answer your question, Ally went back to Savannah. She said something came up."

Ally had left? "Did she say what?"

"Nope. Just that it was something important she had to take care of."

Something to take care of. Probably her family. Not a one of them could get dressed without Ally's assistance. She'd probably be glad to move to Charleston—at least they wouldn't expect her to drop everything every time someone broke a nail. Hell, no wonder she'd said she'd like to have a pet but that she didn't have time to take care of it; it was probably a nice way of saying she didn't *need* something else to take care of.

Still, it stung a bit to think she'd left him in the

hospital and gone rushing home to deal with the crisis of the day.

Jack looked at him closely. "I'm sure she'll call."

"I'm sure she will. It's just irritating that her family has her on call twenty-four/seven."

"You're not in any danger of dying. Maybe she has bigger fish to fry," Jack teased.

"If I'm not dying, when can I get out of here?" He pushed the button to raise the head of his bed into an upright position.

"It's five in the morning, so not for a while. Might as well get comfortable. But the nurses said that if everything checked out, you could go home later today."

Good. He had things to do.

Jack shook his head. "Don't get any ideas. You'll be homebound for the next couple of days at least."

Ugh. But if Ally would come and stay with him...

Jack knew him too well. "*And* on restricted activity. Nothing, um, strenuous."

"You're such a killjoy."

"Hey, I talked Pops out of hiring a home nurse to look after you."

"I'm much obliged." He reached up and felt the bandage around his head. "So how bad was it?"

"A concussion from the boom. There's one hell of a goose egg on the left side of your head. You've got ten stitches above your right temple from where you fell after you were knocked out. It looks like you landed on a cleat and sliced yourself open. Some blood loss, mild dehydration, sunburn. Just enough to mess you up, but you'll survive."

"And the *Circe?*"

"Other than blood in the cockpit and a dent in the boom, she's fine. Pops had her towed back to the docks."

"That's what Ally said." Except then she'd left while he was asleep. What *was* this penchant she had for leaving without saying goodbye properly?

Jack settled back in his chair and stretched his legs out in front of him. "Do you need anything? Water? Painkillers? I can get the nurse for you."

"How about my phone? I could check my e-mail." Call Ally and find out what's going on. No, it's five in the morning.

He shook his head. "Pops would kill me. You're supposed to be resting."

"I'm plenty rested. I feel fine." In fact, he was already itching to get out of bed and move around, and he *would* have, if not for the IV tube tethering him. He drummed his fingers on his thighs, impatient to get out of the small, depressing room. A muffled noise caught his attention, and he looked over to see Jack smothering a laugh.

"What?"

"You."

Jack was the closest thing to a brother he had, so

he wouldn't strangle him. *This* time. "So I'm ready to leave. You would be, too. Why are you here, anyway?"

"Keeping an eye on you. Making sure you stay in that bed. Pops told me to sit on you if I had to." His lips twitched. "I'm still holding out hope you'll push me to it."

"Try it and you'll be the next patient," he threatened. His head did still hurt, even though he wasn't all that tired anymore. "Fine. I'll stay put like a good boy. Unless you have a book there for me, though, you'll have to entertain me. What did I miss yesterday?"

"Not a lot. The *Dagny* passed inspection and rumors are buzzing about her. Pops got the union folks calmed down, and the repairs to the building are almost done. Pretty boring day—until you went missing, of course. That added some excitement."

"Glad I could help." He snorted, then regretted the action as his head throbbed. "I can't believe you had to call out the Coast Guard, though. I'll never live that down."

Jack howled with laughter. "*I* can't believe you got hit with the boom. Maybe we should send you back to sailing school."

"Very funny. The thing jibed out of nowhere. I was a bit distracted, that's all." *Yeah, thinking about Ally.* That was a newbie mistake, daydreaming like that. One he would not make again. Jack's grin didn't fade. "Keep laughing, and the next time you fall overboard, I won't come back for you."

Schooling his features, Jack cleared his throat. "Still…"

"How's Pops?"

"Claiming you're going to be the death of him." Jack grinned again. "But he's found an ally and kindred spirit with Ally. They both think you're too reckless for their sanity."

Chris rolled his eyes. "Ally thinks going swimming less than thirty minutes after eating is too reckless."

"Oh, good. She and Pops can tag team you."

"Don't think I haven't realized that. You're going to have your hands full with the two of them while I'm gone. They'll just feed off each other."

"Maybe I'll go with you…"

They were both laughing when the nurse poked her head around the door. "Well, you seem to be doing much better. I thought I'd pull your IV." She nodded her head toward the light growing stronger outside the window. "We'll get you lined up for some tests, and maybe you can go home this morning."

"That sounds like a plan."

CHAPTER TWELVE

By Sunday afternoon Chris was bored out of his mind. He'd been released yesterday with strict instructions to rest and take it easy, and only by promising to actually do so had he avoided Pops sending a babysitter to his loft to look after him. But being locked in was wearing on him. His head was still tender, and the stitches looked ghastly, but the confinement was driving him crazy.

It was a beautiful day. The sun was shining, no clouds in the sky, and a good breeze moved through his open windows. He could easily think of twenty places he would rather be instead of here, watching TV.

Of course, the fact that he was supposed to be out on the *Circe* with Ally grated across his nerves. Where *was* she, anyway? During the one quick, unsatisfying conversation yesterday, when she called to check on him, her voice had sounded wrong. Flat, like someone had taken all the air out of her. She'd skated over the subject of her family, leaving him to wonder what they had her in the middle of now and if that was the cause of her deflation. Something wasn't right in Ally's world, and whatever it was, she wasn't sharing details.

She'd called earlier this morning—still not sounding quite like herself—saying she'd be up to visit later in the afternoon. He'd offered to send Victor to pick her up, but she'd declined, saying she'd rather drive.

Lord, everything was chafing at him today— even Ally's dislike of the helicopter. Hell, even going to the office was starting to sound like a good idea. At least it beat staring at the same four walls.

He checked the clock. Surely Ally would be here soon, and that would calm his restlessness and need to get out of here. If he had to be trapped indoors, Ally was the one person he'd choose to be with.

Plus, he was feeling a *lot* better.

Where the hell was she? He grabbed his phone, only to hear a knock at the door. Finally. It had to be Ally—otherwise the doorman would have called up.

He crossed the room in three quick strides, his body already awakening at the thought of her. "You have a key, you know," he said as he opened the door, but the sight of Ally's drawn, pinched face stopped him. "Are you all right?"

Her forced smile didn't fool him. "I should be asking you that question. How do you feel?" Ally sounded even more distant, if it were possible, than she had on the phone.

"I'm fine," he answered carefully as Ally stepped forward, and he closed the door behind her. She carried a tote bag—not really large enough to be an overnight bag, but big—clutched tightly to her side.

"You look much better."

Her stilted words had him moving cautiously as he leaned down and kissed her cheek. Whatever was going on with her, well, it wasn't good, that was for sure. She moved stiffly, like she might break, and she seemed to be holding herself together by sheer force of will.

"Chris, I—"

"Why don't you sit," he said at the same time.

Ally nodded and moved to the couch and perched on the edge, placing the large bag in her lap. He sat next to her as she took a deep breath.

"We need to talk. Well, *I* need to tell you something, and I'm not sure how." She sounded cautious, hesitant. Something was wrong.

"Okay." He watched her face closely, saw her mouth twist, and a chill ran through him. "Is it the baby? Is something wrong?"

"No, no." She shook her head, and a curl slipped out of the ponytail. "The baby's fine. In fact, I brought a copy of the ultrasound for you." She patted the bag halfheartedly.

There was more than just an ultrasound in that bag—he'd bet the *Dagny* on it. "Then what?"

Ally chewed on her bottom lip and stared at the coffee table as if it was the most unusual thing she'd ever seen. He realized she hadn't made eye contact with him since she'd walked in the door. Finally she took another deep breath, rubbed her hands across her face and exhaled noisily. "Okay. I'm just gonna say this, so…"

He waited for her to continue.

"I can't do this anymore." Ally's shoulders dropped as she said it, and her eyes finally met his. They were as distant as her voice had been.

She wasn't making a lot of sense. "Do what, exactly?"

"This." She waved her hand between them. "You and me and the whole thing. I just can't do it."

The punch in his gut barely registered as Ally hurried ahead.

"I've had some time to think recently, and you and me—we're just not going to work. We're too different and I can't handle the stress and the worry and…"

He reached out to touch her hand. "Ally, I'm sorry about Friday—I know it worried you—but it was just an accident."

"I understand that. But I can't handle waiting for the next accident. Waiting to hear if you…" She cleared her throat. "Waiting. Look, you love it—sailing, racing, all of it. I understand that, I really do, but *I don't*. And I can't deal with it. I can't compete with it, and I can't handle it, so I'm getting out while I can."

"Did Pops get to you? If this is about the *Dagny*—"

"Pops didn't have to get to me. I got here all by myself." She sighed. "It's all of it, Chris. You and I are too different to get along."

"I thought we were doing pretty well."

Ally got up to pace, giving him a sense of déjà vu. "Yeah, the fireworks, and the chemistry, and the excitement—that's all really great. *Now.* But long-term? No. I want my life to have a lot less drama in it. We're from different worlds—you love the limelight and the thrill, and I'm just an everyday accountant. I can't keep up with you.

"And more importantly, I have to think about the baby. What's best for her."

"And having her parents together isn't good for her?" He saw her wince as he raised his voice, and he tried to tamp down his temper. "Ally, you're not making sense."

"If you're off racing or whatever, then her parents aren't actually together. And I can't be a good parent if I'm always worried about you."

Astonished and not quite getting it, he nearly sputtered before he pulled it back together. "You don't want me to race?"

"I would never ask you to do that. It's too much

a part of you. To ask you to give that up would be asking you not to be *you* anymore and…" She sighed again. "I don't expect you to change who you are. But I can't change who *I* am, either. And that's why this won't work with us."

Ally was taking Friday's scare a bit far. "Take a deep breath and calm down for a minute."

She spun on him, her eyes blazing. It was a nice change from the emptiness. "Don't patronize me. I'm an adult, and I've made my decision. We want different things, and we can't provide them for each other. What kind of *true* relationship could we ever have? You want *this*—" she looked pointedly at his injuries "—and I want…" She stopped, shrugged and picked up the bag she'd let slide to the floor.

Angry, he grabbed her upper arm. "What do you want, Ally? Tell me."

She simply stared at his hand until he released her. He felt like a jerk, reacting like that, but, damn, *where* had all this come from?

Ally pulled a large manila envelope out of the bag and handed it to him.

He knew without opening it he wouldn't like the contents.

Ally took a deep breath to stabilize herself. This was even harder than she'd thought it would be, and the whole conversation was like digging her heart out with a rusty fork. And Chris wasn't making it any easier.

Why'd he have to look at her like that? And why did her libido jump up and dance every time he did? The man was recuperating from an injury, for God's sake, why couldn't he at least look a little less…a little less…well, a little less godlike. He looked remarkably hale and healthy, aside from the stitches over his ear, which made her feel slightly less like a true witch for breaking up with him just forty-eight hours after he got hurt. His sunburn wasn't even peeling—it had darkened into a tan that stood out sharply against his white T-shirt.

This hadn't gone according to the careful plan she'd spent hours thinking about and rehearsing repeatedly in the car on the drive up. She'd let him get to her, and she'd nearly lost what little control she had over herself more than once. She'd come so close to sounding like a complete idiot, too. If she hadn't caught herself, she would have said, "I want someone who loves me more than a boat."

God, it sounded juvenile. She was still jealous of a damn boat. And in reality, it *wasn't* the boat—she just knew she couldn't settle for second or third place in Chris's life. Couldn't be the cheerleader and housemom for his frat-rat, golden-boy lifestyle. She loved him for what he was, but at the same time, she couldn't handle it. She just couldn't put it into words properly.

Saying those things to Chris had been the hardest thing she'd ever done. Handing him the envelope he was now staring at like it was a snake was the second hardest.

He looked at her questioningly and weighed the envelope in his hands. "What's this, Ally?"

"I talked to my lawyer on Friday night." Granted Uncle Joe was her father's oldest friend, but he'd been willing enough to meet with her on Saturday and draw up the documents Chris now held. Of course, if Chris chose to fight her, she'd be doing Uncle Joe's bookkeeping for the rest of her natural life to pay him back the legal fees. "I'm hoping we've moved past the anger and the threats and can discuss this like adults. It's a fair agreement—very liberal visitation, no child support—"

"No child support? Are you sure, Ally?" he mocked.

"I don't need your money to feed and clothe my child."

"*Our* child," he corrected, and she didn't like the snarl in his voice.

"As I said, I don't need money for day-to-day maintenance. There's a clause, though, about extras like braces and dance lessons and college. If you have a problem with any of it, my attorney will be able to work with you to come to an agreement."

"Dammit, Ally." He tossed the envelope onto the coffee table where it landed with a thunk. When he turned to look at her, her breath caught. Was that hurt in his eyes? She gave herself a strong mental shake. No, probably just anger that she'd thrown a kink in his plans.

"We gave it a try, Chris. It didn't work."

"I'd hardly call a couple of weeks a good try," he scoffed.

"It was enough." *Enough to let me fall in love with you. Enough to give you the power to hurt me.* "Take a couple of days to look over the papers. I'm sure you'll see I'm being very reasonable, and I'm only asking the same from you."

God, why did this hurt so much? It was all she could do to keep the tears at bay. She needed to leave. Now. Get distance between them again so she could see straight. So she could let her heart start to heal.

Digging through the bag again, she took out the rest of the contents. A copy of the ultrasound. A T-shirt he'd left at her house. The keys to his loft. The small box containing the necklace. Everything she could find that would remind her of him—save one. Her permanent reminder. The only one she could keep. But with her luck the baby would look exactly like him and break her heart all over again every single day.

Chris didn't say anything, but the muscle in his jaw twitched. She couldn't tell what he was thinking, but she knew if she stayed much longer she'd be lost.

And she couldn't risk that again.

"Bye, Chris." She forced a smile. "I'm glad we had the chance to get to know each other. It'll make things with Kiddo easier." The lie tasted sour in her mouth. Although his silence unnerved her, at the same time it was probably a good thing.

Then he turned those blue eyes on her and her heart seemed to shatter. They were cold.

Barely holding herself together, she turned on her heel and forced herself to walk calmly toward the door. Only once it closed behind her did she give into the tears, and by the time she reached her car, her shoulders were shaking with sobs.

The hollow place in her chest ached, and she took a deep breath, cursing every decision she'd ever made when it came to Chris—all the way back to agreeing to go sailing with him on Tortola in the first damn place. If only she'd known that one decision would come to this painful moment.

But now. *Now* she was thinking straight. Making good decisions. She welcomed back the predicable, rational, reliable Ally she'd lost track of when Hurricane Chris had blown through her life.

Too bad she didn't like that Ally anymore.

The chime of the doorbell woke her up. Seeing Chris had drained her emotionally, and the round-trip drive hadn't helped her physically, either. While she'd managed to get the tears under control, the giant gaping wound in her heart hadn't eased any with the drive home, and she'd gone directly to bed, needing the relief from reality only sleep could provide.

But the room was dark now, and she rolled over to check the clock. Nine-thirty. A little late for visitors, but when she heard the key in the lock she realized this was no average visitor.

Great. Exactly what she didn't need today.

She barely had her feet out from under the covers when she heard her mother's voice.

"Ally, honey, where are you?"

"In here, Mom."

"Why are you in bed so early? Are you feeling all right?"

The simple question brought tears to her eyes, making her glad the room was dark and her mother couldn't see. She wasn't all right. She'd probably never be all right again. "I'm tired. You had three kids. Surely you remember how it was."

Her mother laughed. "That I do."

Waiting for the other shoe to drop always tried her patience, but considering their last conversation, Ally wasn't sure how long she could wait for her mother to dance around the subject. "What brings you by, Mom?"

"I wanted to check on you." She crossed the room and turned on the bedside lamp before sitting on the edge of the bed.

Ally squinted against the light as she pushed

herself to a sitting position. "I'm fine. My doctor's appointment went great, and Dr. Barton says the baby is one hundred percent perfect."

Her mom frowned. "I'm glad to hear it, but I'm here to check on *my* baby, not yours. Are you ready to talk to me again?"

Warily she searched her mother's face, but the brown eyes held only concern. "I don't know, Mom. Did you think about what I said?"

"Of course I did. I just wish you'd said something earlier." She sighed and pushed Ally's hair back from her face, tucking it behind her ears. "I always said you were my little adult. You came out of the womb running the world, so sure of the right thing to do all the time. You never seemed to need me as much as the others." A weak smile crossed her face. "You're my strong one, the one I don't have to worry about all the time. I guess I just got lazy because I knew you'd be there to take it all in hand." Warm hands cupped her cheeks, bringing tears to Ally's eyes. "I am sorry about that, sweetie."

Ally nodded, words trapped behind the lump in her throat. She swiped at the tears on her cheeks.

"I can't promise I'll be able to change overnight, but I will try." With a sigh, her mom wiped at the tears, as well. "And I'll let you handle Erin any way you want to—or not at all. That's completely up to you. If it makes you feel any better, I'll confess Erin is driving me insane, as well. Honestly, you'd think she was the first person to ever get married."

As her mother rolled her eyes, Ally was able to laugh. "Without me to complain at, Erin must be all over you."

"And then some." They shared a moment in silence. "So, are we okay now? I've missed you."

"I've missed you, too, Mom." Though she should feel better now, she felt worse. Without the anger at her family helping to distract her, the pain washed over her in waves. Fresh tears welled in her eyes and rolled down her cheeks.

"Oh, honey, what now?" Her mother wrapped her in a tight hug, and Ally's fragile hold on her control snapped. Sobs shook her as her mom stroked her back and whispered nonsense words of comfort.

Just giving in to the tears helped. It didn't help the hollow feeling in her stomach or the ache that had set up camp in her chest, but she did feel a bit more in control as the sobs abated.

"If we're okay, and the baby's okay, then this must have something to do with Chris."

Ally straightened and nodded.

"Whatever it is, you know I'm there for you. Whatever you need."

So glad her mother was finally being a *mom,* Ally laid her head in her mother's lap and let the whole story flow.

* * *

"You're working poor Grace to death. I sent her home early." Marge brought in a stack of papers and dropped them on his desk. "Those are the financials on the Newport yard. Your grandfather has already had a look and made his recommendations."

"Good." Unfortunately, without Grace here he couldn't get much more done about *that* today. When Marge settled into the chair across from his desk, he realized *he* might not get much more done today, either. She had that look on her face.

Oh, he really didn't need this today. He hadn't slept properly in days—not since Ally had ripped his guts out with her exit from his life—and he was already on edge. Burying himself in paperwork helped precious little, but at least it gave him something he could control, something he could make work.

"You know," she started conversationally, but he wasn't fooled a bit. Marge had something on her mind. "Grace isn't the only one who needs a break. You've been cooped up in here for days, and we're all tired of looking at you. Newport will still be there tomorrow…and Friday. It will even still be there on Monday. Take the *Circe* out or something."

He rubbed a hand tiredly across his face. "I appreciate the sentiment, Marge, but if we want to expand to Newport, we need to get moving before I leave in October." *And it helps pass the time.* "I've got the gala in two days, paperwork from the accident in the yard, and you've just sent my assistant home when I need her. I can't just slip out right now. Anyway, I have a meeting this afternoon—as I'm sure you well know."

"Oh, yes, Grace did mention that." Her nose wrinkled in distaste. "That shark's partner. The little barracuda. Smaller fish to fry this time?"

"Let's just say Dennison is a little overenthusiastic about what I need. The barracuda will do just fine." At Marge's raised eyebrows, he added, "Just a personal matter. Nothing to concern yourself over."

Marge turned a remarkable shade of red. "I've known you practically your entire life and you tell me not to concern myself? That's rich. This meeting is about Ally and the baby."

"Yes, it is."

She waited, but when he didn't offer any additional information, Marge huffed. "That's all you have to say? What is that barracuda up to?"

"Ally and I are in the middle of a custody dispute. Lawyers are the usual accessories."

"I thought you and Ally had come to an agreement already."

He shrugged.

"You're not planning to…to…" Marge went and closed the office door then returned to her seat. "Chris…" she started with a warning tone.

"Don't start. I won't be dragging out the can-

nons again. I'm not my father. I don't plan to fight
dirty."

"Porter said you were getting married."

"That was once the plan, but not anymore. Now
we're back to lawyers."

Marge studied his face carefully, then nodded. "I
see. She turned you down, did she?"

He tossed his pen down in disgust. "You know,
I bet other executives don't have their employees
meddling in their personal lives all the time."

"I wouldn't know," Marge answered cheekily,
making him want to take a hard look at her pension
benefits. "Can't say I blame her, though."

"Gee, thanks for the show of love."

"Oh, I do love you, honey. Any woman would. I
just wouldn't want to marry you." She shook her
head, but her lips twitched.

Fine, he'd bite. "Do I want to know why?"

Serious now, Marge leaned forward in her chair.
"I've known you since you were a child, and I know
you're a good man, but you have to try to see this
from Ally's point of view."

"Ally thinks what I do is dangerous."

"And you can't claim it's not."

"Well, no. But it's not like I'm parachuting into
war zones or something."

"Granted, that would be worrisome, but it's a
totally different situation, as it would be for a good
cause. You've grown up in a world full of men—

I think you're missing a very important point about women."

"Then please enlighten me." It was the only way to get her out of his office so he could get back to work. Talking about Ally wasn't going to help his mood any, either. It only made him recognize how much he missed her.

"I'd bet your boat that Ally's not like the women you're used to. That's why she's gotten under your skin. At the same time, you want her to be like those other women—impressed by who you are and what you do. Ally's not, is she?"

"Ally doesn't know a buoy from a bowline."

"Exactly. I got to spend some time with her at the hospital while you were off getting that thick skull of yours X-rayed, and let me tell you, she was trying to understand and accept your life, your people, and even your boat. Did you do the same for her?"

"Excuse me?"

"Ally was trying to meet you halfway—more than half-way if you ask me. You just weren't holding up your end of the bargain. I'm not surprised she wouldn't marry you. She wants more."

Marge's matter-of-fact tone rankled him in a way she'd never done before. She was stepping way outside of the line, but she had too many years invested in his company and his family for him to call her on it. "Thanks for your concern, Marge, but

I've got this under control. Would you take these files by Billing on your way back to your office?"

Marge stood. "I'll take the files. *And* the hint. Chris, honey, don't expect Ally to settle for second best. She's not that kind of girl and she deserves better. And if you want happiness—for either of you—you wouldn't expect her to. Just think about it."

"Fine. I'll think about it. But right now, I need to think about capital financing and stock options."

Smug now that she'd had her say, Marge left and closed the door behind her. He wondered briefly if she was taking some kind of new medication or something as he tried to focus on the paperwork in front of him.

What "more" could Ally possibly want? He snorted. He'd hardly asked her to "settle" for anything. She and the baby would have everything they wanted. They could be happy together if Ally wasn't such a worrywart and a control freak.

He shook his head and looked at the financials again. The numbers all looked good—everything seemed to add up properly.

Add up.

Ally was a numbers person; everything had to add up properly for her. She liked things in proper columns and rows and nothing about the two of them lined up neatly anywhere. Well, except maybe their bodies. *That* brought a blood-heating mental image.

What had she said about her family? They needed her. So did he, but in an entirely different way.

That thought brought him up short, and the papers in his hand were forgotten. When exactly had she become a need? He'd wanted her since the moment he'd seen her on the dock inspecting the *Circe*. Her impassioned defense of Circe and disparaging remarks about Odysseus had enchanted him much the way Circe had enraptured Odysseus. But *need?* That was a new feeling.

He didn't like it very much, that was for sure. Marge was right that Ally was under his skin, but until this moment, he hadn't realized how much he wanted her there.

He thought of Ally—wearing that shapeless cotton sundress that hid the luscious curves of her body while her hair escaped the braid and flew randomly around her face in the breeze—as she argued her case against Odysseus in defense of women everywhere.

She'd snared him and he'd never denied it. Unlike Odysseus, though, he had no plans to sail off into the sunset and forget her or their child.

Aren't you? It might look that way.

Was *that* it? Did Ally's objections to him taking the *Dagny* around the world go beyond the possible danger? "It's a whole different world," she'd said. Christ. He was as thickheaded as Marge had said.

Ally didn't think she would fit in that world and he'd done nothing to convince her she did. The silly woman thought he'd pull an Odysseus eventually. She'd called Odysseus a player, the original golden boy. No wonder she'd tried to keep herself distant from him.

Tried was the operative word. This whole thing with Ally had spun way off course. She wasn't the only one who'd gotten a hell of a lot more than she'd bargained for that day on the docks. Now he just had to enlighten her.

He opened his drawer and pulled out the manila envelope containing Ally's laughable custody agreement and the necklace she'd returned.

He slid the necklace into his pocket and tossed the papers into the recycling bin.

CHAPTER THIRTEEN

PLAN C WAS A HELL OF A LOT harder than she'd figured—especially when trying to get over Chris had her feeling like a junkie in rehab. Not thinking about Chris was just as hard as thinking about him, and both had her craving him like a drug.

Work didn't help. No matter how deeply she buried herself in paperwork and numbers, the pain in her heart was a constant reminder of what she was trying so hard to forget. She caught up on the backlog at work. She'd cleaned and organized every closet in her house. She began to regret the truce she'd called with her family—at least fighting with them would give her something to do with the long hours. Plus, they were actually taking her new rules of running their own lives seriously, so she didn't have *their* day-to-day business to occupy her. Briefly she even considered making up with Erin— surely her sister could supply her with enough wedding-related drama to keep her busy.

But the dreams were the worst. She could try to

keep Chris at bay during daylight hours, but he seemed to own her subconscious. Heartbreaking, erotic, fanciful—her dreams all had one vivid thing in common: Chris.

With all the work done, she had no reason to stay at the office. Molly was long gone; plans of a hot date with the guy who owned the architecture firm two blocks over had her skipping—literally—out of the door an hour ago.

She opened her e-mail program one last time. The last e-mail from Uncle Joe hadn't helped her mood any: Nothing from him or his lawyer yet. Give it until next week before you worry any more. Easy for him to say. Maybe knowing Chris's signature was on the agreement would help with this whole healing process. Wondering if that horrible lawyer of his was going to make her life hell could be partly to blame for the continuing hollowness in her stomach.

No e-mail from Uncle Joe or anyone else, but a reminder did open up in her window: Get a manicure on the way home.

Well, no need for a manicure now. She'd made that reminder when she was still going to Chris's yacht club thing tomorrow night. Now that she wasn't going, her unpolished, slightly gnawed nails weren't an issue. She'd even given Molly back the lovely red dress she'd borrowed for the event. Instead, she'd spend tomorrow night safely ensconced under the duvet, trying very hard not to think about the announcement Chris was going to make with the official unveiling of the *Dagny*. That thought still made her ill. It was probably a very good thing she wasn't going to be there. There was no way she'd be able to smile and react appropriately while Chris made his announcement.

What did constitute appropriate in a situation like that? Not that it mattered. It wasn't her business anymore. God, this whole situation made her head pound, and she wished alcohol wasn't bad for the baby. She could use a strong drink about now.

She missed Chris. Part of her was willing to do whatever it took, put up with whatever she had to, just to have him for however long she could. Rational Ally was up against a formidable foe when it came to her emotions.

With a sigh, she deleted the reminder for the manicure, wishing she could manipulate her feelings as easily.

Habit took over after that—shutting off her computer, adjusting the office thermostat, turning off the lights, locking the door. She was on the bus before she knew it, and the familiar sights of her neighborhood were almost a shock since she had no recollection of the ride home.

"Have a good weekend," the bus driver said as she got off at her stop.

Yeah, right, she thought, but she managed a polite response.

Fall hadn't arrived on the Georgia coast yet, but it was cooler as she walked down the tree-lined street, letting her mind wander.

The red car in front of her house didn't register at first, but when it did, her heart jumped to her throat and she stopped dead on the sidewalk.

She had to be hallucinating. Or it was a different car that just looked like Chris's. She closed her eyes, cleared the image from her mind, then peeked.

Nope. South Carolina plates. Yacht club sticker in the back window. Her knees nearly buckled. *Oh, God.*

This is why Uncle Joe hadn't heard anything. What part of "contact my attorney" didn't Chris understand?

She approached the car carefully, but the front seat was empty. Taking a deep breath, she turned up the walk to her house.

Sure enough, there—perched on her porch rail and looking too good to be real—was Chris.

Breathe, Ally. She repeated that to herself as she climbed the stairs. Chris sat easily, his back against one of the support posts and his arms crossed casually over his chest. With sunglasses hiding his eyes, she couldn't tell his mood, so she aimed to keep this meeting light.

And hopefully quick. Painless would be too much to ask for.

"Be careful up there. You'd hate to fall and bash your head twice in one week."

Chris pushed his sunglasses up onto his head and grinned at her as he levered himself off the railing. "Well, I certainly don't want to worry you." He sounded cheerful, amused even, and the crinkles around his eyes clawed at her heart, distracting her as she tried to figure out what he was here for.

She scanned the furniture on the porch, looking for evil manila envelopes with lawyers' return addresses, but found none. Chris leaned against the railing, putting his hands in his back pockets and causing the muscles under his formfitting T-shirt to bulge against the fabric. Her mouth went dry and her thighs clenched.

Forget breathing, try focusing. "Okay, I give. Why are you here?"

His eyebrows went up, and she realized how sharp her tone was. "I was hoping we could talk. Should we go in?"

No! Her living room was too small and he filled it far too easily. She needed to breathe, to be clearheaded if they were going to talk. "I think we should talk out here."

She moved to the porch swing and sat, sending it swaying slightly. The movement sent a strong enough signal that she didn't want him joining her there, so he shrugged and lowered himself into the wicker rocker to her right.

"If you wanted to talk about the custody agreement, you should really call my—"

Chris shook his head, causing a lock of hair to slide out from under the sunglasses and fall across his forehead. Her fingers itched to smooth it back, so she twined them together in her lap.

"I don't want to talk about the custody agreement."

That caught her off guard and her mind spun as it searched for possibilities. "Then what?"

He stretched his legs out in front of him, causing the rocker to tilt forward slightly, and leaving only inches between his denim-clad legs and her bare ones. She quickly tucked her feet under the swing. "I thought we'd talk about mythology."

She certainly hadn't been expecting *that*. "Mythology? Seriously?"

He nodded. O-*kay,* mythology was the topic. Why *this* topic was a different question altogether...

"I've been thinking about what you said about Circe and Odysseus."

Oh, dear. "Look, I was just babbling that day. Trying to make conversation, you know?"

"I thought you made some good points. About Odysseus at least. I'd never thought about it from Circe's point of view before."

She fumbled for sensible words. This was surreal, but she'd play along. Maybe she'd figure out where he was going soon. "Well, it was Odysseus's story. He gets the hero treatment."

"I watched the video of the ultrasound. It doesn't look like you're carrying triplets."

Okay. New topic. "I should certainly hope not."

"So unless you have some secret power to turn men into swine I should know about, I think it's safe to say you aren't Circe."

"Um…" The nurse at the hospital had sworn he didn't have brain damage, but now she wasn't so sure.

"And since I don't plan to pull an Odysseus and leave you and the baby behind, can we move past that?"

Mythology riddles were *not* what she needed right now. "Chris, I don't know what you're talking about. I just—"

"I love you, Ally."

Everything froze. Her heart seemed to skip a couple of beats while the happy bubble in her chest inflated at his words. The need to savor that thought—*Chris loved her*—nagged at her, as did the need to throw herself into his arms…

No. She closed her eyes, blocking out the intense blue stare and his beautiful face. It was a wonderful thing, but it changed nothing. *Remember that.* "This won't work."

She opened her eyes in time to see one blond eyebrow arch up. "That's your response when a man tells you he loves you? You sure know how to deflate the moment, don't you?"

"Don't think I don't, um, appreciate the sentiment—I do, really. But love and good sex are two different things—"

Chris smirked. "But they go together quite nicely." She opened her mouth to say more, but Chris continued, seriously this time. "I know you've been burned, but it wasn't by me. You can't judge me based on your ex or anyone else."

That ticked her off. "I'm judging you based on *you* and our history. It's all the information I need to make a decision."

"But, my little number cruncher, did you factor in the fact that you love me and that I love you?"

Ally felt her chin drop and she closed her mouth with a snap. How to answer *that?*

Chris exhaled loudly, an exasperated look on his face, then moved to the swing next to her. "You're not going to help me out here at all, obviously. Fine."

He looked so exasperated, it would almost be funny if the topic weren't so serious.

"I love you. I want to marry you. I want this baby and hopefully more someday. I'm even willing to put up with your family—or run interference for you, whichever you prefer."

The words washed over her, bringing tears to her eyes. God, she wanted to believe him, and from the look in his eyes, she knew he meant what he said. At least he did right now. While it was perfect in so many ways, it also meant nothing at all.

She didn't know what to say, and Chris frowned at her silence. "Maybe this will help convince you." He pulled a folded sheet of paper out of his back pocket and handed it to her.

The film of tears in her eyes made the print blurry, and it took a minute for her to realize she was holding a press release. "Wells Racing Announces Record-breaking Around-the-world Solo Attempt." There was that knot in her stomach again.

"We'll make the official announcement tomorrow night, but that's the press release faxed to all the major papers and sailing press this afternoon."

"That's…that's…that's great, Chris. I wish you nothing but luck."

"How about you read it first?"

What, so the knife in her heart could slice even deeper? But Chris leaned back, setting the swing gently moving again, and didn't say anything more. She blinked against the moisture in her eyes and skimmed the short paragraphs. *Sponsored by OWD Shipyard, world-class racing teams,* blah, blah, blah, *the newly designed* Dagny, *skippered by the internationally known John Forsythe…fifty-nine-day record to beat.*

Wait. Who? She skimmed back. John Forsythe? She looked at Chris questioningly.

"You didn't get to meet John—he wasn't at the last race since he was in Scotland at the International Sailing Federation meeting. Excellent sailor. He's been itching to attempt the record for a couple of years now."

Confusion reigned. "But I thought *you* wanted to break the record."

Chris captured her hand and threaded his fingers through hers. "I do. But not as much as I want you."

Said simply like that, Ally knew he meant it, and her heart expanded until she felt her chest would burst. *He did love her.* Loved her enough to give up the chance to…

"Chris, I can't ask you to do this."

"You didn't. I've never had to take anyone else into consideration before, and it didn't occur to me to try to see it your way. I'm used to being in charge—I forgot we'd have to be a team."

"You'd give up racing for me?" Chris needed racing like he needed air; it wasn't something she could get her head around easily.

Chris's mouth twitched. "I didn't say *that*. This race, definitely. Future races? Well…let's just say it's open to negotiation."

He squeezed her hand gently as he spoke, and this time she squeezed back. She was too happy to say anything at the moment. She just wanted to savor the feeling.

"Ally?"

"I love you."

Happiness lit his eyes, and they glowed a deep Caribbean blue. Tugging her hand, he pulled her into his lap for a kiss that seared through her, healing old wounds as it did. Ally's arms twined around his neck, her hands burying into his hair, holding him close. She never wanted this moment to end, but Chris was shifting awkwardly under her.

She pulled back, breaking the kiss. "Don't tell me I'm too heavy already."

"Hardly," Chris mumbled, capturing her lips again. One arm hooked under her bottom, lifting her slightly as he shifted, then settled her comfortably back on his lap. "I thought you might like this back."

Her necklace dangled from his fingers, the medallion catching the sunlight and sending rainbows over her skin. She felt the smile split her face as he hooked the necklace around her neck.

Chris toyed with the medallion as it nestled between her breasts, and the air around them became charged. Her skin started to tingle and an ache built between her legs. She traced a hand over the expanse of his chest and sighed. "Let's go inside."

Skilled fingers tickled over her collarbone, sending lovely shivers over her skin. With a small smile, Chris helped her off his lap and to her feet. He stood and kissed her gently on the forehead.

Suddenly, everything seemed to click into place. She could do this. Loving Chris might be easier than she thought.

"I'll race you," he challenged.

Well, at least it wouldn't be boring.

* * * * *

Harlequin Presents® is thrilled to introduce a sexy new duet,
HOT BED OF SCANDAL, *by Kelly Hunter!*
Read on for a sneak peek of the first book
EXPOSED:
MISBEHAVING WITH THE MAGNATE.

'I'M ATTRACTED to you and don't see why I should deny it. Our kiss in the garden suggests you're not exactly indifferent to me. The solution seems fairly straightforward.'

'You want me to become the comte's convenient mistress?'

'I'm not a comte,' Luc said. 'All I have is the castle.'

'All right, the billionaire's preferred plaything, then.'

'I'm not a billionaire, either. Yet.' His lazy smile warned her it was on his to-do list. 'No, I want you to become my outrageously beautiful, independently wealthy lover.'

'Isn't that the same option?'

'No, you might have noticed that the wording's a little different.'

'They're just words, Luc. The outcome's the same.'

'It's an attitude thing.' He looked at her, his smile crookedly charming. 'So what do you say?'

To an affair with the likes of Luc Duvalier? 'I say it's dangerous. For both of us.'

Luc's eyes gleamed. 'There is that.'

'Not to mention insane.'

'Quite possibly. Was that a yes?'

Gabrielle really didn't know what to say. 'So how do we start this thing? If I were to agree to it. Which I haven't.' Yet.

'We start with dinner. Tonight. No expectations beyond a pleasant evening with fine food, fine wine and good company. And we see what happens.'

'I don't know,' she said, reaching for her coffee. 'It seems a little…'

'Straightforward?' he suggested. 'Civilized?'

'For us, yes,' she murmured. 'Where would we eat? Somewhere public or in private?'

'Somewhere public,' he said firmly. 'The restaurant I'm thinking of is a fine one—excellent food, small premises and always busy. A man might take his lover there if he was trying to keep his hands off her.'

'Would I meet you there?' she said.

'I will, of course, collect you,' he said, playing the autocrat and playing it well. 'Shall I meet you there,' he murmured in disbelief. 'What kind of question is that?'

'Says the new generation Frenchman,' she countered. 'Liberated, egalitarian, nonsexist…'

'Helpful, attentive, chivalrous…' he added with a reckless smile. 'And very beddable.'

He was that.

'All right,' she said. 'I'll give you the day—and tonight—to prove that a civilized, pleasurable and manageable affair wouldn't be beyond us. If you can prove this to my satisfaction, I'll make love with you. If this gets out of hand, however…'

'Yes?' he said silkily. 'What do you suggest?'

Gabrielle leaned forward, elbows on the table. Luc leaned forward, too. 'Well, I don't know about you,' she murmured, 'but I'm a clever, outrageously beautiful, independently wealthy woman. I plan to run.'

This sparky story is full of passion,
wit and scandal
and will leave you wanting more!
Look for
EXPOSED:
MISBEHAVING WITH THE MAGNATE
Available March 2010